LORD OF THE WOLVES

James Matlack Raney

ISBN: 1539160688
ISBN 13: 9781539160687

Other Books by James Matlack Raney:

Jim Morgan and the King of Thieves
Jim Morgan and the Pirates of the Black Skull
Jim Morgan and the Door at the Edge of the World

For Oma. For my mother. For my sister and brother. For all those who journey.

LORD OF THE WOLVES

The Children of Anorak were born on a spring day when the sun and the moon hung in the sky together.

"It's an omen," the old wolves of the Gray Woods whispered. "A sign foretelling the birth of a great wolf. A lord like his father. A wolf who will grow to defend the honor of the Gray Woods."

On the day of the whelping the whole pack gathered in the circle beneath the oldest Tree in the woods. Even Lady Frost Feather the Owl came, circling down from the blue sky.

"Greetings, Lord Anorak," said the owl, bowing her silver-feathered head to the Lord of the Pack.

"Greetings, Lady Frost Feather," said Anorak, bowing in return. But his proud yellow eyes never left the she-wolf before him. She lay in the grass, eyes closed from the pain. She was Lady Summer, Lord Anorak's wife. Her pain was the suffering of childbirth.

"I came as fast as I could," said Frost Feather, flapping down from the branch to land in the grass beside Lady Summer, her big owl eyes wide and unblinking. "Pups born under *both* a sun and a moon? It's a sign indeed, Anorak. It bespeaks of great things." She almost added, *or terrible things,* but kept that part to herself.

The birthing came soon. The first pup born was so big that every wolf in the pack gasped. His paws were already the size of a pup a season old. His fur was already gray. Though his eyes were closed he managed to stand on his own, rearing back as if to howl at the sky.

Lord Anorak rose up with pride. As solemn and lordly as he was, his tail wagged at the sight of his first born son. "This one shall have a name from the old times," he said, "from the days of the First Wolves. Orion. He shall be called, Orion."

Next came a pup with fur white as snow. She was already beautiful. The she-wolves laughed and bayed. They foresaw her becoming lady of a pack one day. But Frost Feather the Owl noticed that this pup did not sniff at the air as she crawled about on the ground. But she said nothing about this.

"Glimmer," said her mother. "Like a sparkle of morning dew."

Then came another male, this one only half as big as his brother and only just smaller than his sister. A black stripe ran down the fur on his back, from his withers to his tail. The moment he touched the grass he began to kick about as though jumping for joy to be alive.

"Kicker," said Lady Summer. The wolves in the pack laughed.

Last came a pup smaller still, with pied fur of brown and white and black. This one curled up in a ball the moment she touched the cool evening air. She was already sniffing at everything around her.

"This one's nose is special," said Lady Frost Feather. "She's already lost in the scents upon the wind."

"Windy," said Lady Summer. And the old wolves smiled.

"It is a proud day for the Gray Woods," said Anorak. He nuzzled his four pups and his wife. Then he lifted his head and turned to the pack. "It is a day to give thanks to the Trees, the goddesses of the Old Forest." He reared back his head to howl. The pack howled with him, until Lady Summer moaned in pain again. Frost Feather the Owl gave a startled squawk.

"Wait!" she cried. "There is one more."

The wolves went quiet. Their eyes fell on Lady Summer just as the fifth pup climbed into the world. At once the pack could see why this one came last. He was only a third the size of the first wolf, smaller even than his sister who came before him. He was a runt. And worse, one of his legs was curled up beneath him like a bird's wing. He crawled onto the grass with three legs alone. He was lame.

All the joy and happiness fled the clearing beneath the Tree. The pack knew what must be done. What Anorak and Summer would have to do.

"Anorak," whispered Lady Summer, exhausted from her labor. "What's wrong?"

"The fifth pup, milady," said Anorak, his words catching in his throat. "He has been born lame."

Lady Summer began to whimper. The Old Forest was a hard place, full of danger, full of enemies, full even of magic. It was a hard enough place to be a pup. It was too hard for a pup with three legs. Some packs decided right away and sped lame runts from the woods. Others just waited for them to die on their own.

Lord Anorak would be merciful and make it quick. He closed his eyes and opened his jaws. But before he could do his unfortunate deed, Lady Frost Feather stayed him with a wing on his shoulder.

"Anorak, wait," she hissed. "Look!"

When Anorak opened his eyes and peered down at the little runt, he found the most amazing sight: The pup's eyes were open as well. They were staring back at him.

"Owl's eyes," whispered an aged voice from the circle of wolves. It was Long Tooth, the oldest wolf in the woods, shaking his head in disbelief. "The runt has owl's eyes, milord – big eyes open from birth. I've not seen a pup born with those for moons upon moons upon moons."

"Owl's eyes," whispered Lady Frost Feather. "Eyes that can see the mysteries of the Old Forest."

"But what good are they," asked Anorak, "if the poor creature won't live long enough to use them? Runts rarely live long, Lady Frost Feather. Lame runts hardly live at all."

But even as Anorak said this, the lame pup's eyes shifted from his father to his mother. Lady Summer smiled at the pup. The pup seemed to smile back. He crawled for her belly where his brothers and sisters were already feeding on her milk.

At first, the other pups refused to let him in. He was not strong enough to fight his way through. But then the big pup, the one that had come first, kicked with his paws. He was already powerful enough to move all three of his siblings at once. And he made room. The little runt squirmed in close to his biggest brother and began to drink.

"Oh, Anorak," said Summer.

"Well I never," said Lady Frost Feather, a smile curving just at the edges of her beak.

"Alright," said the lord with a sigh. "We shall wait and see. But we won't name him right away. We shall wait, and if he lives, only then will he be named."

But Lady Frost Feather had already hopped over to where the young pups fed. She reached out with a silvery wing and gently stroked the fur of the lame runt with the owl eyes.

"Watcher," she whispered. "Just a suggestion, milord and milady. If this pup lives, you should call him Watcher."

1

Watcher sat on a hill beneath the fur gray sky, listening for the hunt through the pines. Far away, he heard a Great Crown crashing through the thickets. He heard the hunters baying at its heels. His breaths grew deep, as though he too ran with the pack, making the red snow and taking the first share. Those were Watcher's wildest dreams, as many and as delicate as the snowflakes that drifted down on his snout and melted away – beautiful wonders not meant to last.

"How many Great Crowns are there, Windy?" Watcher asked his sister for at least the third time. "Who in the pack is closest?" Windy sat beside him and Glimmer on the snow-dusted hill, while Kicker lay behind them, facing the other direction and sulking, as usual. The litter was almost a full season old now, wolflings shedding their pup's soft fur.

"A clutch, and then another clutch," said Windy. She held her dappled snout to the air. Her eyes fixed to the gray sky, as though the moon held her under a spell. *A clutch and then another,* thought Watcher, leaning forward, his heart a-thumping faster and faster.

"But that must mean—"

"There is a chieftain among them."

Glimmer reared off her haunches and pranced about, throwing up snow with her white paws. "And who's closest, Windy?" she asked, all but howling. "Who's closest?" But Watcher knew before Windy could answer in her dreamer's far-away voice.

"Orion," she said to the air.

"Orion! Orion!" Watcher and Glimmer shouted together, laughing aloud. Watcher did his best to prance beside his second sister without falling over. It was never easy on three legs. But when Glimmer raised her paws in the air she didn't push against Watcher to knock him down; for Glimmer was as gentle to him as the spring winds.

"There was never a pup in the Forest like Orion," said Glimmer.

"And there will be no wolf like him either!" Watcher shouted. But at once he wished he had not shouted so loudly. Kicker snorted with his snout in the snow, blowing up a steamy white cloud. It was never good to have Kicker in a foul mood with the rest of the pack away. Watcher knew that better than anyone.

"Will you three runts just quit your yapping already?" Kicker growled. "I'm trying to take a nap before the long lope. And besides, the pack won't be able to hear each other bay for all of Three Legs' and Dull Snout's noise."

"Sorry, Kicker," said Watcher. And even though Kicker wasn't looking, Watcher thought it best to bow his head and sit back down beside Windy. It wasn't so bad when Kicker called him names. It was far better than neck biting or ear grabbing or snout grounding, wasn't it? But somehow, when Kicker growled *Three Legs,* it always made Watcher's lame paw quiver, the one curled up under his breast like a bird's wing. But it wasn't so bad.

But Watcher did wish Kicker would stop calling Glimmer *Dull Snout.* If there was anything in the Old Forest worse than a lame leg, it was a dull snout. Glimmer was so good at so much else, Watcher

2

thought. She was fast and strong and kind. Almost every night Watcher prayed to the Trees that his sister's smell would improve, if for nothing else, so that Kicker would just stop teasing her about it.

"You sound as grumpy as old Long Tooth, *Scat Kicker,*" said Glimmer. "You're just jealous."

Watcher cringed and dipped his snout almost to the snow. Why did Glimmer always have to fight back? It just made things worse.

Kicker leapt up, a rumble in his throat. "Wolflings aren't supposed to hunt for two seasons," he snarled, jabbing his snout into Glimmer's and backing her down. "That's part of the Ancient Law, *Dull Snout.* Even Long Tooth says so."

"But Orion is no ordinary wolfling!" Glimmer refused to bow her head. "Long Tooth says that too."

"Then why aren't I out there? Why am I not invited on the hunt a season early? I'm almost as big as Orion!"

Glimmer coughed a laugh. "Maybe my snout *is* dull, Kicker, but my eyes work just fine. If you were born in a litter of Orions, you'd be the runt, not Watcher!"

Watcher groaned. He snuck a glance back at his bigger brother, whose black fur stripe bristled on his back. Kicker coiled up to spring on Glimmer and drive her into the snow to make her swallow that insult whole. But Windy, still lost in the cold gusts that whirled through the pines, spoke first.

"The hunt draws near. Only a short lope away. It is the chieftain. A Chieftain of the Great Crowns runs this way!"

The littermates went silent, even Kicker. He stepped to the edge of the hill, tasting the wind with his snout, twitching his ears. But only the rustle of the pines shivered in the Gray Wood. After a long cold moment, he sighed.

"There's nothing out there, Windy."

"The hunt draws near," she said again, "but—" Her snout trembled. Windy's eyes grew moonround in her trance, as though seized by some terrible vision.

"But what?"

"There's a scent on the back of the hunt. Behind it. chasing it. A dark scent. A foul odor. It smells like the first taste of a storm. It's brewing fast. It's coming! I – I can smell red snow in its wake!"

Watcher shivered. The cold suddenly bit through his fur. He bowed his head low and inched closer to Kicker, as did Glimmer. "What is it, Windy?" he asked. "What could make a smell like that?"

But Kicker just snorted at Watcher and shook free of the others. He snapped his teeth in Windy's ear, finally breaking her trance. "Quit crying, Watcher. Windy's just smelling ghosts again, as usual. The hunt's not coming this way and no storm is either. *Nothing's* coming this way. This is the most boring hill in the entire Old Forest and I'm stuck on it with you runts when I should be out hunting." Kicker turned away to go back to his sulking, but threw a last barb over his shoulder. "Stop smelling at ghosts, Windy. You're scaring the Three Legs."

"Something *is* coming, Kicker," Windy said softly. She looked out over the pines, as though she could see what she had smelled. "And there *are* ghosts on the wind. I can smell them."

Watcher shivered again, as though his fur had stopped shielding him from the wind. "Maybe we should find another hill, Kicker," he suggested. "Just to be safe."

"Well then make yourself useful for once, Three Legs, and go find us one!" Kicker backpedaled and shoved Watcher down the hill with his strong hind leg, sending him tumbling head over heels in the snow.

2

Lying at the bottom of the hill, Watcher heard his sisters snapping at Kicker for being so cruel. But it was best to just do as Kicker asked. *I am the runt after all, aren't I?* he told himself. And besides that, if the hunt did pass this way, and if he did find a safer hill for the litter, wouldn't that be something to tell his father? Wouldn't that be something to make his mother smile? Wouldn't that be something to make Orion proud?

So Watcher put his snout to the snow, smelling for a safe place. His nose was not nearly as strong as Windy's, but then again, *no wolf's* nose was as good as hers. Watcher wished he could smell like that – even if it meant smelling the ghosts. If he could smell like Windy, what would it matter that he had only three good legs?

Watcher ambled his way through the trees toward the next hill, trotting with his awkward lope. Kicker said it looked more like falling forward than running. That was probably true. A lame leg might as well be no leg at all.

But halfway up the hill, where a green patch yet poked through the white dust, a bird zipped past Watcher's face. It was a fat sparrow, moving fast through the air, careening through the pine branches. Watcher followed it with his owl eyes.

The sparrow spiraled up and landed on the very end of a slender pine branch, which bobbed up and down beneath its weight. Watcher laughed. Then he began to wonder, as he often did about such small things. *How did such a fat sparrow even manage to fly? How could such a small branch hold it?* The wind teased Watcher's fur as he stood there pondering. His big eyes wandered down from the thin branch to the thick trunk of the Tree. *The wind is bigger than the bird,* he thought, *even though I can't see it. And the Tree is bigger than the branch. The wind and the Trees are big enough to hold up all the birds in the world.*

Watcher laughed again at this funny thought. But when his eyes finally wandered back to the fat sparrow, he found only bobbing pine needles where the bird had been. It had flown away. Then Watcher realized he had not really been watching. Not listening. Not sniffing. Not paying attention.

He heard his sisters first. Then even his brother. They barked his name from the hilltop behind him. They called it over and over. They called for him to run.

Thicket branches snapped. Snow crunched beneath hooved feet. Watcher froze on the green patch and slowly turned his head.

The beast charged him at full gallop. Its fur hung like brown vines from its body. Its nostrils flared as wide as its crazed eyes. Its hooves shook the ground beneath Watcher's paws. But more terrifying still was the great crown upon its head. Bony spines reached to either side longer than a wolf from tail to snout, ridges like the hills in the forest from tip to tip.

It was the Chieftain of the Great Crowns, tearing through the forest. How many wolves had been trampled to death under hooves such as those? How many had old Long Tooth said? Watcher wondered what it would feel like when they crushed him.

That thought broke the ice on his bones. Watcher scrambled backwards, falling as he turned on his lame paw. He dug his three good legs into the snow to keep pushing forward. The Great Crown thundered after, churning the brown earth from under the snow as it barreled up the hill. Watcher wanted to scream, but the only sound he could make was silence as he pictured his bones smashed to dust beneath the hooves bearing down upon him.

For a moment, as he flung himself forward, Watcher thought he might just be fast enough to escape, that he might prove Kicker wrong about him. But his lame paw betrayed him at the top of the hill. He tripped on a root with no way to catch himself. He tumbled snout-first into the snow, rolling onto his back in time to see the chieftain crest the hill.

Even in terror, Watcher's eyes refused to shut. Thus they saw the Tree save his life. The Great Crown's antlers struck a reach of low hanging branches, becoming ensnared. The chieftain thrashed and bucked. It bellowed and roared. Snow burst beneath its hooves. Pine needles and cones rained down on its head.

Watcher took the chance to run again, but he did not get far before the chieftain tore loose. It charged. Watcher knew he would not be so lucky again. Maybe it would be a blessing, he thought in that awful moment, to free the pack of the burden that was a runt with three legs.

But a sharp bay cut through the air. A lone wolf bounded over the hill. His coat was thick as the snow in deepest winter, gray as the clouds that bring the storms. His legs were strong. His teeth were sharp. With a leap in his chest, Watcher knew he would not die this day.

It was Orion.

The wolf did not hesitate before the chieftain. He chased the Great Crown down and leapt into the air, latching his teeth onto the beast's throat. The Great Crown took but a few more steps before it crashed to the snow. A wave of white dust and brown earth washed over Watcher. The chieftain's snout slid to a stop just before his trembling paws.

All was quiet amongst the Trees again. It was a long moment before Watcher even heard the thump-thump-thump of his rushing blood.

A familiar face rose up from behind the Great Crown's antlers, smiling down on Watcher with red on this teeth, a laugh on his tongue, and a wag on his tail.

"Well good morning, little brother," said Orion. "Now Kicker's really going to be in a bad mood. You got to go hunting before he did."

3

"What's going on here?" demanded a voice from over the hill. "What's happened, for the Trees' sakes?" Watcher's father and mother, Lord Anorak and Lady Summer, appeared, followed by all the lieutenants and hunters from the Gray Woods Pack. But there was so much baying and yapping that Watcher's father couldn't get an answer. The wolflings had come down from their hill and stood beside the fallen Great Crown, churned earth and pine needles strewn in its wake. Watcher's mother rushed to her children, sniffing and licking them one at a time.

"Aw, mother," said Kicker, trying to escape his mother's snout in front of the hunters. But Orion just laughed when his mother licked his face. Watcher nuzzled into her coat when she came near, as did his sisters. There was no other feeling in the world to Watcher like his mother's warmth.

"Someone answer me. What's happened here?" Watcher's father finally demanded again, silencing the excited babble. Watcher swallowed hard and reluctantly pulled himself out from behind his mother. He didn't want to tell his father that he'd wandered off, chasing another bird or bug, almost getting himself killed again. But one of the lieutenants saved him the trouble.

"Milord," said the wolf, staring at the Great Crown with moonround eyes. "It's a chieftain. Someone's brought down a chieftain!"

Watcher's father and all the pack gathered close to the fallen beast, sniffing at it and the red snow that slowly spread around it. They looked to each other, then at the wolflings, their mouths agape and their tongues still. Watcher was sure he'd never seen anything surprise his father before. His father knew *everything* in the woods – every creature and every law. The only wolf who might know more was old Long Tooth. But even Lord Anorak had gone silent.

"Father, forgive me. It was—" Watcher opened his mouth to say what happened, when his brother cut him off.

"It was Watcher and me, father," said Orion, bowing his head low. But that smile still snuck over his jaws. "Watcher stood beneath this Tree. He stood with great courage, Father, like a warrior! He lured the chieftain forward until its crown became stuck in the branches. I was then able to sneak up behind him and bring him into the red snow. I couldn't have done it without Watcher's help."

Watcher held his breath through the entire story. He might have gone on holding it forever until Lord Anorak smiled with a smile that looked so much like Orion's. He looked over his sons with wise eyes. He bowed his head, and all the pack bowed with him, to Orion, and to Watcher. Watcher trembled so hard he thought he would fall over on his lame leg. The pack was bowing to him – to him! Orion was still smiling that smile. Watcher bowed his head to his brother. His brother bowed his head back.

Then the Gray Woods Pack gathered in the circle about the chieftain, forming a ring around the tree atop the hill. Watcher's father bowed his head, snout to snout with the Great Crown, and spoke. "Mighty Chieftain, lord among your people, this day you ran with courage. We take pride in your red snow and the strength it will lend our pack. It was the Trees who sent us, and to the Trees we shall return."

After he had spoken, Watcher's father nodded to Watcher and Orion. They were to have the first shares. Watcher couldn't stop shaking. He was lame. He was a three legs. For the Trees' sake, he was the runt of his litter! He was lucky to eat at all. If he had been born to another mother and another father, to another pack – but here he was, about to have the only first share he might ever have in his life – until he saw Kicker.

Kicker's eyes were moonround and fixed on Watcher's face. Watcher knew that look. It was the look that came before neck biting and snout grounding. Only this time it was worse. So much worse. Watcher took only one step toward the chieftain.

"Father, I – I want to give my first share to Kicker, Windy, and Glimmer," he said. "It was their idea for me to come to this hill. They deserve the first share, not me."

"Watcher, you can't—" Orion began, but his father barked sharply.

"Orion! Watcher's share is his to do with as he pleases. He is a Gray Woods Wolf, as are you. He may make his own mind."

Watcher backed away, keeping his eyes to the snow. He already knew the looks on his littermates' faces. Kicker's would still be full of storms, but dulled enough to make Watcher feel better. And safer. Windy, and especially Glimmer, on the other hand, would have the sad eyes they usually wore for him. But Orion's gaze was the one Watcher feared the most. It would not be mean or sad, only disappointed. Watcher's own eyes stung. They burned with hot water as the joyful trembles in his body faded away.

In the end, he managed to lift his head to watch his littermates take their shares. Only Windy was not biting. She stood frozen beside the Great Crown, her nose in the air, twitching. Her eyes had gone wide in her scent trance yet again.

"It's coming!" she said. "The darkness I smelled. It's coming!"

Only then did Watcher hear the baying of more wolves over the Trees. And in the distance he saw them coming; clutches of dark bodies charging through the woods.

4

The scent of the red snow is strong, Long Tooth had taught Watcher and the others when they were pups. *It is the strongest of all scents. When it possesses a wolf's nose, he will smell nothing else.* But it was fortunate for the Gray Woods Pack that they had Windy, for her nose was special. Even over the intoxicating power of the red snow it could smell the coming of the Lone Rock Pack. For that is who came for them.

Neither Watcher nor any of the other wolflings, not even Orion, had seen another pack with their own eyes before. They'd been taught from the time they could walk to honor the boundaries between one pack's territory and another's. But they'd all heard old Long Tooth's stories of the Lone Rock Wolves. Tales of red fur and red snow. Tales of war.

"Keep the circle around the chieftain," commanded Watcher's father. "Put the young ones behind us."

"Father," said Orion, raising himself to his full height, already bigger – and maybe even stronger – than Lord Anorak. "Let me stand beside you. I can fight!"

"Me too, father!" trumpeted Kicker. "I'm ready!" He tried to puff out his chest and raise his head high, but next to Orion, Watcher thought he looked like a pup playing at being a wolf.

"You both heard me," said Anorak. "If I can help it, there will be no fighting today. Keep still behind the wolves and stay quiet. The rest of you hold your ground and hold your tongues. No battling unless first attacked. We shall see if words might do more than teeth."

Watcher made himself as small as he could, which was already smallest of the litter. He crouched between Orion and Kicker. Windy huddled beside him, but Glimmer, who was as big as Kicker and came up to Orion's shoulder, stood beside her brothers. Watcher could hear all their heartbeats hammering away. He thought his own might go wild, leap out of his throat and run away like a terrified squirrel. But there was one heartbeat of the litter's that pounded strong and steady.

"Stay beside me, little brother," whispered Orion. "I'll look out for you."

"Aren't you scared? Scared of the red fur and the red snow?"

"A little. But I know a secret that helps."

"What's that?"

"The wolves that are coming, their fur can turn just as red as mine." Orion smiled with teeth that had felled a Chieftain of the Great Crowns. Watcher scooted just a little closer in the snow towards his big brother. *There was no pup like Orion*, he thought. *There will be no wolf either.*

The Lone Rocks came, clutches strong. They charged up the hill through the Tree trunks and skidded to a stop in the snow, just down the hill from Watcher's father and the ring of Gray Woods wolves. Their lips rolled back over their fangs. Their midnight fur bristled. Growls rumbled in their throats. From their midst strode their lord, flanked by the she-wolf and his first lieutenant. Long Tooth had told Watcher stories of them all. The she-wolf was Dark

Fleece, with a soul like winter. The lieutenant was Long Claw, and Watcher could see his namesakes gleaming in the snow. But worse than either of them was the Lord of the Lone Rock Pack – Bone.

His fur was like a night with no moon. His fangs curved like thorns. He stood as tall as Watcher's father, but there was none of Anorak's kindness in his eye – his lone eye. The place where the other eye should have been was only a black pit, white bone piercing the ragged skin about its edges. Watcher could not tear his big eyes away from it.

"Anorak," said Bone, "Lord of the Gray Woods Pack." Bone refused to bow. He spoke the words as though he was choking on sick meat. His hard voice made what little courage Watcher possessed melt, even hiding beside Orion.

"Bone," replied Watcher's father, tilting his head – but never lowering his eyes. "Lord of the Lone Rock Pack. What brings you to us?"

"What brings me here? Why, I was about to ask you the same thing, Anorak. You're standing beside our kill. We've come to give out the shares."

"Your kill? Perhaps your mind is going dull, Bone. But I don't see your tracks leading to or from this red snow."

"This is true, Anorak. Truly, you possess a lordly mind and lordly eyes. But this kill was made on *our* land. Therefore, it belongs to *us!*"

"Your land?" A trace of a growl stole into Watcher's father's voice. "Perhaps your snout has gone as dull as your mind, Bone. The Trees between the rivers are clearly marked by me and belong to the Gray Woods Pack, as they have since the time of my father's father. You know the Ancient Laws. You know—"

"The Ancient Laws?" Bone snarled, his voice echoing through the woods. Watcher felt the wolves about him dig in their heels and tremble with quiet growls. "You and your family have always been the first to spout the old ways when they serve your purpose, and quick to forget them when they do not! What do the Ancient Laws say about stealing, Anorak? For you know as well as I that this land once belonged to the Lone Rock Pack. And I say it still does!"

"Your father's father lost these lands when he raided the territory of the Grey Woods Pack, Bone. Your father made the same claims as you, moons and moons ago, when we were both young. He went to war over it – or have you've forgotten how that ended as well?"

Bone's good eye twitched. His lightless fur bristled higher. "Oh, I remember, Anorak. I will *always* remember. But things change, oh great Lord of the Gray Woods. The Lone Rock Pack grows and grows. Our young are strong."

"Whereas the Gray Woods Pack grows weaker and weaker." This time Dark Fleece spoke. She inched a bit further up the hill, staring at Watcher's mother with a cruel smile on her lips. "It is whispered amongst the Trees that you have given birth to a lame leg and a dull snout. That you let them *live*. Your will is as weak as your blood, Summer."

Watcher felt a prick on his insides, as though he'd run his heart through a bramble brush, ripping and tearing it as he went. *Even the other packs know about me. They know about my leg. They would have let me die for it.* Maybe it would have been better if the Great Crown and run him down, Watcher thought.

"You would be wise to mind your tongue about my litter, she-wolf," said Watcher's mother. He had never heard her voice shake so. He had never seen her fur bristle. "There is more to a wolf than teeth and claws. The strength of the Gray Woods Pack will show itself true before all is said and done."

"Enough talk!" roared Bone. "Give us the Great Crown, Anorak. Or we will turn the snow on this hill red as the setting sun."

"Great Crown?" said Anorak. Watcher heard a smile on his father's voice. "Oh, do you mean our *chieftain*?" Watcher's father stepped aside. When Bone and his pack saw the length and breadth of the antlers and the size of the beast within the ring of wolves, their eyes went moonround and even their snarls failed.

"Your pack has brought down a chieftain?" said Long Claw. It seemed to Watcher he still did not believe.

"Not my pack," said Anarok. "My *son*."

It was only then that Bone, Long Claw, and Dark Fleece saw Orion atop the hill, and Watcher was sure that their bristling fur all but fell flat. Watcher's father was a powerful wolf, powerful enough to stand against any lord. But Orion, only a wolfling, already looked strong enough to best the world.

"Do you still doubt the strength of our blood, Lone Rocks?" asked Watcher's mother.

But Bone only heaped more hate over his surprise. His lips trembled. His fur bristled again. When he spoke, his words were a rumble.

"This is *our* land, Anorak. That is *our* kill."

"Then come and take it, Bone," Anorak replied.

"Be careful what you ask for, Anorak."

Watcher's chest nearly burst. He was sure a war was about to break out all around him. But before the wolves could come to fighting, a shrieking voice descended from above, falling out of the gray sky to land on the very same branch where Watcher's fat sparrow had sat only a short while ago.

"Hold! Hold! Let there be no fighting here today between you ridiculous wolves! What in blazes is going on?" said the voice.

"This is none of your concern, Frost Feather, you old *crow*," said Bone to the bird, who was not a crow, but an owl. Her feathers might have once been brown, but they had turned silver with the years, and upon her head they formed horns like those of the Great Crowns. Long Tooth had once told Watcher that Lady Frost Feather was far older than even he was, and that she had been the Keeper of the Ancient Laws in the woods since Long Tooth's father's father had loped through the Trees. But Watcher knew this best about the owl: she'd always been kind to him and taught him everything he wanted to know about the Old Forest.

"Not my concern? Not my concern?" Frost Feather ruffled her gray wings and nearly twisted her head around in a full circle. "I am the Keeper in these woods, Bone, you furry fool. It's *all* my concern. And it is my duty to make such business the concern of all Forest Folk, from the Great Fields to the Fallen Tree Bridge."

"Lady Frost Feather, you are most welcome here," said Anorak, bowing his head to the owl. "It seems the Lone Rock Pack has forgotten where their borders lie."

"Another lie!" growled Bone. "We remember well where our true borders—" But Frost Feather cut him off with a sharp twill.

"I have ears to hear, Bone, you wretched dog. I have heard your bellyaching until those ears have burned from it. Perhaps you do remember where your father's father's lands once stretched, but you have forgotten that we owls were blessed by the Trees with eyes round enough to see the world, and deep enough to hold all we have seen in the well of our minds. I watched your father raid the Gray Woods and I watched him fall in defeat. And I watched *you*, Bone, you and all the hate in your heart. For his crimes, your father lost his borderlands to a pack more deserving of their riches."

"A *better* pack? You think following some *laws* make a pack better or more deserving?" raged Bone. "I say *strength* is the only true test of a wolf's worth. And the Gray Woods Pack grows weak. I demand a challenge with Anorak, that we might stake our claim and win back what is ours. I have the right!"

"Indeed you do, Bone," replied Lady Frost Feather. "But you don't choose the times for such things. I do. As the owls and the birds always have. And if there are two things I know about wolves, Bone – and I know a great deal – it is that wolves can't think straight around red snow or under a full moon. Therefore, a challenge shall never be held before either. That is the law! Or perhaps I should let the Far Runners know you have broken that one as well?"

At mention of the Far Runners Bone finally ceased his raging. *Far Runners.* Watcher thought about them the way he thought about a dream: something that was both real and not. But Watcher could still hear the growl thrumming in Bone's chest. He could still see the hate roiling in the Lone Rock Pack's eyes.

"If not now, when, you old witch?" Bone finally muttered.

"In but another day we shall have the night with no moon," said Frost Feather. "And such black nights are when you idiot wolves have about you the most of what little wits the Trees felt necessary to plant in your tiny heads! Perhaps then you will see the wisdom of waging war with words over teeth, Bone. All heart, are wolves, the Tress help us! All heart and no mind at all!"

"My lieutenants and I will meet you at that time, Bone," said Anorak, again bowing his head, but keeping his eyes on his enemy.

"So be it," Bone replied. He did not bow his head at all but only barked to his pack. They turned with him, running off through the snow and the Trees, back to their own lands.

When the Lone Rock Pack was finally out of sight Watcher breathed again, for what felt like the first time since the Great Crown had nearly trampled him. His body ached as though he'd loped to the Wide River and back again. But Orion was still smiling, and he nuzzled his snout against Watcher's.

"See little brother? Nothing to worry about. Not with father here now. Not with me here for moons to come."

As safe as his brother's promise made him feel, Watcher couldn't help but notice Frost Feather flap down from her branch and land before his father. He couldn't help but hear her words to the Lord of the Gray Woods Pack.

"I will be there at the challenge, Anorak," said Frost Feather. "But be on your guard. When you hollowed out Bone's eye as a young wolf, you hollowed out his heart. He has filled it with hate. His roots are twisted, and I fear what fruit they will bear. Beware! Beware!"

5

The Gray Woods stretched all the way from the Twisting Creek in the east to the Wide River in the West. It was home to countless Forest Folk. Its Trees nested flocks of birds. Its glades crawled with squirrels and badgers. The Great Crowns ran in clutches amongst the pines, whose trunks were as gray as the wolves who called the woods home. Even in the spring a mist the color of storm clouds lay thick over the land. Thus the Woods had always been gray, and always would be. It was a good land, a far-reaching land, and through its Trees Lord Anorak and his pack ran.

Long lopes like this one were the hardest for Watcher, especially in winter when the snow lay deep. He picked his way the best he could through the white divots and icy ridges. But as always, his lame leg dragged in the snow, slowing him down. He tumbled head first into the ground time and time again.

But he never gave up and he never stayed down for long. For Watcher had a secret fear about these long lopes, one that he never told even Orion or Glimmer. He was terrified that one day he would reach the place where his pack's scent last lingered, only to find them long since moved on, leaving him alone – ridding themselves of his burden. So whenever Watcher fell he sprang up right away and kept on running.

Watcher was the last pup in his litter receive his name, as with all other things. Old Long Tooth had said this was because his mother was waiting to see if he would die. But he didn't. "There was just too much in the world for you to see to die so young," said the old wolf with a laugh. "Even then you would watch every bird and every bug that crossed your path, as if it was the most interesting thing in the world. We thought perhaps the Trees had made a mistake, and that an owl had been born in a wolf's body – an owl with a broken wing." And so they called him Watcher – after they were sure he would live.

You gave birth to a lame leg and a dull snout, and you let them live. Dark Fleece's words echoed in Watcher's ears. Had he been born to the Lone Rocks they would not have waited for fate to take its course. Runts and cripples were burdens to the pack. But as thankful as Watcher was for his family, sometimes his heart felt as lame as his leg. Today he'd been given a chance at the first share, but he'd never tasted it. *And I never will,* he reminded himself. *But just be thankful for what you've got, Watcher!*

Watcher was so caught up in his own thoughts that he didn't notice Windy until he'd nearly run her over. It was the first time Watcher could remember catching another wolf on a long lope.

"What are you doing back here, Windy?" he asked. "Are you hurt?" Watcher could tell right away that something was wrong with his sister, but it was not with her body. As she waded through the deep snow, marked with the footprints of the pack, she kept looking back over her shoulder, her snout trembling in the air.

"I can still smell it, Watcher," she said. "I can still smell the dark *something* in the air, no matter what Kicker says about it. It's *chasing* us."

"You mean Bone and the Lone Rocks?" Watcher remembered Frost Feather's words. *Beware! Beware!*

"Yes. But there was something wrong with that Bone's smell. Something terrible! His scent still lingers, lurking on the wind, closing in."

Watcher didn't know what to make of that. So he stayed by Windy's side and they ran the rest of the way together, until at last she seemed to calm down and the evil smell on the wind seemed farther away.

By the time Watcher and Windy finally reached the pack the old wolves had already eaten the shares brought back from the kill and most of the hunters and lieutenants were cleaned and lain down for the evening.

Watcher's mother waited for him and his sister beside a rock at the front of a clearing, which sat at the foot of a tall hill, marked by a fallen tree. "Finally home," she said, leaning over to lick both of their faces. Watcher's mother always waited for him, no matter how long it took for him to catch up.

"Hello, mother," said Watcher. "Where's Orion?" Watcher's mother shook her head and laughed.

"I hope you'll ask so eagerly for me one day. But there's no escaping bath time, especially not after your big day."

"But I need to talk to him. This is important!" He wanted to ask Orion about what Windy had smelled. It always made him feel better to talk with Orion.

"So is getting clean, Watcher. Now come on. You won't see your brother for a while anyway. Soon he will go up the hill to speak with your father."

Watcher looked past his mother and over the fallen tree. The setting sun's red light was creeping through the clouds past the mountains to fall on the hillcrest. There Watcher could see the great silhouette of Lord Anorak, sitting tall on his haunches and staring out toward the horizon.

"What are they going to talk about?" Watcher asked. His mother didn't answer right away. Something about her quiet unsettled Watcher more than a little.

"That's between them," she said after a while. "What's between us right now is a good cleaning. So come on with you."

"Well, tell me all about it, Watcher," said his mother as she gave him his bath. All his siblings were already finished and lying with the wolves in a ring at the foot of the hill, waiting for Long Tooth to tell a story.

"All about what?"

His mother laughed again. "So, you've already forgotten about your adventure with the Chieftain of the Great Crowns, have you? No wolf has brought down a chieftain alone since before my mother's mother's time."

"Oh, that."

Watcher looked away as his mother cleaned around his lame leg. He hated when she cleaned there. Hated when she had to touch it.

"Is that all you have to say about it? *Oh that?*"

"Well, I-" More than anything, Watcher wished his brother's story had been true. He wished he *had* planned to have the Great Crown's antler's ensnared in the branches. He wished he had *truly* earned a first share. "It wasn't really a plan to lead the Great Crown under the Tree. It just sort of happened." Watcher hung his head. But he heard a quiet smile in his mother's voice.

"Watcher, let me ask you a question. Were you there when the chieftain charged?"

"Yes, mother."

"Did you stand under its hooves as it came for you? Keeping just out of reach, so as to not be killed?"

Watcher thought back. Those few breaths seemed to have lasted a whole day and a whole night. He could remember every moment. "I guess so."

"And did the chieftain's horns indeed become ensnared in the branches of the tree as it charged after you? Allowing your brother to make his run?"

"It did slow him down, now that I think about it."

"Well, then it is sounds very much like what your brother said actually happened, doesn't it?" Watcher looked up and found the smile he'd heard in full bloom on his mother's face. Her eyes were wise and gentle, like the sunrise. Watcher couldn't help but wag his tail.

"I guess it does, doesn't it?"

"So then, why did you give away the first share your father offered you?"

Watcher's tail stopped wagging. He looked back to the snow between his paws. After a moment he said: "I can't hunt. I can't fight. I can't *really* earn my own share."

"Watcher—" his mother began. But Watcher asked a question – *the* question – before she could finish.

"Why did you let me live, mother? Lady Dark Fleece said today that everyone knew that you'd let me and Glimmer live. She said it made our blood – our pack – weak. So why did you?"

There was quiet after his words. Watcher smelled a change come over his mother. It wasn't anger exactly, and Watcher again wished he possessed Windy's snout so he could know for sure. But after a while, when he thought she might say nothing at all, his mother leaned down and whispered to into his ear: "follow me now, my son."

Watcher's mother led him around the base of the hill, away from the fallen tree and the rest of the pack, until the other wolves' voices faded away. Watcher followed her large, perfect tracks in the snow, marring them with his dragging sets of three.

They went on for a while, out of the clearing and into the shadowy woods. In the back of his mind Watcher wondered about his mother's change in smell. A sudden terror welled up in his chest. *What if she's changed her mind?* he thought. *What if I am a shame upon her blood?* For a moment, Watcher saw himself lying in the red snow, that very night, his mother at last relieving her disgrace with the mercy of her teeth. She was a she-wolf and Lady of the Gray Woods Pack. Watcher thought even Lady Frost Feather wouldn't stop her from doing it.

By the time his mother called a halt, Watcher's three good legs were shaking. He told himself that he would at least have the courage not to run – as though he could escape if he tried.

"Watcher, look at me."

Watcher could hardly stand to. But at long last, when he had felt neither his mother's bite nor heard her speak again, he did. There were no bared fangs looming over him. Just the sunrise in his mother's eyes. She had not changed her mind about him after all.

The two of them stood in another small clearing at the roots of a tall Tree. It was not just any Tree, but a great pine, taller than all her sisters, stretching her green raiment to the fur gray sky.

"Look at this goddess of the forest, Watcher. Is she not glorious?"

"Yes, mother," Watcher said, only just finding the courage to speak again.

"It was under this very Tree that you and your littermates were born. Now, look here. Down in the snow." His mother's voice fell back to a whisper. She led Watcher to the roots, where a clutch of cones lay in the white dust. She took one of the brown things in her teeth and shook it. Little bits dropped out, like brown snowflakes on the ground. "Do you know what those are, Watcher? Those little brown nothings on the ground?"

"Just bits of a cone?" Watcher guessed, but his mother shook her head.

"They are the Children of the Trees."

"These? These little kernels?"

"Yes. Not all of them take root. Some of them blow away in the wind, never to be seen again. Some grow into the bent woods like those in the lands of our cousins to the north. But some of them become goddesses of the forest, like this one, and they give life to all the world."

Watcher looked up from the seed, no more than a speck on the snow, to the branches that spread out above him. He found his mother also facing the Tree, her head bowed low.

"Could you ever guess that such a child could grow to be such a lady, Watcher? I couldn't, not until my mother taught me the same lesson when I was just a pup. No one knows the end of a story before it's told. And I, for one, would rather give the story a chance before passing judgment, wouldn't you?"

Watcher could not fight the hot warmth flooding his eyes. "Yes, I would," he said. He nuzzled up close to his mother. She licked him soft on the top of his head. Then the two of them walked back to the pack, side by side.

6

When Watcher reached the fallen tree his mother left him and went to join the lieutenants and the hunters. The sun was nearly set, tracing a burning red ribbon across the darkening hillcrest. It was almost time for another of Long Tooth's story, and Watcher was supposed to go sit with the others in the ring to wait. But in the fading glow he saw a shadow climbing the hill behind him. Orion was going to speak with Father.

A flutter of curiosity stole into Watcher's chest. He snuck a glance at his littermates sitting beside the fallen tree, Glimmer whispering to Windy and Kicker pretending not to care. They hadn't seen him yet.

With a dash of the courage that so often sent Watcher chasing bugs and burrowers in the summer, he crept up the hill. Right before the crest he managed to find a hiding spot in a nook between two rocks, where he wedged himself just as Orion sat down beside Lord Anorak.

"Were you waiting for nightfall to come sit beside me, Orion?" Anorak growled, but Watcher could hear the laughter behind the rumble. "I could feel myself growing older and grayer as you crawled up the hill like a timid bug."

"So is it a race then, Father?" Orion said with a happy bark, jumping on his feet. "Or are you finally going to give me a chance to pin you again?"

Invisible teeth nipped at the back of Watcher's throat. When the litter had been even smaller than they were now, still covered in their puffy fur, Anorak had wrestled and raced them all. Even Watcher. He would use one paw to bat Watcher around or pin him to the snow. How it had made Watcher laugh.

But now the litter was getting older and bigger. Wrestling and racing had become training. To hunt and to fight. Watcher still loved to sit by as Orion and Father went round and round. It was glorious – even frightening. But as with most things, that was all Watcher could do. Watch and wish.

"Don't tempt me Orion," said Anorak, snapping playfully at Orion's snout. "You may be big and you may be strong, but the old wolves still have their tricks."

"I'm learning your tricks, Father," said Orion. "One day you won't be able to pin me anymore!"

"That day may already be here. But calm down, Orion, and sit for the Trees' sake. We have words alone to share tonight."

Orion finally settled again on the snowy hilltop. He and Father faced the West, where a rift in the gray sky had torn over the White Mountain, loosing what was left of the falling sun's red light.

"Do you see them, Orion?" Anorak asked. "The Great Pack in the Sky? There are so few days in winter when they show themselves. But do you see them tonight? Running over the Mountain?"

Watcher couldn't help himself. He poked his head a bit further from the rocks, risking sight by the wolves at the bottom of the hill. He had to see. Only once before had Lord Anorak shown his children the Sky Wolves, back in the spring. But here they were again in white and gray, the shapes of great wolves' heads in the sky, racing across the last edge of the sun in gold and red and purple.

"They are the spirits of the great wolves sent into the sky's endless fields. There it is always spring. There they can run and not grow tired. There they never need howl for the lack of a friend."

"You'll be there one day won't you, Father?" asked Orion. Watcher certainly thought so. There was no other wolf like his father. None except for Orion.

But Anorak only laughed and shook his head. "No, my son, I don't think so. When I leave the woods I will do so with my head held high, and I shall know no shame when my body returns to the roots of the Trees. But there shall be no lope to the sky for me."

Watcher's heart skipped a thump. He thought he saw Orion's shadow shift nervously on the hill. It was hard for Watcher to imagine a Gray Woods without his father. *But why wouldn't the Trees send him to join the Sky Pack?* The same question must have leapt onto Orion's face, for Anorak said:

"Don't fear for me, my son. Didn't I just tell you that when I leave the woods I will do so without shame? Orion, what were the first lessons I taught you and your littermates from the Ancient Laws?"

Watcher remembered. His father hadn't taught him many lessons – not as many as his brothers and sisters anyway – but this one he had taught them all. He whispered the words to himself as his brother said them aloud.

"First: the Trees gave birth to the wolves. Not to rule over the Forest, but to give it order. Second: the other creatures of the Forest, the Forest Folk, are older than the wolves and wiser, so they are to be respected, especially the Great Crowns. And third: wolves are not like the other creatures. They do not burrow and they do not nest. The have no hole. The pack is their only home."

"The pack is their only home," Anorak repeated. As he spoke, the sun finally fell beneath the world and the Sky Pack seemed to disappear into the night. "Orion, when I do leave the woods I will not go to the sky because I have done only what a wolf *should* do. And I am proud. I am proud of this pack. I am proud of my wife and her children. I am proud of you. From the day you were born all the old wolves foresaw the time when you would take my place at the head of the Gray Woods Pack. That is why we gave you an old name, like mine, from the time of the First Wolves."

The skipping thump in Watcher's chest beat even harder now. Every wolf in the pack knew Orion would be the next lord, and perhaps only Kicker was unhappy about it. But there was something at the edge of Anorak's voice. Watcher could hear it. He could smell it on his father's fur. Something that would threaten that sure vision of the future.

"As proud as I would be to leave these woods knowing you would take my place, my son, I would be prouder still to see you ramble before that day comes."

All the breath slipped from Watcher's lungs. He sat frozen still between his rocks. Only his lame leg, hanging slack beneath his breast, dared to quiver.

"Ramble, father?" Orion said, his voice just as shaky as Watcher's body. "Ramble where? What pack in all the Forest is as noble as the Gray Woods Pack? Choose another wolf to be your successor, but don't cast me out!"

"Still yourself, Orion. Listen. I'm not talking about casting you out. I'm talking about the Far Runners."

A quiet fell over the hilltop at the mere mention of the name, as thick as the night taking hold of the world. Now Watcher understood.

"The Far Runners are the greatest pack of Wolves in the world," Anorak continued. "Only the strongest. Only the fastest. Only the most true. They keep justice between the other packs. They parlay with the older, wiser creatures of the Forest. It is said they even entreat with the Trees themselves. My son, when I see you I see a wolf that might grow to become greater than me. I see a wolf that can do *more* than what a wolf *should* do."

Even as his chest went hollow and his throat turned into a tight knot, Watcher knew his father was right. *There was no pup like Orion,* Glimmer had said. How right she had been. Watcher felt suddenly tugged in two, as if two wolves seized him at once by the snout and the tail to tear him apart. He wanted this for his brother, maybe more than Orion wanted it for himself. But if this dream were to come true, it would mean Orion would go away. It would mean he would leave Watcher behind.

"If I were to go, Father, who then would take your place here?"

"I can't say for certain, really. At least, not yet. But I think Kicker will grow to be fast and strong. He is eager and willing to learn. Perhaps he will take my place."

Fear stabbed Watcher like a sharp thorn in the soft pad of his paw. Orion's shadow took another start in the darkness.

"But Kicker doesn't love Watcher or Glimmer, Father. What about them? You know what he did to Watcher earlier today."

"I know how you feel about your brother, Orion. But as I said after the hunt, Watcher is a Gray Woods Wolf. Three legs or not. He must learn to look out for himself. He must learn to make his own way."

"But Father—"

"Peace, Orion." Orion's father cut him off, but not unkindly. Not with a growl. "I meant to honor you with this talk, not trouble your mind. Just sit here with me for a while. Don't speak about this with your littermates or with the other wolves. No need to dwell on it too deeply for now. There's still time, my son. Time to see and to learn and to decide. There's still time for nights like this – you and me, sitting together, father and son. It's not as though I'm leaving the woods tomorrow."

So Orion sat in quiet with his father upon the hilltop as Watcher slunk back down the hill. His mind was tumbling like a rolling rock. Watcher had nearly been killed by a Great Crown earlier in the day. Then Windy had smelled her *darkness*. And Bone and his Lone Rocks had challenged his father. But none of those things terrified Watcher more than the thought of his father leaving the woods and his brother rambling away. Of being left alone.

7

Winter nights in the Gray Woods were as quiet as a frozen river and lonesome as the moon. The bugs that Watcher loved to chase in the spring were gone. The birds were huddled silent in the Trees, save for the owls who kept the watches of the night. But the pack had each other, and the snowy evenings were the perfect time for Long Tooth's stories.

Long Tooth was the oldest wolf in the woods. His fur had gone thin, his teeth and claws brittle, his once bright eyes dulled by time. But Watcher thought that perhaps only Frost Feather the Owl remembered more, for Long Tooth was the teller of a wood's worth of tales.

Watcher remembered every story Long Tooth had ever told. Sometimes he dreamed he was the hero wolf in the tales. Not a runt. Not lame. Strong. Fast. Loved. But that night, behind Watcher's troubled eyes, all he could see was Orion. His brother could be a great wolf, Watcher knew. A wolf of legend. Not for pretend, like Watcher's daydreams. For real.

That night, as the crescent moon rose over the ring of wolves lying at the foot of the hill by the fallen tree, Long Tooth went far back in time for his tale – all the way to the beginning. That night he told the story of Romulus, the first wolf.

"Long, long ago, when all the Forests in the whole world covered but a single hill and a single field, and the Moon had yet to turn her face from us in the sky, Father Earth brought up from the dirt the beasts of the field – the Forest Folk." Long Tooth's old voice was quiet but strong. When he told his stories it was rare to hear another wolf dare to breathe.

"They were many in number and vast in assortment, but the first of the Children of the Earth were the Great Crowns, the bucks and the does. Their feet were light and their legs were strong. The crowns upon their heads were as curved and as beautiful as the branches of the great Trees. These were the crowns of princes and princesses, for they were the nobility of the young world. Father Earth took great joy in watching them leap up and touch the sky. The sound of their laughter filled him with pride.

"At first, the Forest Folk ate only the dirt from the ground, for that is from whence they came. And even the Trees, the old goddesses, watched over the Great Crowns and the others as mothers would. But one day, tired of the same old dirt day after day and lacking anything better to do, one of the young princes tasted a leaf from a low hanging branch. Its taste was sweeter than the purest water. Its sustenance gave him power to leap even higher and farther. So he brought his brothers and sisters leaves to taste and, before long, the Great Crowns had abandoned the dirt for the grass of the clearings and the leaves of the Trees.

"The Trees called out to Father Earth to control his children, but he was an indulgent father. He could not deny them this unexpected pleasure. So the Trees turned to the Sun and the Moon, rulers of the day and the night. But they replied: "what have we to do with the goings on upon the land?"

"So at last, when nearly everything that was green had been stripped from the earth and all was as brown as the dirt itself, the

Mother of all Trees, the oldest and most powerful goddess, took action. She too gave birth to creatures of the forest. Her children were the wolves.

"The first and greatest of the wolves was Romulus, father and lord over all others. It was to him the command was given to bring balance back to the world. If the Children of the Earth were to enjoy the green of the Trees, then the Children of the Trees were to enjoy the red of the Forest Folk.

"At first Father Earth was angry at the Trees. But he could not destroy them, for not only were the old goddesses almost as strong as he, but if they were gone, what green things would his children enjoy? So he tried to destroy the wolves instead. He sharpened the crowns and hooves of his children to make the red fur on the wolves. He rolled his rocks down his hills to crush them. He plotted with the Sky to create winter and freeze them solid. But the Trees had born their children well.

"The wolves could run and not grow tired. They could see in the night as though it were day. They could smell the Forest Folk, no matter how carefully hidden. But most importantly of all, Romulus had the power to make the Trees the wolves' home. If a wolf was in trouble, surrounded by sharp antlers or threatened by rolling rocks, all Romulus had to do was howl and the Trees would open up their wombs again to hide the wolves inside until danger had passed.

"And so, for a time, balance seemed to return. The green things grew again. But, as Father Earth had underestimated the hunger of his children, so had the Trees underestimated the thirst of theirs. The red that flowed from the Forest Folk began to drive the wolves mad. They could not stop themselves from feeding. The Great Crowns gave up their fighting and ran in terror. The Sun was horrified by the killing. Even the Moon was forced to turn her back on the woods. Father Earth was so heartbroken for his children that he cried tears that flowed through the land and became the rivers and creeks. But as long as the wolves could hide in the Trees, neither the Great Crowns, nor the Sky, nor the Moon, nor Father Earth could stop them.

"Yet in this darkest time, when the forest was threatened to be flooded with the red and drowned, it was not any of the old goddesses or gods who found a solution. It was Romulus. He too looked upon the heedless destruction wrought by his people and was ashamed. He knew they had been born to bring order, not chaos. Romulus realized that the wolves had become too powerful, that their power had to be weakened to restore balance again.

"So Romulus went to the top of a tall hill, all alone. He growled at Father Earth in challenge. He snarled at the Sun in disrespect. He flashed his teeth and claws at all the Great Crowns. So angry did he make all his foes that they turned on him as one. But when they came with their winter winds, thunderous lightning, and sharpened horns, Romulus refused to howl. He refused to use his gift to hide in the Trees. He left himself out in the open. He let them strike him down so that his own red watered the earth.

"Then Father Earth, the Sun, the Moon, and the Great Crowns understood what Romulus had done. The wolves no longer had a home. They could no longer hide from the dangers of the world. They had been made mortal again. By sacrificing himself, Romulus had restored balance once and for all.

"In honor of Romulus's great deed, Father Earth still cries tears to water the earth and remind us of his courage. The Moon still turns her back on the world to remind us why he died. And the Trees took Romulus's spirit and set it loose in the smoke caused by the lightning from the sky, letting it travel to the endless blue fields, to remind all creatures what the Lord of the Wolves had done."

When Long Tooth finished his story all the wolves in the pack were quiet. Watcher could hear his blood thrumming in his ears. For a moment he imagined himself running with that

First Pack – whole and perfect, running right beside Orion. He imagined it so hard that for a breath he almost believed he could be fast enough to chase Orion down if he ever left, to join him with the Far Runners.

Then Watcher's father rose and stood in the center of the ring, standing tall under the blue light of the moon. He spoke to the pack and said: "This is why wolves have no home but each other. This is why we must respect the Great Crowns and all the other Forest Folk. This is why we must each strive for greatness, that perhaps one among our number might one day rise through the Trees to run in the endless blue fields with the Lord of the Wolves."

As Watcher's father spoke, his eyes passed over his pack. But before they could reach Watcher they came to rest on Orion. There they stayed, so full of pride and hope that Watcher thought they might burst into light.

Watcher was glad for his brother. But his soul became quiet. His burning blood cooled. The soft place within him that was as lame as his leg ached again, like a freshly formed bruise.

8

Watcher said goodbye to his father and mother the next afternoon. The pack gathered in the circle by the fallen tree as old Long Tooth asked the Trees for good fortune. Watcher's father told them all not to worry, that between he and Lady Frost Feather they would talk some sense into "that rascal, Bone." Watcher's mother left all her children a lick on the cheek. But she gave Watcher two, one on each side of his face.

The moment their parents had left, Watcher and the others ran all the way to the top of the hill to watch them go. Lady Frost Feather flew above the party, off into the distance until she was nothing but a dark speck against the gray sky.

Watcher lay next to Orion in the snow, the two of them competing to catch the last glimpse of their parents through the Trees. It was the only game Watcher could ever win. Glimmer sat nearby with Windy, who seemed to have fallen ill since last night. She had hardly spoken a word since telling Watcher about the dark smell. Even then she held her uncanny nose to the air, tracking her parents' scent for as long as she could. Behind them all, Kicker lay in the snow, looking off in the other direction, toward the White Mountain, still pretending not to care.

"So what were you really doing out there?" Orion asked Watcher after neither of them could see Lord Anorak or Lady Summer anymore.

"Out where?"

"Out on the hill beneath that Tree. Yesterday. You know, when the gigantic Great Crown nearly trampled you to pieces? Remember?"

"Nothing really. Windy could smell the hunt drawing near. So I was looking for another hill to sit on."

"Stop lying, Watcher," growled Kicker, without bothering to turn over or even lift his head from the snow. "That's why you went, but that's not what you were *doing.*"

"I don't remember asking you, *scat kicker,*" said Orion dangerously.

"Besides," added Glimmer. "Watcher wouldn't have even been there if you hadn't kicked him down the hill. How would you have felt if he would have been killed?"

"Well he wasn't killed, was he?" said Kicker. "The Great Crown ended up stuck in those branches and *Orion the Almighty* got his chieftain. If anything, the two of you should be thanking me."

"Well, you did get your first share, didn't you?" Watcher heard a growl under Orion's breath. Kicker must have heard it too, for he wisely said nothing, allowing himself only a small snort in the snow, announcing itself with a brief puff of white. "So," said Orion again, turning back to Watcher. "What *were* you really doing?"

"I was watching a sparrow land on a tree."

Orion smiled and managed a laugh, but his eyes never left Watcher's face. If there was one thing that Watcher loved most about his oldest brother it was that. He always waited to hear not just what Watcher watched, but what he *saw.*

"And?"

"Well, at first I thought it was strange that such a fat sparrow could even fly, much less sit on a slender branch and not break it. But then I was thinking, it's not really the bird that's flying, is it? The wind is holding it up. And it's not just the branch that's holding the bird when it lands. It's the Tree. Then it didn't seem strange to me at all. I don't think small things can hold big things, at least not for very long. But the big things, things as big as the wind and the Trees, they can hold all the small things. Maybe forever."

Watcher and Orion sat quietly for a while, first looking at each other, then out toward the gray horizon. Orion seemed to hold on to Watcher's words in his closed mouth, as though tasting them on his tongue.

"The big things can hold the small. Maybe forever," he said after a time. "I wish I saw birds and Trees the way you do, Watcher."

"Oh yeah, *big* things and *small* things," Kicker threw in from behind them. "Watcher's as wise as an owl."

"I've had just about enough of you!" Orion snapped, moving to get up. But Watcher stayed him with a look. It was better if they didn't fight. Watcher knew Orion would win. But later *he* and Kicker would be alone, and Kicker would make *him* pay for it. When nothing happened, Kicker huffed up another spurt of snow.

"Maybe they should have named you *Snorter*," said Glimmer, throwing Watcher and Orion a wink.

"Can I ask you a question, Orion?" said Watcher, after the litter had gone quiet again.

"As long as you don't expect an answer like one of yours."

"What do you mean?"

"It's like I was saying - I wish I could see the world the way you do. The way Father does."

For all his life Watcher had only been compared to other creatures, be they clumsy badgers, creeping bugs, or even the owls. But he'd never been compared to another wolf before, much less his father, the Lord of the Gray Woods. Moments like those made Watcher all the more sure that his brother was the greatest wolf in the woods.

"You probably do see the world like Father, Orion, and just don't know it," said Watcher, after he'd stopped trembling with joy. Then he swallowed hard and asked his question. "Do you – Do you want to be like Father? Do you want to rule the Gray Woods?"

Orion sat quiet and still. Watcher could tell his brother was wrestling with his words. That made Watcher queasy inside. He and Orion had held secrets *between* each other before. But never *from* each other. That's what Orion was wrestling with now. Watcher was sure of it. Whether or not to tell him his secret.

"I don't know if I can be like Father," Orion said after a while, his eyes to the snow. "I just want to be the best wolf I can be."

"Oh, just stop already, will you?" said Kicker, still staring off toward the mountains. "Everyone knows it's only a matter of time before *Almighty Orion* runs the pack."

But Watcher saw it then. It passed over his brother's face like a blue-lit cloud across the moon. It was something he rarely ever saw in Orion's eyes. It was doubt. Maybe it was even fear. *He does want to go,* Watcher thought. A cold trickle crept down into his stomach like freezing ice.

"So you don't ever think about leaving?" Watcher said, not much more than a whisper. An ache began to burn in his chest. "You don't ever think about *rambling.*"

When Orion said nothing and only kept staring into the snow, Watcher felt hot tears melt the terrible cold that had settled over his soul. *You can't leave!* He wanted to cry out. *You can't! You can't leave me alone!* He suddenly realized that all of his littermates were now staring at Orion with him. Even Kicker had finally lifted his head from the snow and turned back to face them. Only Windy, still lost in her trance, seemed oblivious.

"Ramble?" Kicker said, disbelieving.

"That's crazy, Watcher," said Glimmer. "Why would Orion ever ramble? He's going to be the next Lord of the Gray Woods."

"The Far Runners," said Watcher. It broke his heart to say it. For even as Orion opened his mouth to deny it he could see in his brother's eyes that it was true – and that it was what he wanted, in his deepest soul, more than anything.

"Nothing's been decided," said Orion, fumbling for his words. "We were just talking. I—"

But before he could finish a loud whimpering whined over the hilltop, so loud and so frightened that it startled the wolflings into forgetting all other worries for a moment. It was Windy. She shook as though she'd fallen beneath the ice into the river's cold waters.

"It's still there!" she shrieked. "It's still there and it's getting stronger!"

"It's just Windy smelling her ghosts, again," said Kicker, though he stared at his sister with moonround eyes of his own.

"Shut up, Kicker," snapped Orion. "Glimmer, wake her from her trance. Bite her if you have to!"

Glimmer tried to nuzzle, then shove her sister awake. But after a clutch of tries she gave in to Orion's advice and took the spotted scruff of Windy's neck in her jaws, giving it a firm squeeze. Windy flinched and yelped. She fell over and her eyes finally returned to the snowy hilltop above the fallen tree, until she squeezed them shut, as though trying to forget whatever she had seen.

"What was it, Windy?" said Watcher, gathering close to her with the others. "What's wrong?"

She lay trembling for another long moment. But at last she opened her eyes again and sat up, casting her glance toward the gray horizon where Watcher's father and mother had run.

"It's what I smelled before. The *something*. The darkness. It's come back. But it's getting worse. It's getting *bigger*. And it's not just on the horizon. It's coming closer. It's coming here." Glimmer curled up beside Windy to keep her from shivering, nuzzling her gently.

"Don't worry, Windy," said Orion. "Father and mother will be back soon. We'll tell them about it. They'll know what to do."

"It's just the ghosts," whispered Kicker again. But Watcher wasn't sure that even Kicker believed that this time.

Watcher looked to the horizon with Orion. For a moment he felt he could see the darkness that Windy could smell, crawling across the sky toward the hill where they stood. He hoped and prayed that Father and Mother would be back soon. But in the back of his mind, all he could wonder was that if Orion were to one day ramble, who then would save him from such terrors? For a three legs could never stand against such things alone.

9

Watcher woke with a start in the middle of the night. The hour was dark and the woods beyond the clearing were deepest black, for it was the night the moon turned her back on the world. All around Watcher the Gray Woods Pack slept in twos and threes by the fallen tree, beneath the rattling rumble of old Long Tooth's snores.

Windy's whimpering had woken Watcher up. Even with Glimmer curled up beside her she trembled in the grasp of some nightmare. *It was that smell,* Watcher thought. The one she'd sensed during the hunt. *She'll be better once father and mother return,* Watcher told himself. At least he hoped so. *Father will know what to do. He always knows.*

Watcher stretched, yawned, and gave himself a scratch behind the ears with his good leg. He was about to close his eyes and go back to sleep when he heard an owl's soft hooting. A Tree branch just beyond the clearing rustled. Watcher squinted in the moonless night. He couldn't quite make the bird out in the dark. But there was another soft hoot and the branch shook again. *Could it be a black owl?* Old Long Tooth had once told Watcher that there were owls with feathers so black they were the color of night. But Watcher had never seen one before.

He couldn't help himself. He got up and padded toward the Trees, silent as a shadow through the rows of sleeping wolves. *I'll have to be careful and quiet if I'm going to sneak up on it,* he thought. He heard another hoot. Another branch rustled, this one even deeper in the woods. Watcher sniffed at the air. There was a faint trace of owl, all right. But he was upwind from the bird and once again wishing he had Windy's snout.

Watcher followed the soft hoots, smell, and bobbing branches through the thick Trees, farther and farther from the pack, determined to track down the black owl. But finally he came to stand under a wagging branch where he could hear no more hooting and saw no other bending limbs. *I missed her,* he thought. He was about to turn back for the pack when he caught the scent of another creature lurking beneath the owl's smell.

Watcher scrambled to escape. He was a step too slow. A crushing weight slammed him to the ground. Sharp teeth bit the scruff of his neck. He yelped, but the jaws that held him shoved his snout into the snow, snuffing out his cry for help.

"See what happens when you watch birds instead of your surroundings, *Three Legs?*" a voice hissed in Watcher's ear.

Kicker.

Watcher gave up struggling and squirming. He lay still as his older brother ground his face so far into the snow that his nose touched the cold dirt underneath. *I won't fight it,* Watcher thought. *It's easier that way.* The harder he fought these pouncings the longer they lasted and the worse they got.

"You're not strong enough to defend yourself, Three Legs. So you have to stay vigilant at all times. Father, mother, and Orion have babied you for too long. If Orion rambles and I become the lord of the pack, I won't be so easy. You'll have to learn to pull your own weight!"

Kicker finally released Watcher's neck and let him up to breathe. When Watcher glanced up he found his brother covered in old straw and faded feathers. Kicker had rolled himself in a fallen owl's nest. That's how he had deceived Watcher's snout.

Something hot welled up within Watcher's chest, like a bubble rising up in a river. He knew better than to let it burst. But Kicker had bit his neck raw and had used his love of birds against him, so out it came.

"That's big talk coming from a pup who hasn't even hunted yet, *scat sniffer.*"

Watcher regretted the words the moment they slipped off his tongue. Kicker's fur bristled down his back. His lips peeled away from his fangs. Watcher cowered in the snow as his brother stalked forward.

"You just wait, Three Legs. One day. One day there won't be a father, or a mother, or another brother to rescue you. One day you'll have to stand alone." Kicker coiled up to strike. "We'll see how well you stand on three legs then. One day—"

"But not today."

The new voice startled the growl from Kicker's throat. He was suddenly scrambling as desperately as Watcher had a moment ago. But like Watcher he too was a step slow. Orion leapt from behind a tree and flattened Kicker, turning him over on his back and exposing his belly, snarling into his face. Glimmer and Windy trotted into the clearing behind him, coming to stand beside Watcher and licking the red fur Kicker had left on the back of his aching neck.

"See what happens when you focus on a creature weaker than you instead of minding your surroundings, *scat sniffer?*" Orion's growl filled the clearing. It turned all Kicker's swagger into whimpering yelps. It even frightened Watcher. "I'm tired of all your whining and neck biting, Kicker. Perhaps I need to teach you a lesson that won't heal so quickly. Perhaps I should leave you a scar to help you remember it."

Orion reared back to bite. A panic welled up in Watcher's chest. This wouldn't make things better. It would only make them worse. He was about to say as much when Windy interrupted them both.

"Stop, stop! Be quiet! We must all be quiet, please!"

Orion ceased his snarling and begrudgingly let Kicker up. But his fur still bristled. He came to stand beside Watcher and Windy, whose snout was up in the air and whose eyes had gone moonround yet again.

"Here she goes with her darkness and ghosts again," said Kicker bitterly. But one look from Orion and he clapped his teeth shut.

"It *is* the darkness," said Windy, her whisper rising high and awful. "But it has not come alone. It is no longer just a *something*. The darkness *is* wolves. There are wolves in the woods!"

"Gray Woods Wolves?" asked Glimmer. Her ears pricked up and her lips trembled. With her dull snout she was blind to the forest beyond her sight. "Could it be Father and Mother returning?"

"No," whispered Windy. She began to shake from nose to tail. "I can no longer smell Father and Mother. *Their scents are gone from the wind.* The wolves that come are like shadows. I have smelled them only once before. At the red snow of the chieftain."

"Lone Rock Pack," said Orion. If Watcher had thought he'd seen his brother's fury before, he learned he was wrong. Orion's bristling fur rose even higher. He seemed to grow twice in size. His lips drew back from his teeth. They looked sharp enough to bite through flesh and bone like snow.

As if called by the sound of their name, the woods erupted with the bays of wolves. They were horrible sounds – snarls, growls, and yelps. They froze Watcher's blood and turned his bones to ice. They rang out from direction of the clearing by the fallen tree.

"We're under attack!" cried Orion. "Those cowards!" Orion whipped about in a circle like a giant gone mad with rage. "Kicker, Glimmer, come with me. We're going back to fight. Watcher, stay here with Windy. I'll come back for you after we've run those gutless dogs off!"

Kicker and Glimmer looked to each other. Then Watcher thought he saw Kicker look to him, his eyes wide and round. It was as though he was looking to Watcher to talk Orion out of this, to talk Orion out of taking him to war. For all Kicker's bluster he was afraid, and Watcher could hardly blame him. Watcher was terrified. But it wasn't Watcher who saved them. Another voice floated down through the trees, calling for Orion to stop.

"Stay your anger young prince, as impossible as it might be after you hear what I have to tell you." Lady Frost Feather flapped down from the black sky and landed in a cloud of scattered snow, blocking the litter's path back to the clearing. One of her wings was close to broken, its feathers raked, bent, and torn loose.

"What's happened, Lady Frost Feather?" asked Glimmer, her voice shaking. "Where are our mother and father?"

"Treachery. It was treachery." Watcher heard Frost Feather's agony in her voice. He suddenly wished he were deaf instead of lame. He didn't want to hear what she was about to say. "When your father and mother arrived at the challenge, Bone would hear no words. He wanted to fight. The Ancient Laws are very clear. Such a fight was within his rights. But it was to be wolf against wolf, one against one. But when your father began to fight, when his back was turned–"

Watcher wanted to wretch. He could picture it all in his head. His father facing Bone. His mother looking on. The Lone Rock Pack sneaking in from the shadows. He and his littermates began to whimper. Even Orion. His big brother reared back to unleash his howl to the black night when Frost Feather silenced them all.

"Silence, silence! I know your pain! And I know the wolf's need to share it with the world. But you must not howl, or you'll all die! The Lone Rock Pack has rolled themselves in fallen nests or crawled through badger's tunnels to mask their scent. They snuck up even on me, and nearly had me killed as well. I only just escaped. The entire pack followed your mother and father's trail back to the Gray Woods, to the clearing where your pack slept. I thought I would be too late to save any of you, but the Trees have been kind, and here are at least you five. The last litter of the Gray Woods."

The last, Watcher thought. The words burned like red fur beneath biting teeth. *But what now?*

"Revenge!" Orion growled, as though he could hear Watcher's thoughts. "There is only revenge!" Slather hung from his jaws and his yellow eyes went bright and hot as the summer sun.

"You are truly a great wolf, Orion," said Frost Feather. "You are your father's son. But not even you can fight an entire pack on your own. If you go back tonight, you go to your death. Will you take your brothers and sisters with you? What would your father do, mighty Orion? How would he lead?"

Orion stopped circling and pacing. His breaths came in ragged gasps. He looked over Kicker, Glimmer, and Windy. But it was only when his gaze fell on Watcher that his bristling fur lay flat again and his blazing eyes cooled. Orion opened his mouth, as if he were going to ask Watcher a question, but it was as though he had forgotten the words.

But somehow Watcher knew the question, and somehow he also knew the answer. His father's words came to him like a dragonfly skipping over the grass. "The wolves have no home, Orion. The have only the pack. The pack is their only home."

Orion stared at Watcher for a long moment, then hung his head until his nose touched the snow between his paws. "What can we do, Lady Frost Feather? Where can we go?"

"Tonight you must flee the Gray Woods. Do not dawdle. Do not stop for rest or water or food. Bone has sworn to put all of the Gray Woods Pack to the red snow and claim these lands for himself. He has sworn revenge for the shame done his pack in his father's time.

And Orion, neither he nor Dark Fleece lied when they said their pack had grown in strength. I wouldn't have believed it if I didn't see it with my own eyes. The Lone Rocks are more than a pack now. They are an army!"

Watcher and the others went quieter still. Watcher pictured Bone – the black pit in his eye threatening to swallow him whole – standing before an endless river of midnight furred wolves. Slather dangled from their jaws. Fangs glistened. Watcher thought the fear was going to gobble him up from the inside out.

"But Lady Frost Feather, we've never been beyond the Gray Woods before," said Glimmer. "We don't know anywhere else."

"And we don't know any other wolves. We can't just go running into other pack's territories," said Kicker. "Where can we go?"

"I understand your fears, young ones. I need time to think myself, and time to ask for guidance. Here, smell my feathers." Frost Feather hopped up to Windy, lending her good wing to Windy's snout. "Can you smell the scent of my people, young one? Can you smell the scent of my home?"

Windy breathed deeply of Lady Frost Feather's wings. "Yes, I can smell it." Then she turned her snout to the wind again. "And I can smell it on the air as well. It's faint, but I can just make it out."

"Follow the scent to the Council of the Flyers. I must let my wing rest tonight, for it is nearly broken. I won't be able to keep up with you. But I will meet you there soon if I can. Not all the birds know the ways of wolves, but they are wise in the Ancient Laws. They will give us guidance."

Lady Frost Feather hopped closer to the wolflings, closest of all to Watcher. "You five were born under the sun *and* the moon. Did you know that? We all hoped it was a sign of a new golden age. But I always knew it might have been an omen of darkness. Now I see that for true. But take hope in this: whether it is for light or dark, wolves born under such a sky are wolves born with a destiny. *All of them.*" Frost Feather's big eyes fell on Watcher, and she held him in her gaze for a long moment. "Now go, and take my sorrows and tears with you."

With that the litter began to run. Orion led the way, his big head and shoulders hanging low. His tail all but dragged in the snow behind him. Windy ran beside him, her nose leading the way, with Kicker and Glimmer after. As Watcher followed his throat burned and his eyes stung. Flashes of his mother, his father, and an army of Lone Rock Wolves swirled behind his eyes. But Frost Feather flapped slowly above his head on her wounded wing, whispering to him a few last words.

"Do not give in to despair, my little wolf-son. May your three legs have the strength of four tonight. I saved this last for you alone. Your father's final words were these: He must watch out for him with his eyes. He must see for him the way."

"I won't hold Orion back," Watcher said to the owl, running as fast as he could. "I won't slow the others down."

"No, you don't understand. I don't believe these words were meant for your brother. I think they were meant for you. You have owl's eyes, Watcher. They can see mysteries and secrets if you let them. Use them to look out for the others. Use them to find the way!" Then Frost Feather flapped up to land on a tree branch and rest.

There was no time for Watcher to dwell on her words or what they meant, for if he was to survive the night he had to spend all of his thought and strength on running for his life.

10

The stench of red snow covered the woods. Watcher choked on it. He could taste it on his tongue. It was everywhere. This was no red snow of an honorable hunt. It was the red snow of treachery. It was the red snow of his pack. Of his family.

Tears wet Watcher's fur, slowly freezing into white whiskers as he loped through the woods. Though Frost Feather had warned him and his littermates to run as silently as the snow falls, he could not keep from whimpering. Behind his big owl eyes Watcher could still see the sunrise on his mother's face. He could still feel her warmth as she cleaned him. Her soft snout nuzzling his cheek. Holes broke open within Watcher where his father's voice and old Long Tooth's tales had once been. But knowing that his mother would never again be there waiting for him when he finally caught up with the rest of the pack was the deepest hole of all.

Watcher crested a small hill and found his littermates stopped in the snow. He was about to ask why they'd paused when he followed their eyes. The snow in the clearing by the fallen tree had turned so red it was nearly black. Dark shadows of Lone Rock

Wolves prowled the Gray Woods, baying and howling, driven glee-fully mad by the red snow.

They were all gone, Watcher thought. Long Tooth. The lieu-tenants and the hunters. All of the Gray Woods Pack but the five wolflings upon the hill had left the woods.

Glimmer's whimpers were loudest, louder than even Watcher's. But none of her brothers silenced her. Frozen tears clung to the fur on their faces, even Orion's. But Orion wasn't whimpering. Some brew of a growl and a howl welled up within his chest.

"Betrayers," he rumbled. "False wolves. They have no honor. They have forgotten the Ancient Laws and the Trees that bore them."

Watcher could see that fury light again in his brother's eyes. Orion's fur bristled. He edged toward the slope of the hill that led back to the red clearing and the Lone Rock Pack. *He wants to go back*, Watcher thought. *He wants to fight*. This terrified the tears from Watcher's eyes. What would he do without Orion? He'd lost everyone. He could not lose his brother as well. *Watch out for him*, Frost Feather had said. *Help him see the way*. Had his father's last words really been meant for him? Whether they were or were not, Watcher would not let his brother run to his death.

"We need to make it to the Wide River," Watcher said quietly. "The border of the Gray Woods. Maybe if we cross the river we'll be alright."

"What would you know about it, Watcher?" said Kicker, his snout falling toward the snow. "What do any of us know about any-thing anymore?"

"Frost Feather said that Bone wanted our territory, the Gray Woods. Our territory ends at the Wide River. Perhaps they won't come after us once we're beyond it."

"But Lady Frost Feather also said that Bone wanted revenge on all the Gray Woods Pack," said Glimmer. Her eyes were still fixed on the clearing below. "She said he wanted to put us all in the red snow. What if he doesn't stop at the river?

"Then," said Orion, still staring down the hill with teeth bared, "we will fight."

"We'll find out soon enough what they'll do." Windy's far away voice startled Watcher and the others. "The Lone Rocks know they did not put all the Gray Woods Pack to the red snow. They've caught our scent. They're coming!"

Panic hammered hard in Watcher's breast. He turned to Orion again, pleading. "Let's at least try for the river. Then we can go to Frost Feather's people, to the Council of the Flyers. Orion, please."

"What will it matter?" cried Kicker, his eyes moonround with fear. "We can't all make it anyway."

Watcher knew what Kicker meant by *all*. He meant there was no way a three legs could outrun full grown wolves. But Watcher had made a promise to Frost Feather. He wouldn't hold back his brother or his littermates. He wouldn't slow the pack. For the second time that night he remembered his father's words.

"I'm a Gray Woods Wolf, Kicker. I can make my own mind. And I say we try for the river."

Watcher looked to Orion. All the wolflings did. "I can carry you," Orion said quietly.

Watcher shook his head. "You have to lead the way, Orion. I won't slow you down."

The sound of baying carried up the hill. The call of hunters and war.

"We make for the river," said Orion at last. "No stopping. No turning back, not even to fight." And with that they ran.

Watcher never ran so fast in his life. He fixed his wandering eyes to his path. He picked his way through the Trees and the snow drifts. He smelled Orion in front, slowly pulling farther and farther away.

Yet careful as he was, and though his good front leg burned down to the bone from the effort, Watcher still fell, time and again. Each time he got back up. Each time he sensed he was farther behind. Each time he felt the Lone Rocks draw closer and closer.

Watcher caught Bone's oppressive scent on the wind. It smelled of rotted wood and spoiled flesh, of hate and rage. Bone's ragged growls to his lieutenants and hunters grew loud in Watcher's ears. The sounds and smells of the Lone Rock Pack drowned the scent of his littermates. Watcher cried out with fear when he realized he had lost them.

Distracted, he tripped on a root hidden beneath the snow. The black night and white snow spun all about him as he rolled down a sharp hill into a ravine.

When Watcher lifted his head he knew he was lost. The dark shapes of the Lone Rock Pack appeared between the pines, only a stretch behind him. He tried to get up, but his good leg all but crumpled beneath him, exhausted. Watcher's slather dripped into the snow from his panting mouth.

How could he have ever thought he would escape? *Kicker was right.* He was a lame runt. He was weak blood, just like Lady Dark Fleece had said. But Watcher had made a promise not to slow the others down. So he did not cry for help.

He decided to sit back down and wait for the end. He closed his eyes to say a prayer to the Trees. "Keep my brothers and sisters safe," he whispered. "Help Orion find the way. Help him become a lord of wolves, like he should be." When Watcher finished his prayer he turned away from the hill where the Lone Rocks were coming. He didn't want to be afraid.

Snow soon crunched and branches snapped from the top of the ravine. Then the bushes exploded in a cloud of white dust. A wolf flew through the air, landing in the ravine beside Watcher. But it was no Lone Rock.

Orion.

"You *are* a Gray Woods Wolf, Watcher," he said. "But so am I, and I won't leave you behind!" Before Watcher could say a word he felt Orion's teeth seize the scruff of his neck lift him into the air.

Watcher had seen his brother run before. He had thought it was the most glorious sight in all the woods. But Watcher had not known what speed was until that night. *I'm like the sparrow,* he thought. *Like the sparrow on the wind!* The Trees flew by in a blur. Snowy hills rose and fell under Orion's feet like a ripple on the river. The sound of the Lone Rock's baying and the smell of Bone's hate fell away. Orion flew and flew until the river came into sight.

Watcher caught a breath in his throat. Kicker, Glimmer, and Windy were already on the ice, creeping across the frozen water. Beyond them was only the darkness of unknown Trees: the border of the Gray Woods' territory. Watcher had never expected to see it in his entire life. He always thought he would live and die in the Gray Woods between the Winding Creek and the Wide River.

Barking snapped from just a hill behind. The Lone Rocks drew close. Orion broke from the treeline and reached the icy river-bank, setting Watcher down so they could walk across together.

The ice felt like hard ground beneath Watcher's small paws. But when Orion stepped upon it, the river groaned. The ice moaned and even snapped like a Great Crown tearing through a thicket.

"What is that?" asked Orion, looking down between his paws. "Is the river angry at me, Watcher? Is Father Earth trying to tell me something?"

"I don't think so," said Watcher. "It's the same sound the river makes when spring is coming. When–"

"The ice is breaking," Orion whispered. "But not now, will it? The river is big – like you said – that which is big will hold that which is small?"

"The river *is* big, Orion. But I think the ice is not."

"And I'm the fat sparrow."

"Just go slowly. You can make it!"

But slow was not a choice. A wolf's howl pierced the night. It was not the call of a lowly hunter. It was Bone. Watcher knew he shouldn't, but he couldn't keep from turning over his should and glancing back. Shadows blacker than night slipped through the Trees, careering for the river's edge.

"They'll stop at the border." Watcher whispered, his body trembling. "They'll stop." It was as much a prayer as anything else. But the look in Orion's eyes said otherwise.

"They're not going to stop, Watcher. Keep going. Don't look back. I'll slow them down. I'll put as many to the red snow as my teeth can manage. And Bone. Especially him."

Orion turned to go back to the snowy shore. Watcher didn't know what to say. His brother couldn't fight an entire pack. Watcher couldn't make himself think of his brother in the red snow, not like his father and mother. Orion's first step back to the shore put a crack in the ice, splashing cold river water through the fissure at his paws.

Just then a picture formed behind Watcher's eyes — a mad image — like something from a story. He had an idea.

"Orion! They *will* stop at the river. We'll make them stop. Follow me!" Watcher began to run on the ice. But he didn't head toward the far shore. He went downstream like the fish he liked to watch in the summer. The ice not so much as budged beneath his runt weight. But when Orion followed, it rumbled like distant thunder.

"Watcher, they're getting closer!" Orion shouted. But when Watcher turned and ran back the other way, just a bit closer to the other side, and the cracks in the ice began to spread, Orion understood. "Watcher, I see!" he shouted. "I see what you see! Come on!"

Once more Orion scooped Watcher up in his jaws and began to run. Back and forth along the ice he went, even as the Lone Rock Pack poured down the hill and out of the Trees, rushing toward the river.

"Orion of the Gray Woods!" roared Bone, his voice like falling stones. "Do not run from me. Your father and mother died beneath my teeth. They offered you up to me as a sacrifice if I would spare their lives and leave them with even a corner of their precious Gray Woods."

Watcher yelped as Orion's teeth bit harder into his scruff. He felt his brother's pace slow on the ice. "It's a lie," Watcher whispered.

"Don't listen to him, Orion. Keep running. Let him fall into the cold water under the ice. That will be revenge enough!"

And so Orion ran, faster and faster. Many times the ice nearly broke under his own feet, dropping him and Watcher both into the dark water. But he was too quick to fall into his own trap.

The first of the Lone Rock Wolves approached the river. They began to slow, fearful of the ice, until Bone lashed them with his tongue.

"Do not stop or slow, you cowards! Onto the river with you. Bring those pups to me. No wolf of the Gray Woods Pack shall escape my vengeance!"

But when the Lone Rocks stepped onto the cracked ice they fell through with shrill yelps and splashing paws. They thrashed in the cold water. Only one or two of those that first followed made it back to shore.

Bone reached the riverside and shoved two more of his soldiers onto the ice. But they too fell into the dark waters and did not come back up. The cracks had spread far down the river in both directions. The ice had wholly broken and the water began to flow. The Lone Rock Pack, even under the horrible glare of their lord, backed away from the banks and refused to go any further.

Orion finally reached the far shore, where Kicker, Glimmer, and Windy waited at the edge of the unknown woods. But as Watcher was set down on the snow he heard Bone's voice chase them over the broken ice.

"Do you think you've escaped? Do you think you've gotten away? We will go to the rock crossing, little pups. I know these lands well, for they were once my father's father's. We won't stop at the river. We won't stop for any obstacle. We won't stop until every Gray Woods Wolf lies in the red snow. There's nowhere in the Old Forest you can hide. There's nowhere you will ever be safe from me!"

11

Sleep kept just out of Watcher's reach. Every time he closed his eyes he saw only the empty black pit in Bone's face. He felt as though he were falling into its lightless depths. At the bottom lay the clearing by the fallen tree, carpeted with red snow. So Watcher gave up trying to rest and kept a lookout over his sleeping brothers and sisters instead.

The litter had run all night and into the morning. They had pulled at Tree branches to knock down old nests and rolled in their sticks and straw. They had crawled through holes left by big badgers. They rubbed the scents of other creatures into their fur to mask their trail.

"This was my idea," Kicker had grumbled.

"You mean when you attacked Watcher?" Glimmer had snapped back.

"If I hadn't done that, we'd all be dead! So don't bark at me, *dull snout!*"

"Quiet!" Orion had snarled then. "Especially you." He had glared at Kicker. "Not another word unless it's of use."

Watcher had known they were all tired and angry. But nevertheless Kicker had finally gone silent. Yet even on the run for their lives, with all their family gone from the woods forever, Watcher still felt Kicker's eyes upon him. If anything they were filled with more contempt than ever before.

As for Watcher, he had tried to run as much as he could. Whenever he fell too far behind Orion would appear to carry him. Watcher couldn't bear to look at the others as he dangled in Orion's jaws, especially not Kicker. So instead he set his eyes on the unknown woods about him.

The Trees in this part of the Old Forest grew crooked and bent. Their needles were more brown than green. The thickets and brambles beneath their branches spread thick and untamed, as though no Forest Folk ever ate them and no wolves ever trampled through their tangles. It was an unkempt, unwatched, and empty land – save for the smells.

As frightening as the journey was for Watcher, he knew it was worse for Windy. She could smell the wispy traces of wolves long gone on the Trees. Of battles and red snows from moons and moons ago. Of dangers and dire warnings crawling through holes, slithering along the ravines, cresting the hills of this strange land.

"Windy, are you alright?" Watcher had asked when he saw her flinching from the shadows. "Is it the Lone Rocks?"

"No," she had replied, her eyes and nose darting in every direction. "The Lone Rocks have fallen further back from us. I think it took them longer to ford the river by the rocks than Bone thought. No, it's these woods, Watcher. Something is wrong with them. It's like no creatures have been here for a long, long time. It's like a forgotten place."

But finally, when even Orion had begun to gulp for air and pant with a lolling tongue, the wolflings had stopped to rest. They found a thicket that grew in a thorny ring beneath a bent Tree, whose branches dipped down to the snow. There they tried to sleep through the day until the gray light grew dim and evening approached again. But fitful sleep escaped them.

"I'm hungry," Kicker had said, snorting up another puff of snow, once they were all up and ready to lope again. Kicker sounded sulky, but Watcher's stomach was growling too. The feast of the Great Crown Chieftain had been the last thing they'd eaten.

"I haven't seen any Great Crowns or even any mice or squirrels since last night," said Glimmer. "I haven't seen anything."

"Or smelled it," said Windy. "Not anything alive, anyway." Watcher shivered at Windy's words. *The ghosts are real,* she had said to Kicker.

"We couldn't hunt them even if they were around," said Orion. "Fresh red snow would call every wolf for stretches and stretches. The Lone Rocks would find us more easily. Maybe the wolves of this land. And we are trespassing."

"The wolves of this land have not come this way for a long time," said Windy. "The marks of their territory have gone thin."

"Maybe they're all gone," said Kicker. "Maybe we can claim these woods for *our* territory. Orion and I can mark the Trees."

"So close to the Gray Woods? To the Lone Rocks?" Orion scoffed. "Don't be such an idiot, Kicker. We wouldn't last a moon. We'll go to the Council of the Flyers like Frost Feather said. They'll help us find a new pack to join."

"And what pack will take *all* of us, oh mighty Orion?"

Watcher hung his head as his two brother continued to bicker within the ring of thorns. Once again he knew what Kicker meant by *all* of them. There was a reason Watcher had never expected to ramble. Rambling wolves had to earn their way into packs. That would be hard to do on three legs. But as Glimmer gave Watcher a nuzzle to make him feel better, he caught Windy in the corner of his eye. She had gone silent and still, her nose twitching in the cold breeze.

"What is it, Windy?" Watcher whispered to her. "Is the Lone Rocks? Have they found our trail?"

"No," she answered in her dreaming voice. "There is a creature nearby. His scent is faint. I almost didn't smell it at all. His smell is like the rest of this place – all but forgotten – but it is not so foul. It's like a smell that should *not* have been forgotten."

As though pulled by her nose, Windy got up and left the thicket without another word, following a scent that Watcher could not smell.

"Orion," Watcher said, interrupting the fight between him and Kicker. "Windy's smelled something. We need to follow her!" Watcher didn't wait for the others. He hopped up onto his three legs and pushed through the thicket behind his sister.

Windy wound slowly and carefully through the Trees and the brush. It seemed to Watcher as though the scent was trying to escape her. But she would not let it go.

"What does she smell, Watcher?" asked Glimmer, coming up beside him. She peered anxiously this way and that. "Can you smell it too?"

Watcher opened his mouth to say that he could not, when he caught a fleeting touch of *something* on the wind. *What was that?* It was an old flavor, like the scent of long buried earth kicked up from beneath a badger's paws. "I *can* smell it, Glimmer!" he said. "Just for a moment I did. It's like – it's hard to say what it's like. But I smelled it!"

"Oh, wonderful," grumbled Kicker from behind. "Now Three Legs thinks he can smell ghosts, too." But that was all he dared say, for Orion ran just beside him.

After going a little farther Windy's direction grew truer. Her pace quickened. She began to run. Watcher and the others ran behind her until they came to the base of a tall Tree. It was the tallest, straightest Tree Watcher had seen since they'd come to these woods. Her needles were still green like spring. She reminded Watcher of the goddesses from the Gray Woods, like the one where his mother had taught him the lesson about the Children of the Trees.

At the base of the Tree was a large mound of piled brush, pine-cones, and needles. From beneath its clutter the smell grew strong enough for all the litter to sniff it. *There's something under the brush,* thought Watcher. *Something alive.*

Windy had come to a stop a few lengths from the pile, just beneath the furthest reach of the great Tree's outstretched limbs. But Watcher had caught the scent of the creature, and it wasn't enough for him just to smell. He had to *see.* So he slowly limped under the Tree, inching his way to the brush.

"Watcher, wait," Orion whispered from behind him. "We don't know what it is."

"It's not dangerous," said Windy, still in her far-off way. "At least, not in the way of red fur or red snow. And yet–" But she did not finish.

Watcher reached the brush and prodded it once with his nose. No sooner had he touched it than the pile shivered. Its center bloomed like dirt above a digging badger. Old needles, branches, and twigs fell away as two great horns, curved and twisted, rose up over Watcher. A many-pointed helm of a Great Crown appeared. Watcher fell on his seat, nearly rolling over backwards to scramble away as a huge buck shook off his covering and stood tall beneath the Tree.

Glimmer and Kicker leapt away. But Orion bristled his fur. He pinned back his ears and unleashed a growl that would have frightened any creature of any forest. But Watcher, startled as he was, his little heart thumping, immediately came between Orion and the buck.

"Orion, wait!" he said. "Look."

There was something different about this buck. Standing out in the open, his smell reminded Watcher of the last night of summer, or of the first day of spring. Like ice melting and flowers blooming. The smell of spring seemed to rush from the buck's hair, filling the space beneath the Tree.

The creature stepped forward and, when he did, the snow seemed to melt away from his hooves, revealing green grass underneath that seemed to reach up and entwine his feet. He was old, Watcher saw, old like Frost Feather or Long Tooth. Perhaps even older still. His golden fur was touched of silver. His eyes were blue moons behind white clouds. When he spoke it was with a voice like crunching leaves in the fall.

"Hail, Children of Anorak, sons and daughters of the Gray Woods."

"How do you know who we are?" asked Orion. His fur had gone flat. He stood still beside Watcher and Windy, his mouth hanging open.

"Are wolves the only creatures with noses that smell? Are owls the only Forest Folk with eyes that see? I am a Child of the Earth, young prince. Our lands are not your lands. Our ways are not your ways."

"Who are you?" asked Watcher.

"I have had many names, young prince, for I have lived a long, long life, moons longer than perhaps I should have. But when last I still had strength to leap the fields, they called me Lord Gold Hoof, the Long Seer."

"I'm not a prince, Lord Gold Hoof. I'm the runt," said Watcher, as though it wasn't obvious.

"I have seen great rivers that began as bubbling springs, little wolf. Only those that walk a long way discover the truth of the matter. Only the old find out, and I am very old."

"Lord Gold Hoof," said Glimmer, coming a few steps closer and bowing her head. "We have not seen any Great Crowns for a long while. Where are the others? Where is your family?" But it was Windy who answered in her dreaming voice.

"He's alone. He's been alone for a long, long time." An invisible thorn pricked Watcher's chest for the buck. Gold Hoof had no pack. He had only this Tree and the brush beneath it to keep him warm. Watcher wondered if one day the big buck had returned from leaping to find all his pack gone, with no trace of their scent to follow. It was the very thing Watcher feared for himself.

"This one was born with a great gift from the Trees. She too is a far seer, though she sees with her nose, through the winds." Gold Hoof bowed to Windy, and she finally woke from her Trance, sitting down in the snow as though she were quite tired. "I received such a gift from Father Earth. But my sight is different still. And I have seen much. You all have my sorrows and my tears for what you have lost. Bone has committed a great crime against the Old Forest."

"But how could you know about that?" said Kicker, barking a bit harshly for Watcher's taste. But the buck hardly seemed to notice.

"I'm too old for running and leaping any more, young wolf. Mostly I sleep here under this Tree. But when I close these blind eyes, I still run in my dreams. I run farther there than I ever did when my body was strong. On the night of the no-moon, I was drawn in my dreams to the Gray Woods. I saw Bone's treachery.

"The wolves were born to bring balance to the Forest. But Bone believes he is more than a wolf. He believes he is a wildfire, that which clears away the old and brings the new. But he does not know the consequence of his actions. He will burn out of control. His fire will bring only death."

"He must be stopped," said Orion, staring into the snow, a growl at the back of his voice. "Our parents and our pack must be avenged."

"That is one path, Prince of the Wolves," said Gold Hoof. "But two fires simply burn twice as much, twice as fast. At least, that is what I have observed. But there are other paths."

"You – you've seen these other paths?" asked Watcher. "You've seen things that haven't happened yet?"

Gold Hoof just smiled and said: "Spring follows winter and summer follows spring. Is it predicting the future to know that what has come before will come again? It's easier to think about it that way. I could tell you more, but you have already tarried here too long. You must be on your way to the Council of the Flyers. But we have not met by chance, and before you go, I must mention one other thing.

"The Flyers watch over the Old Forest and keep the Ancient Laws, from the Great Fields to the shadow of the White Mountain. And perhaps they could find you a pack to join within those stretches. But one night in my dreams I ran to a place beyond the Old Forest. It was past the Fallen Tree Bridge, through the Haunted Forest, and over the White Mountain. I descended into a Far Valley. It was a good place, teeming with creatures of the earth. But it lacked balance – for there were no wolves. I thought to myself: *if good wolves were to find this place, what a wonder it might be. It would be something new!* Can you imagine, young ones? Renewal without fire? Even I have never seen such a thing."

"Over the White Mountain?" said Orion, trembling at the thought, the way Watcher would tremble. "No wolf has ever gone so far, not even in Long Tooth's stories. Is that even possible?" But Gold Hoof answered that question with only a smile.

"You should go now, young wolves," he said, sounding very tired. "Bone and his pack still seek you. And whatever path you choose, they all lead through the Council of the Flyers."

Kicker couldn't trot away fast enough. And though Orion seemed like he wanted to ask another question, after a moment he shook his head and said nothing. He bowed to the buck and walked away, followed by Glimmer.

"Goodbye, little Far Seer," said Gold Hoof to Windy.

"Goodbye, Gold Hoof," she said, bowing to the buck as he bowed back. When she turned to go, Watcher made to follow her, but after a few steps he stopped and turned back. There was something he had to say, and he felt he couldn't leave without having said it. He ran back to the tall Tree with his awkward lope, stopping before Gold Hoof's legs, who stood there as though he'd been waiting for Watcher to do just that.

"I'm sorry," said Watcher. "I'm sorry you're all alone. If you were a wolf, I know you could come with us. I know my brother would let you come."

"Thank you, Deep Eyes," said the buck. He dipped his head low, until his antlers nearly touched the ground and his snout nearly pressed against Watcher's. "You have owl's eyes, young one, but do not think them to be your only gift. Pain and sorrow are like rains that come in spring, little Watcher, and there will be more of both to come on this journey. I fear not all of you shall see the end of it, that perhaps one or more might fall. But do not let hate and anger grow in the wake of such times. Look how terrible that has made Bone. Let something better take root. Something truer. And when it grows, it will grow strong. Goodbye, Watcher."

"Goodbye, Gold Hoof."

Then Watcher ran away, fighting the warm wetness that threatened to spill onto his fur. For even giving such dire warnings, the buck's eyes had reminded him of the sunrise, and his mother.

12

Watcher and the others followed Windy and the scent from Frost Feather's wing for another day and night. When they finally reached a tall hill at the edge of the Forgotten Woods, as Windy called them, they needed only their eyes to know they had found the Council of the Flyers.

Three boulders stood atop the hill, scarred and worn by the wind, rain, and time. A column of birds circled above the stones, stretching all the way to the gray clouds. Watcher's owl eyes grew even bigger and rounder. His mouth fell open, but any words to describe the beauty of all those wings riding the wind escaped him.

Orion led the others up the hill to a clearing before the stones. Three great birds sat in hollowed-out nooks, one for each boulder, silver in all their ancient feathers. One was a crow with black upon black eyes. The other was Lady Frost Feather the Owl. But in the middle sat what must have been the oldest and grayest of them all. It was an eagle, and when he saw the wolves enter the clearing atop the hill he screamed loudly to the sky. The column of circling birds descended in a roar of flapping wings. It sounded like the pounding of a summer storm on Tree leaves above Watcher's head.

When the birds had all landed they went silent as the stones upon which they sat. The three, Lady Frost Feather, the crow, and the eagle, bowed their heads to the wolves. The littermates bowed back. Then the eagle spoke.

"Greetings, Orion of the Gray Woods, and to his brothers and sisters. I am Storm Talon, head of this council. You already know Lady Frost Feather. And this is Moon Caw the Crow. We welcome you to the Court of Stones, to the Council of the Flyers, and we offer you our condolences for your loss. The Lone Rock's breach of the Ancient Laws was most – upsetting."

Orion stirred where he sat. A ripple seemed to pass down the fur on his back. Watcher knew what his brother was thinking and what he was feeling. When a wolf pack – when a mother and a father and all their kin – had been betrayed to the red snow, it was more than *upsetting*. But Orion clenched any such words behind his teeth and bowed his head. "Thank you, Storm Talon," was all he said.

"We know that you have come to us for wisdom and counsel. We have spoken amongst ourselves and we have all come to the same conclusion."

Lady Frost Feather gave a sharp squawk and slapped her wings at her side. Troubled thoughts seemed to brew behind her big eyes, Watcher thought. He heard more than a few feathers ruffle from the birds upon the stones. But Storm Talon silenced them all with a long cry and a snap of his beak.

"We have *all* agreed on what it is best for you," the eagle repeated, "and what is most in keeping with the Ancient Laws. But before we go further I will introduce Ash, lieutenant of the Bramble Woods Pack, who we have invited to join us."

Another wolf trotted into the clearing before the great boulders. This Ash was all gray with no white in his fur. He wasn't a particularly large wolf either, Watcher thought, especially not for a lieutenant. He couldn't have been any bigger than either Kicker or Glimmer. Yet he seemed very calm to Watcher, almost sleepy, with a slow smile spread over his lips as he bowed to the wolflings.

Watcher looked to Windy. Her snout quivered as she took in this new wolf's smell. Watcher wasn't sure he liked the look in her eyes as she tested it.

"Greetings, Ash," said Storm Talon. "Thank you for coming on such short notice."

"The Bramble Woods Pack is always at your service, Storm Talon," said Ash slowly, as though it was a small favor, that smile still on his face.

"Forgive us, lords and ladies of the council," said Orion. Watcher saw his brother try to hide the flash of concern in his yellow eyes. "But until yesterday, we'd never been beyond the Wide River. We'd never left our home in the Gray Woods. None of us have ever heard of the Bramble Woods before, or of their pack. How long of a lope is it to their territory?"

"You will be happy to know, young Orion," said Storm Talon, spreading his wings gladly. "That you have hardly any ways to go at all. You have just come through the far border of the Bramble Woods on your way to the council."

The Forgotten Woods? A cold tendril sprouted in Watcher's chest, crawling down his legs and into his tail. His brothers and sisters stamped their paws in the snow beside him. Orion's fur once more rose and fell, as if in a gust of wind. When the young wolves looked up to Lady Frost Feather, she could not meet their eyes.

"Forgive me again," said Orion. This time there was no hiding the growl at the edge of his voice. "But I'm not sure you understand what has happened. The Lone Rocks have grown in size and strength. They have become an army! They raided our territory without fear. They killed every wolf in our pack but us. Even our father and our mother. Bone has sworn to put all of the Gray Woods Pack to the red snow. He could be just behind us. When we travelled through these Bramble Woods we were never challenged by sentries or guards. The markings at their boundaries have grown old and faded, as though no wolf has been there in ages. The Trees were brown and there was hardly a trace of any Forest Folk at all."

There was more rustling of feathers and even a disquieted murmur over the boulders. But it was Ash, the lieutenant, who answered Orion. "You have only seen a small portion of our territory, my young friend," he said calmly, as though hardly offended by Orion's accusations. That easy, sleepy smile never left his face. "In the spring those woods will grow healthy again, I assure you. Many stretches of our land are so green you might think you've never before seen the color. And though we may not be as famous as our illustrious cousins in the Gray Woods once were, we have our defenses. And they are strong." Only then did the smile fade from Ash's face. A cold gleam in his eyes replaced it. Watcher wasn't sure he liked that look. Not at all.

"And they'll take ramblers?" said Glimmer all of a sudden. She bowed her head to both the council and Orion, her voice quiet. "They'll take *all* of us?"

Watcher's breathing quickened. He'd been so unsure of the birds' plan to send him and his littermates with this Ash that he'd forgotten his first fear. He was a three legs and Glimmer was a dull snout. They were never meant to ramble. *What if Kicker was right? What if this Bramble Woods Pack would take only Orion, Kicker, and Windy? What then?*

"Fear not, young wolf." That smile returned to Ash's face. "We honor the Ancient Laws in the Bramble Woods. We, like the Gray Woods Pack, believe that *all* wolves can serve the good of the pack, no matter their strength. Or their size." Watcher couldn't be sure, but for some reason he thought Ash wasn't saying that for him or for Glimmer. He thought the lieutenant had stolen a glance at Orion. *So what does he really mean?* Watcher thought. *His tongue says one thing – but that smile says something else.*

But Orion hadn't been paying attention to Ash. His snout and his eyes pointed to the snow between his paws. A growl was building behind his teeth.

"And what about Bone?" he said. "What about his army of Lone Rocks that still pursue us? Even if these Bramble Woods Wolves can protect us, what becomes of him and his crimes?"

"The wolf prince speaks true, Lord Storm Talon," said a young falcon, perched near the back of one of the large stones. "The Lone Rocks still pursue those that remain of the Gray Woods Pack. They loped far down the Wide River to the stone crossing. They stopped at the eastern border of the Bramble Woods to hunt and feed. But they do not look to be returning to the Gray Woods. They look to press further still, and to capture the wolflings."

The cold vine crawling through Watcher's body wound even tighter, down to his bones. He tried to push the image of Bone's empty eye from his thoughts.

But Storm Talon only folded his wings, glaring hotly at the falcon who had spoken out of turn. After a long sigh he turned back to the wolves and said: "Bone has violated the Ancient Laws, it is true. But many wolves have died already. He shall be told to return to the Gray Woods with his Lone Rocks. He shall be given a stern reminder that there are consequences to violating the Law."

"A reminder? *A reminder?*" Orion's growl became a roar. He rose up onto his feet and lifted his eyes to where Storm Talon sat perched upon his boulder, terrible again, his fur bristling and his teeth gleaming. "Bone raided our lands. He betrayed and murdered my father and my mother. He slaughtered our pack. Now he has chased us into yet another pack's territory, and all you will have for him are words?"

"You forget yourself, *wolf*," screeched Storm Talon, snapping his beak again. "The words we use shall be very stern indeed! We are the Keepers of the Ancient Ways. We are here to remind you wolves of justice, not to dispense it."

"Then fly to the Far Runners!" Orion cried. "Tell them what has happened. Tell them that our pack must be avenged!"

"Even the Far Runners know that there must be wolves in the Gray Woods, Orion. If *only* your father or mother had fallen to the red snow, we would fly at once and tell Great Paw, Lord of the Far Runners, to come and oversee your vengeance. But wolves bring balance to the Forest. There must be wolves in the Gray Woods. Even if they were once of the Lone Rock."

"So you're just going to give them what they stole? You're going to let them get away with treachery?" Orion snapped his jaws and raised his tail.

"You will accept our judgment, Orion!" screeched Storm Talon, pointing his wing. "Or it shall be in regards to you that a message shall be sent to Great Paw."

Watcher got up and went to Orion's side. He nuzzled against his brother's fur until Orion looked down at him. "Maybe there's another way," he said. "What about what Gold Hoof said?"

Looking into Watcher's eyes, the storm in Orion's slowly calmed. His fur flattened and his eyes fell to the snow. Sadness flooded Watcher's body. Twice now he had seen his brother covered with shame, and how Watcher wished he could take it away and wear it for himself. But after a time Orion lifted his snout and spoke to the birds again.

"Along the way here we met an old buck of the Great Crowns. He seemed as old as the Trees themselves. He spoke of a place beyond the Fallen Tree Bridge, over the White Mountain. He said there was a Far Valley in the lands there, a place where no wolves had yet marked their territory. What if we were to go there?"

At this Lady Frost Feather lifted her eyes for the first time, a glimmer of something other than sorrow or trouble at their edges, perhaps even hope. But Storm Talon and most of the other council were already cawing and flapping in outrage.

"You've been meeting with that old fool, Gold Hoof," said Storm Talon. "How long before he finally walks from the woods? The Far Valley is a myth. Nothing but barren wilderness lies beyond the White Mountain. You wolves have been thrust from youth to adulthood in but a night's time. And for this I am sorry. But you must learn the difference between hopes and dreams and the harsh winter of truth. You were born into the Old Forest to bring balance *here*. And *here* you must stay. That is the Ancient Law!"

Orion opened his mouth to yell back at Storm Talon again, but this time it was Glimmer who whispered into his ear to stop him, having come up on his other side.

"I know how angry you are, Orion. I'm angry too. I want Bone to pay for what he's done just as much as any of you. But this pack says they'll take all of us. *All of us.* That Ash has seen Watcher's leg, and he said nothing. What other pack will do that for us? The pack is a wolf's only home, Orion. And we don't have one. But maybe we could. Maybe, for now, that's enough."

"I don't like his smell," said Windy quietly, coming up beside Watcher and casting a glance at Ash. "It's not that it's evil, not like Bone's. But it is faint. Almost forgotten. Like their woods."

"You don't like the way anything smells, Windy," said Kicker, last to join the others in their small circle. "But Glimmer's right, Orion. What other pack will take all of us?" He stole a glance at Watcher, one that made Watcher feel as though all the shame Orion had born had indeed been his fault from the beginning. "Look at that lieutenant. He's smaller than I am. You could become lord of that pack easily. Or maybe – maybe you could still join the Far Runners and *I* could become their lord. Then one of us could challenge Bone, couldn't we? Then one of us could take revenge."

Watcher wanted to say something. He wanted so badly to say that he had believed the old buck's story and that they should keep running, past the Fallen Tree Bridge and over the White Mountain, all the way to this Far Valley. But what if it wasn't there? What if it *was* only a barren wasteland? How much more shame would he bring on Orion then? Maybe it would be better to join this pack. Then maybe he would stop being such a burden on Orion. So Watcher only looked to the snow between his paws and said nothing. After a time, Orion spoke loudly enough for all the council to hear.

"We will go with the Bramble Woods Pack." There was no joy in his voice when he said it. He kept his head low as he and the others followed Ash from the hilltop of the three stones, under the shadow of the great boulders.

13

Watcher hated the Forgotten Woods. That was a better name for them than the Bramble Woods, he thought. The shrubs and leafy Trees had been picked down to the bark long before winter, the way the crows picked skeletons down to the bone. There were so few tracks and only faint scents of either Forest Folk or wolf. For the entire journey behind Ash Watcher saw not one hunting party or patrol. Bone and his Lone Rocks could slip through this forest in but a day, with nothing but the snow and brown tangles to slow them down.

Why are we going this way, Orion? Watcher wanted to ask. But he already knew the answer. Kicker had repeated it so many times. *No other pack will take us all.* Which really meant: *No other pack will take a three legs and a dull snout.* The truth was, Watcher knew, they were following this Ash because of him. And even if Orion believed in the Far Valley beyond the White Mountain, he certainly didn't think Watcher could make the journey there.

The only good thing Watcher could find about the morning was that his brothers and sisters weren't loping so fast and he could keep up. Ash seemed to be in no hurry. He trotted along easily at the head of the line. But all the while, as Orion ran just behind, he kept looking over his shoulder, not at Watcher, but back to the Gray Woods – back toward Bone and revenge.

Don't leave me, Orion, Watcher thought. *Please don't leave me here and forget about me, like everything else in this wood has been forgotten.*

"There's something wrong in these woods," Windy whispered to Watcher, coming up beside him as though she'd heard his thoughts aloud. She cast her eyes up to the barren Tree branches, gnarled and bent like bony claws. "It's more than that they've been forgotten. It's more like they're hiding something. A secret."

"A good secret?" Watcher asked. But Windy couldn't say. Only Glimmer seemed to hold any real hope for this place, Watcher thought. She longed for the comfort of the pack again, for Mother and Father. Watcher couldn't blame her for that.

At last the wolves entered a clearing, where Ash slowed his trot to a walk. But he led them not to a circle of waiting wolves – and hopefully a few warriors a might bit bigger than Ash himself – but to the mouth of cave that sunk into the earth. It was a black hole, lightless beyond the sharp rocks that ringed it like teeth, tattered roots poking out between like leftover shreds of meat.

"What's this place?" said Orion, coming to a stop just beyond the Trees, sniffing warily at the hole. "Where is your pack?"

"Just up ahead," said Ash, that smile still on his face. "The Bramble Woods Pack is down there." He nodded to the cave. Orion looked back to Windy, his eyes full of disbelief. But she sniffed the air and nodded back to him.

"They are down there," she said. "All of them. They smell like Ash. They smell *odd* like him."

"I don't want to go down there, Orion," said Watcher. He could hardly look at the cave without remembering Bone's ragged, empty eye, for it too was like a tooth filled maw as deep and threatening as any hole in the earth. It made him shake down to his paws. It made him think of Mother and Father and the red snow. "I don't like the way it feels. I don't like the way anything in these woods feel."

"Not enough birds to chase after, Three Legs?" said Kicker. But even he had taken two steps back from the cave. Orion growled a warning at him to watch his tongue, but Kicker said: "Well where does he want us to go? Back to the Gray Woods? Back to Bone's waiting teeth and claws? Where else could we go?"

"To the Far Valley," said Watcher.

Kicker sniffed. But Glimmer came around from beside Orion and nuzzled Watcher gently. "You heard what the Council of Flyers said, Watcher. They said there is no Far Valley. That old buck couldn't possibly know what lies beyond the Fallen Tree Bridge or the White Mountain, could he? It's just a story. This pack is real. And they'll take us in. Lame leg, dull snout and all." She whispered the last part, as though afraid Ash might still change his mind. "Isn't that at least worth a look?"

A voice in Watcher's head was shouting at him not to go into the hole. But in Glimmer's eyes, those that reminded Watcher of his mother's, he saw how tired and scared she was. He saw how much hope that she had, that they might be able to stay here. So he nuzzled Glimmer back and said: "Just a look."

Ash went ahead and one by one the Gray Woods litter followed him down into the cave. As Watcher came last, he couldn't help but feel like he was falling into the dark emptiness that had once been Bone's eye.

Watcher quickly realized that the cave was more than just a divot in the earth. As the wolflings came down a steep path, a web of tunnels and chambers opened up before them. Not all of it had been formed by Father Earth. There were marks of claws, teeth, and snouts on the walls. This cave had been hollowed, Watcher thought, the way badgers made their homes, with dirt pathways stamped flat by the marching of many paws.

Gray light cut through cracks in the roof, falling like moonlight through clouds in ghostly shafts. Through these beams Ash led the siblings down the central tunnel to a round opening encircled by twisting roots, the limbs of a great Tree that reached far into the Earth. Watcher suddenly felt upside down in the world, beneath the ground when he should be above it. There was no sun and no wind down here, no grass and no leaves. There was no room to run or to leap or even to breath. It was no place for a wolf.

"I don't smell any badgers or mice, Watcher," Windy whispered in his ear, testing the tunnel's dull air. "I don't think the Bramble Woods Pack found this place."

"I know," said Watcher. "I think they dug it out themselves." He had never even heard of such a thing, not even in Long Tooth's tales.

"There are many wolves in these tunnels. They all smell like Ash. But there's something else down here, Watcher. Some other *creature*. Maybe more than one. It smells like a wolf, but then not like one at all."

Watcher shivered at his sister's words as they crossed under the twisting roots and into the largest chamber yet. *What creatures could she mean?* "Keep your eyes open wide, Watcher," Windy added before going quiet again. Her words were like Lady Frost Feather's – the last words of his father – a warning for Watcher to *watch*. But he no longer knew what he was looking for.

The wolflings trotted to the center of the chamber. Watcher felt like he was back in front of the Council of the Flyers all over again. Three wolves sat on dirt mounds at the back of the chamber, lit by three shafts of gray light punching through the roots of the Tree, which grew tall just above the cave. They were not large wolves, the three, not like Orion was or Watcher's father had been. In truth, they were very nearly the same size as Ash.

In the cave's dim light Watcher could hardly tell the three apart, but for the wolf in the middle. His eyes glowed rounder and wider than the others beside him. They were like owl's eyes. *They're like my eyes,* Watcher thought.

"Greetings, cousins from the Gray Woods," said the middle wolf, the one with the big eyes. "I have been told by the Council of the Flyers who you are: Kicker, Windy, Glimmer, Watcher, and Orion. My name is Crag." Watcher followed Orion's lead as he dipped his head to Crag. But Crag did not bow in return. "We don't do that here," he said. "It is an old and tired tradition."

"You don't bow, milord?" asked Orion.

"Nor do we call any one wolf 'lord,' cousin. It is also an old and useless term. Every wolf here is a lord and a lady."

"Then, you do not lead this pack?" Orion asked.

"Do you always ask so many questions of your hosts, Orion of the Gray Woods?"

"No, mil—" Orion caught himself.

"See? You don't even know what to call me without the Ancient Ways leading your tongue. How silly. So I shall introduce myself again. Perhaps pay attention this time. I am Crag."

"Greetings, Crag." Orion's words came out tight and thick.

"Ah, so you can do it after all. Well done. We accept your greetings and we accept you, cousins. Welcome to our home."

"Home, milord?" asked Kicker, looking around the cave. Watcher was also a little confused. When the Gray Woods Wolves had taken in a rambler, which they had done twice that summer, Anorak had always said: *Welcome to our pack.*

"Do *all* of you so frequently speak out of turn? Or are only the biggest and strongest of you so rude? That is not unexpected though, is it? But in answer to your question, yes, this is our home. We no longer bother loping and loping, day after day. Such customs are ways of the past. We are doing something new."

"But—" Orion began. But Crag spoke over him as though he had not heard him.

"Which one of you is Glimmer?"

Glimmer stepped to the center of the cave floor, bowing her snow-white head, as they had been taught.

"I see you will have to unlearn all the unnecessary habits foisted upon you as a pup, young Glimmer. But it won't take long. You're going to be very happy here. Is it true that you have a dull snout?"

Orion took a start. Watcher could feel his brother's muscles twist and tighten beside him. That was not a question any wolf asked another. But Glimmer, swallowing hard, managed an answer.

"Yes, mil— I mean, Crag."

"But I suppose you have many other strengths, don't you? You seem to me well knit, strong and fast."

"I'm as fast as any wolf my age. And I can fight, just as good as the boys."

"But of course you can, my dear. Welcome to our home." Crag panned over the litter until he came to Watcher. His big eyes were so round and unblinking. They glimmered in the shaft of light that fell on his head through the Tree roots in the dirt ceiling, like two glowing ponds in the gray light. Their gaze was heavy on Watcher's face. "And you must be Watcher. No need to ask you about your leg, is there?"

Watcher thought Orion was going to charge Crag where he sat, challenging him right then and there for leadership of the pack. But though he trembled, somehow Orion held fast. Watcher hung his head. "No, milord."

"But I have heard that you have eyes for the world. Owl's eyes, they say. Is that true?"

"I – I suppose so."

"Don't be afraid to speak highly of your strengths, Watcher. This is not the Gray Woods. You are welcome, and safe, here."

"I'm sorry, mil–, Crag," said Orion at last, barely keeping the growl from his lips, "but I'm not so sure we are safe. Your boundary markers have grown faint. The Forest Folk, what little of them are left, have eaten much of your lands down to the dirt. Bone and his

Lone Rocks are chasing us. They may be in your lands even now. You must—"

"I *must?*" Crag snapped. For the first time, Watcher thought he heard a snarl on the smaller wolf's voice. "What do you know of what a wolf *must* do, Orion of the Gray Woods? Your father did all things wolves must do, didn't he? Where did that get him? An unfortunate, but not unexpected, end."

"How dare you! What do you mean by that?" Orion had no trouble leaving the 'milord' this time. And he also had no trouble forgetting not to growl, his fur bristling.

"I mean those that live by the tooth, die by the tooth," said Crag. If he was worried about a fight with Orion, as Watcher thought he should be, it didn't show. "They always do. But don't take us for fools, cousin. This cave is not so easily discovered by uninvited guests. We have lived in the world. We know it is a harsh place. We are not unprepared."

With that, three more wolves stepped into the light. They emerged from the shadows behind the mounds. Watcher nearly fell over backwards at the sight of them. They were lean, their thin, taut muscles riding just over their bones. Their fur seemed shorn to Watcher, as though bitten and gnawed nearly to the skin. Their yellow eyes were sunken into their heads, small, sharp, and biting. And their teeth – *their teeth!* – curved out from withered lips, as though all these wolves were born to do was snarl and bite.

"It's them," Windy whispered to Watcher, making herself small beside him. "It's the *creatures.*" When Watcher tasted the air with his nose, he knew what Windy meant. Perhaps these things had been wolves once before, but their scent no longer spoke the truth of it.

"You see, we are most safe here, cousins. So again I tell you: welcome to our home."

14

A sh led the wolflings to a chamber that was to be their room in the Bramble Woods Cave. The dirt ceiling crawled with tangled roots like spider's webs, lit by a single shaft of gray light. With every moment Watcher spent in the cave, he felt as if the tunnels and chambers were growing smaller and smaller, falling in on him and threatening to entomb him in darkness forever.

But no sooner had they had arrived in the room and sat down to rest their tired bodies and aching paws, and before Watcher could tell Orion how much he wanted to leave, another wolf appeared behind Ash in the tunnel.

"Orion, Kicker, and Glimmer," he announced. "Crag has called for a hunt to celebrate your arrival. He has requested you assist the pack."

"All of us?" said Kicker. Watcher noticed that even in spite of the cave and Crag's *creatures*, his brother couldn't help but wag his tail at the thought of finally joining a hunt. Glimmer, however, seemed just as concerned as Watcher by this sudden request.

"A hunt?" she said. "Now? We're only one season old, and we've been running all day and all night for almost three days. We haven't eaten in four. We're all tired, but Orion is exhausted. He needs rest to get his strength back."

"But how can he regain his strength on an empty belly?" said the wolf. A slow smile, nearly a reflection of Ash's, crossed the second wolf's face. "He shall have food and rest enough after the hunt. All of you shall. You three bigger wolflings will join us now." The wolf then nodded toward Watcher and Windy. "Your smaller brother and sister will stay behind for the time being. But don't worry, grow a little bigger and you'll get your chance."

"Why not let Kicker and Glimmer go and let Orion stay?" said Watcher. He knew his big brother was tired. But he also wanted a moment alone with him, to tell him they should leave. "He carried me in his jaws for more than half the way here. He really is more tired than the rest of us." Watcher was embarrassed to admit the fact that he'd been carried in front of the new pack. But if Ash and the other wolf cared at all, concern never slipped upon their faces. They kept smiling those strange smiles, as if there was nothing wrong with such a thing as being carried at all.

"He looks strong enough to have carried you the *whole* way," said Ash. "Even in our little cave we've heard word of the great young hunter, Orion of the Gray Woods. Crag would be very disappointed to miss a demonstration of his prowess." Watcher looked to Glimmer. She opened her mouth to argue again when Orion interrupted them both.

"Don't worry about me, Watcher," he said, getting back up with a small groan. His big shoulders were slumped and his tail hung low between his legs. Somehow he managed to give Watcher a shadow of the smile he usually wore. "You know I don't even need half my strength to bring down a good sized buck, right?"

Watcher tried to return the smile, but he couldn't force it onto his lips. He watched his brothers and sister follow the other wolf and Ash down the tunnel, until they disappeared in the shadows, leaving him and Windy in the dark chamber.

Watcher lay on the dirt floor of the dimly lit room, watching a column of black ants march along a half-buried root sticking out from the wall. He wished there were other creatures to look at down here, under the earth. Birds especially. But there were nothing but bugs besides him and Windy. He was trying not to worry, trying not to feel like he was going to drown under the dirt, but his brothers and Glimmer had been gone with the hunt for a long, long time. Too long.

So he watched the ants and tried not to think dark thoughts. Back and forth the ants marched, creeping by like the moments Watcher spent in the cave. They never stopped to rest. They never played or wrestled. They never ran. It wasn't that Watcher didn't appreciate ants. He rather liked bugs. But he liked it most when animals did something big and great and unexpected – when they did something he had never seen before.

You can learn hard work from ants, Watcher's father had told him once, when he caught him staring at them one summer day. *You can learn much from all the Forest Folk. But ants aren't wolves, Watcher, and neither are birds or badgers. Learn from the Forest. But in the end, learn to be a good wolf, my son."* Watcher would never forget that lesson. It was the only one his father had given just for him. Just for a father and a son.

"I can't smell the air beyond this cave, Watcher," Windy said after a long time of silence and waiting. It surprised Watcher, for he thought perhaps she'd fallen asleep. But she was sitting up then, her patchy ears alert and voice atremble. "I can't smell the ghosts that would speak to me on the winds outside. I can't smell the Trees. I can't even smell Bone and all his darkness, whether he's near or far. I can't breathe down here."

Watcher sat up beside his sister. The fear in her voice made his good leg quiver, because he felt it too. "Then let's go outside for a while, Windy. Let's go right now." When Watcher said it, he realized that his chest was aching for the fresh air like his stomach would rumble for food.

"*They* won't let us, Watcher." Windy's eyes flicked to the tunnel that led from their chamber. Barely moving in the shadows beyond were two wolves. They sat to either side of the entrance – like guards. "They don't smell right. *None* of the wolves here smell right. They smell like the Forgotten Woods. They smell like they've forgotten how to be wolves. But worse, there's a taste of those *creatures* on all of them, Watcher. Those *creatures* haven't just forgotten how to be wolves. I can't even be sure they *are* wolves anymore. All except for Crag, Watcher. He smells like a wolf alright. He smells like Bone."

"Like Bone?" Watcher all but yelped. He and Windy were speaking very softly, and Watcher found himself suddenly worried that the wolves at the end of the tunnel were listening. So he whispered as low as he could. "I don't like this place any more than you, but Crag doesn't seem anything like Bone. He's small. Like us."

"He smells like him, Watcher. Just a hint. Like a hint of the *darkness*."

Watcher shivered, even though the air in the cave was warm without the winter wind. He tried to think of anything but Bone. He tried to make himself feel better about any of their situation at all. "Crag did let us join their pack, Windy. He let me and Glimmer join, even with her nose. Even with my leg. That must make him a little like father and mother, doesn't it?" Just mentioning his parents made Watcher's throat hurt.

"Maybe," said Windy. "But he doesn't smell like them. And he doesn't look like a pack lord, does he?"

"No, he doesn't," Watcher admitted. "Actually, I thought – for a moment – I thought he looked a bit more like me. Except without a lame leg." A tremor went through Watcher's chest just then, for a moment picturing himself running at the front of a great pack.

But he splashed that image away, like running his paw over the surface of still waters.

"I thought so too," said Windy. "But how do you think he became the lord? Do you think he could win a challenge?"

"Maybe there's another way besides a challenge to be a lord."

"There's always a challenge, Watcher. Always."

Watcher went quiet again, thinking hard about all of this, when a great commotion rose up in the tunnel outside the chamber. The hunters had returned.

Wolves filed past the shadows beyond the tunnel, shreds of red meat in their jaws. Watcher's stomach growled. He and Windy were about to risk leaving their chamber when Kicker and Glimmer arrived. They ran down the tunnel, laying a share each at Watcher and Windy's feet. But hungry as he was, the looks on his brother and sister's face spoiled Watcher's appetite.

"Where's Orion?"

Kicker and Glimmer shared a round-eyed look. They cast furtive glances over their shoulders, back down the tunnel where the two guards still sat. "Everything's fine," Kicker said loudly. "Just eat up!"

Watcher snuck a glance to Glimmer. She nodded back. He understood. The guards *were* listening. Even though his stomach was twisting and turning with worry, Watcher forced himself to gobble down his dinner. While he and Windy smacked their lips on their food, Kicker and Glimmer gathered close, whispering right into their ears about what had happened.

"Crag and the others led us north," Kicker began, "not far, to a place where the Trees were still green and some grass poked through the snow. It must be the last place in their territory where the Forest Folk still live, where there are Great Crowns. But even still it took us all morning to track down a good-sized buck and his cohort. Most of the wolves could hardly track, much less hunt. When we started the chase not another wolf was even a length behind Orion. Not even–" Kicker's eyes snuck back and forth in his head, as though the shadows were creeping. The words caught in his throat.

"Those *things*." said Glimmer, shivering. "Those wolves."

"The *creatures*," Windy whispered.

"Yes," said Kicker, even more quietly than before. "They were with us. Two of them anyway. They never spoke. They never bayed. They never howled. Even when they saw the buck they never even moved until Crag commanded them. But when he did release them – I've never heard snarls like that before. Even so, they couldn't catch Orion. He brought down the buck on his own and put it to the red snow. I saw it clear. He made the kill. We waited for Crag to bow his head and speak the blessing, but he did not. So then Orion went to take his share, but they denied it to him."

"They didn't give him the first share?" Watcher blurted a little too loudly, earning himself a fierce glare from Kicker. "But that's against the Ancient Laws," he whispered.

"No, Watcher, it's worse than that," said Glimmer. "They didn't only deny him the first share. They denied him *any* share."

"The pack first," said Kicker. "That's what Crag said when Orion asked for his rights. Then he said something to those *things.*"

"They turned on Orion to block him from the kill," said Glimmer. "Orion was going to fight them, but I couldn't bear to see it, so I asked him to please, please just wait. I never knew they wouldn't give him anything, I swear! He's come so far with us and he hasn't eaten since the Great Crown. He must be so hungry. I'm so sorry." Glimmer began to whine and cry until Kicker shushed her with a sharp snap.

"Quiet down, will you? You don't want them turning those *things* on us, do you?"

"Where is Orion now?" Watcher's heart thumped hard within him. He couldn't catch his breath. *What have they done with my brother? What have they done?*

"When we got back to the cave," Kicker continued, "Crag told Orion to come with him. To talk with him. But I don't know. I don't know what's happened."

Windy began to sniff the air, breathing it in as deeply as she could. "I smelled him, when the hunt first returned to the cave. But now his scent is gone. But it's so hard to smell under the earth."

"His smell is gone?" Glimmer seemed as though she might fall over and begin to howl. "Is he–? I mean, those *creatures* went with him. Could they have–?"

"I don't think so," said Windy, nuzzling her sister to calm her down. "There's no smell of red dirt in the cave. Even down here we would all be able to smell that. But for whatever cause, I can't smell Orion."

Where could he have gone? Thought Watcher. *What could they have done with him?* He was about to ask Kicker these things when a voice barked from the chamber entrance, surprising them all. Watcher's question caught in his throat. Kicker and Glimmer spun, as though afraid of an attack. But all they found behind them was Ash, that sleepy smile lazing on his face. He was smiling at Watcher.

"Watcher," he said, "you need to come with me."

"He needs to come with you where?" said Kicker, ill-disguising the growl at the back of his voice.

"Nothing to worry about, cousins," said Ash happily. "Crag just wants a word with him, that's all. Probably just to get to know him a little. I'm sure he'll do the same with all of you at some time or another. Just making you feel welcome to our home."

Watcher looked to each of his brothers and sisters before following Ash, but Glimmer's frightened eyes spoke loudest to him of all. They repeated the message given to him by Lady Frost Feather and Windy.

Keep your eyes open, Watcher. Keep your eyes open wide! But now that message meant something different and terrible. It meant he needed to find Orion. It meant he needed to find a way out of this cave.

15

"Hello, Watcher."

Crag sat in the center of the great chamber, the three mounds and the crisscrossing beams of gray light behind him. He looked past Watcher to the twisted tree root entrance and flicked his head, dismissing Ash without a word.

"Greetings, milord." Watcher dipped his head out of habit. Crag clucked his tongue against his needle teeth.

"Watcher, don't make me remind you again. There's no bowing here. No Lord This or Lady That. We're all equals in this cave. Even us runts."

Watcher tried to hide his surprise, but his big eyes went even wider before he could dip his head back to the floor. Crag laughed at this in the dark chamber, roots spearing through the dirt roof above his head like the upside down antlers of Great Crowns.

"Surprised, my young friend? At what, I wonder?"

Watcher said nothing. But he now knew Crag was more like him than he first thought. After the silence had hung thick as fog for a long while, flattening Watcher's fur and making his insides wiggle like an earthworm, Crag spoke again.

"I don't suppose you've ever heard of a runt leading a pack before, have you, Watcher?"

"I've rarely heard of runts being kept in a pack at all, much less becoming lord," said Watcher. "Not even in old Long Tooth's stories."

Crag clucked his tongue again. "Watcher, how many times do I have to tell you? I'm not *lord* of this pack. In this pack we all have a say. But we can't all speak at the same time, can we? So, I just speak *for* the pack. That's all. I'm the opposite of a lord. I'm a servant."

Watcher thought about this for a long moment. He thought about the way Ash had led him and the others straight to Crag when they'd first come to the cave. About how Crag had sent Ash off with nothing but a flick of his head. About how Crag had called forth those *creatures*. That seemed like a lord to Watcher. And what was it Windy had just told him? *He smells like Bone.*

"I can see there's no fooling you, Watcher," Crag said, a laugh on his voice. "You don't believe me, do you?"

"No, milo—, I mean, Crag. I mean, yes, of course I believe you!" Watcher's words stumbled out all wrong. But Crag just laughed even louder. He stood up and walked across the dirt floor toward Watcher.

"Watcher, you – especially you among all your brothers and sisters – don't have to be afraid of me. Here, let me show you something."

Crag came close. He was less than a head taller than Watcher, and certainly not any heavier. At first, Watcher thought Crag was breaking his own rule and bowing, but he was only twisting his head so that Watcher could see the back of his neck. The fur there was patched and thin, barely concealing rows of pink scars on the skin underneath.

Red Fur, Watcher thought. *Or what happens after more red furs than a wolf can count – clutches and clutches of them.* The back of Watcher's neck tingled where it too had been bitten. From where Kicker would take hold of him and shove his snout in the snow.

"I can see it on your face that you know what those are," said Crag. He was looking at Watcher again. He was looking *into* his eyes. "Yes, I can see that you know well. I was indeed the runt of my litter. Who knows why or how I was allowed to live. But I did. For so long I thought perhaps it would have been better if I hadn't. I thought that every time they bit my neck it would have been better to die. Every time they drove my snout into the snow and the dirt. Every time they held me down and laughed. My *brothers.*"

Kicker's face flashed in Watcher's mind. That look on his face. The look that came before the red fur. *When I am lord of this pack,* he had said. *You will have to learn to pull your own weight.*

"Oh, the older wolves would come along every once in a while and break it up," Crag went on, pacing circles around Watcher in the chamber, moving in and out of the shadows between the shafts of light. "But only after the damage was done."

For the briefest of moments, like a hummingbird zipping over a blossom in summer, a thought stole into the place behind Watcher's eyes. A thought of *him* standing over Kicker, not Orion. It was *him* readying to teach his brother the lesson that would not so easily heal.

"How – how did you make it stop?" Watcher finally asked.

Crag smiled. Watcher didn't have Windy's nose. But he had his owl eyes. That smile reminded him of another wolf. It reminded him of Bone.

As Watcher dropped his eyes back to the ground, he caught the flicker of another wolf in the chamber. It slunk along the wall behind the crisscrossing lights, breathing quiet as a mouse. Watcher's heart nearly stopped and sent him from the woods. It was one of the *creatures.*

"I will show you how I made it stop, Watcher. I will show you my secret. It is something you must see to believe. Try to keep your eyes open for as long as you can."

Watcher shrunk. He couldn't stop himself from sliding back toward the tunnel behind him, his ears flat and a whimper welling up in his chest. *Something bad is about to happen,* he thought.

"Ripper," Crag called to the shadows. "Hunt."

A burst of teeth and claws tore through the light, gnawed fur atop sharp bones. It leapt over the mounds and cleared the chamber in two strides. Watcher screamed and fell back toward tunnel. He toppled over on his lame leg to his back, exposing his belly. The *creature* was on top of him. Mouth open. Fangs bared to put Watcher into the red dirt.

"Stop!"

Crag's voice echoed in the chamber. Watcher whimpered on the dirt floor, waiting for the bite. The wolf called Ripper loomed over him. Those sunken eyes were locked on Watcher's throat. The forever smile of long teeth in its withered snout glistened with dangling slather.

"Ripper, retreat."

The wolf gave Watcher but one more sniff before trotting back across dirt floor, where he sank again into the shadows. Crag let Watcher stand back up, shivering on his three legs, panting as if he'd just loped the entire length of the Gray Woods.

"You see, Watcher," Crag said, "like you, I too saw things other wolves didn't see. I thought things other wolves didn't think. And in doing so, I saw what I had to do. What must be done.

"At first, I thought the key was the first share – that share which is given to the strongest wolves and keeps them stronger. But then I realized that it was *all* the shares. Even the strongest wolves must eat. I may have been a slave to my brothers. But we were *all* slaves to our hunger. That's the way the Trees made us, or so they say, to desire the red the way the Great Crowns desire the green.

"So I thought and I thought. I watched and I watched. I took special note of the badgers and the way they made their tunnels and their holes. The way unsuspecting wolves fell into them sometimes when they ran. Then I found the beginnings of a cave – this cave – and I knew my chance had come. See, look what I have done."

Crag beckoned Watcher to the wall, where there was another hole in the dirt, encircled by the winding roots. This one was not aimed to the sky, but down deeper into the earth. Crag put his eye to the wall. Watcher thought he heard the whisper of a coughing laugh escape under his breath. Crag stepped aside and made room for Watcher. A smile – that awful, Bone-like smile – threatened at the corners of his mouth.

Watcher put one of his big eyes to the hole. There was a small chamber at the bottom. Its far side, where the entrance should have been, was nothing but a pile stones and dirt. A shape moved in the darkness. It was a wolf. Watcher knew that shape. He could smell the familiar scent creeping up through the hole. It was Orion.

"You've trapped him!" Watcher all but shouted. He couldn't help himself. But Crag didn't seem to care. "What are you doing to him? Why?"

"You may not believe me now, Watcher, but I'm helping your brother. I'm helping your family. Most of all I'm helping *you*. Right now your brother believes that he earns his share by his strength. By his speed. By his skill. How will he ever put the pack first that way? I must teach him that he earns his share through *obedience*. He will only receive food when he learns to obey the voice of the pack. Then he will become a servant of the pack, like me."

Watcher slowly crept back from Crag, shivering from snout to tail, trying to hold back the whimper in his throat. He flicked his eyes to the *shape* slinking behind the light – Ripper. Watcher thought about the *creature's* gaunt face, withered fur, and bony frame. He thought about the way its fur looked as though it had been scratched and gnawed nearly to the skin.

He starved them, Watcher thought, horror rising behind his eyes. *These creatures were not born this way. Windy was right! They had once been wolves – until Crag turned them into something else.*

"Who were they?" Watcher asked.

"Now they are called Ripper, Biter, and Tearer. They had other names once, long ago. But honestly, I've forgotten them. How displeased my mother would have been if she knew I had unlearned the names of my own brothers."

"Your brothers?" Watcher could no longer keep the revulsion from his face. "Crag, this is wrong! This is evil! This is against the Ancient Laws!"

"The Ancient Laws?" Crag suddenly roared. "What do the Ancient Laws do, Watcher, but reward the strong and forget the weak? Allow the big to terrorize the small?"

"Not Orion!" Watcher cried. "Never Orion. He's my true brother. He loves me!"

"For now, perhaps, while you're both young. But I promise you this, Watcher. I promise you that one day he'll forget about you. One day he'll believe that he is too great for your small company. The strong *always* forget the weak, Watcher. The big *always* pin down the small. They climb upon us, like these mounds, to stand even that much taller than the rest. The only way to stop it is to pin them first. To turn their strength into yours. To make them your slaves."

Watcher wanted to close his ears so he couldn't hear Crag's voice. But behind his owl eyes, his thoughts returned to the last day in the Gray Woods. To when he learned Orion might leave and join the Far Runners. Might leave Watcher all alone. *No, no, no!* Watcher said to himself. *Don't listen!*

"You see, my brothers will never forget me, Watcher," Crag continued. "They'll never abandon me or betray me. I've taught them how to put the pack first. I've taught them to obey. Don't you see? Of all the Gray Woods wolves, I knew you would be the one to understand. You and I are the same. I've waited and waited to meet a wolf like me. And now that you're here, I'll do for you what I did for myself. I'll do for Orion what I did for my brothers."

Watcher wanted to scream and howl for help. But who would answer? Orion was down in that hole, soon to be driven mad by hunger. Soon to scratch and bite his fur when his belly burned. To shrink down until his ribs showed through his once glorious fur. That smile that Watcher so loved on his brother's lips would become the grin that was forever carved onto Ripper's.

"No!" Watcher finally shouted. "I won't let this happen!" But how could he, just a three legs, overpower Crag and his *creatures*? How could he free his brother and escape?

Watcher was still searching for an answer when a great clamor rose up from the tunnel beyond the chamber's entrance. Wolves barked and yelped in fear and confusion. Ash reappeared at the hole. For the first time since Watcher had met him that easy smile was gone from his face.

"I told you we were not to be disturbed," Crag snapped. "What's all that racket?"

"Wolves, Crag! Wolves at the cave entrance! Dark wolves with midnight fur. They're attacking us. I think it's the Lone Rocks!"

Watcher saw Crag's face quiver and melt into a horrified mask. Bone had tracked them after all, even to the cave. He'd come to fulfill his promise and put all the Gray Woods wolves into the red snow.

16

"Ripper, Biter, Tearer!" Crag screamed into the cave. "Defend!" The terrible *creature* burst from the shadows at the back of the chamber and flew down the tunnel toward the fighting. Just behind him, Watcher heard the two others – Crag's two other brothers – pounding after him on the dirt pathway.

But Crag did not lead them, not the way Watcher's father would have led the Gray Woods Pack against the their enemies. Instead he began to whimper, pacing this way and that on the chamber floor, asking the Trees, the Sky, and Father Earth to hide him. He paced all the way back behind the gray-lit mounds, hiding in the shadows where he had kept his former brother, Ripper, until all Watcher could see were the glints of his big tear-filled eyes.

Watcher wasted no time and sprang from the chamber into the tunnel, running as fast as his three legs could carry him. Bramble Woods Wolves were everywhere, running, yelping, and howling. The cave had fallen into chaos. At the main entrance – that black hole like a tooth-filled mouth – the *creatures* and a few of the pack's bigger hunters blocked the path into the tunnels, battling hard. But framed in daylight on the other side, clutches of midnight-furred Lone Rocks raged against them. Watcher could smell their fury. Their snarls drowned out the cries of the Bramble Woods Pack. Teeth and claws were already drawing red.

Over the baying and growling of battle, Watcher heard one of the Bramble Woods Wolves yell out: "We'll give them to you! For the Trees' sake we'll give them to you! Just leave us be!"

Watcher knew who *they* were – he and his family. But Crag's brothers had begun to fight, and Crag was not there to call them off. They fought as though they felt no pain. They attacked as though they felt no fear. It was because they truly felt neither, Watcher knew. It was because they weren't wolves anymore. Crag had turned them into something else, something more like ants. But not even they could hold back the Lone Rocks forever.

Watcher started back down the tunnel. He knew he had to find Kicker, Glimmer, and Windy before the cave's defenses fell. Fortunately, he only went a little further before he found them. All of them were breathless with moonround eyes. Kicker and Glimmer's fur was mussed and patched with red. They had been fighting as well.

"What happened?" Watcher asked.

"The guards at the mouth of chamber tried to drag us up to the front," said Kicker. "They wanted to give us over to the Lone Rocks."

"But Kicker and I wouldn't let them," said Glimmer. Her words shook on her tongue. She shivered from ear to paw, as did Kicker.

"You have to follow me," Watcher said, already backing down the tunnel. "We don't have much time. The Lone Rocks will break through any moment."

"What we have to do is get out of here," Kicker growled. "There must be another tunnel that leads above ground somewhere."

"We can't go yet. Now without Orion."

"Where is he, Watcher?" asked Windy. "Why can't I smell him?"

"Crag trapped him in one of the chambers. There's no time to explain. I think I know where it is. We have to get him out." Watcher thought his brother and sisters would follow him at once. But Kicker didn't budge. He only moved to shake his head.

"There's no time," he said. "Orion will have to take care of himself."

Watcher couldn't believe his ears. "Kicker, this is Orion we're talking about. This is our brother!"

"I know who he is!" Kicker snarled, baring his teeth, still specked with another wolf's red. "But you remember that night in the Gray Woods as well as I do. Lady Frost Feather told us not to go back for the others. She told us we would only fall into the red snow beside them. Even Orion listened to her. He would do the same thing for us."

For an instant, for just a breath, Watcher thought he saw Glimmer and Windy hang their heads beneath Kicker's will. Watcher felt his own ears start to lie flat. But he too remembered that night of their first escape, lying helpless at the bottom of the ravine, waiting to die. He'd told Orion not to wait for him. Not to come back. But his brother had come regardless. *I am a Gray Woods Wolf,* Watcher said to himself. *I make my own mind.*

"Then go," said Watcher. "But I'm going to dig Orion out." This time he didn't wait and he didn't look back. He ran back toward the central chamber, keeping an eye out for a sharp, nearly hidden turn to the left, just before the Tree-root entrance. He'd seen it when Ash had led him to meet with Crag. It was his only guess – his only hope – where he might find Orion.

As the turn drew near, Watcher discovered with joy that he did not run alone. Glimmer and Windy were just behind him. And after them, another length back, came Kicker. His brother refused to look at Watcher. He ran with his hard eyes fixed to the dirt beneath his paws.

But Watcher had no time to worry about snout groundings or red fur on the back of his neck. Just up ahead was the sharp turn. Watcher nearly tumbled past it he was running so fast. But he scrambled down the tunnel, which came to a dead end, one that looked newly burrowed.

"Orion!" Watcher called through the wall of dirt and stone. "Orion are you there?"

For a moment there was nothing. Only silence. Watcher nearly panicked. There was no time to search the rest of the tunnels in the cave. The Lone Rocks were coming. But just before Watcher gave up, a muffled voice cried out through the wall.

"Watcher? Is that you? What's happening? Where are the others?"

"The Lone Rocks are here, Orion! They're breaking into the cave. We're all here to get you out."

"We'll never dig through this in time," Kicker hissed, looking over his shoulder. The sounds of snarling and baying grew louder and louder behind him. "The Lone Rocks will be through the entrance any moment!"

"Kicker's right," Watcher heard Orion say from behind the wall. "Save yourselves. Leave me."

"I'm not going without you!" Watcher shouted. "Is there no weak place in the wall? Remember the ice, Orion. It looked thick as the river, but it was only a thin layer on top."

"I've been trying to dig out through the bottom corner, over here." Orion's voice moved to the far side of the tunnel. "But I've hit a stone. I can't go any further. It may be hopeless, Watcher."

But Watcher had stopped talking and had gotten to doing what he did best of all – looking. He found the stone that blocked Orion's way. It was indeed too big for any of the wolves to move. But, he also saw that it was resting on a smaller stone, one that could fit in Watcher's jaws. Watcher remembered the fat sparrow on the branch. He remembered the ice beneath Orion's weight. If the small stone was moved, the big one would fall a bit as well.

Everything on top of it would come down too. The hole wouldn't form at the bottom. It would open at the top.

"Hold on, Orion! I think I know what to do." Watcher began to scratch and claw at the dirt around the smaller stone. He had to make a space big enough to get his teeth all the way around it. In only a moment Glimmer and Windy seemed to understand what Watcher was up to.

"Watcher, let me," said his bigger sister. Both she and Windy began to clear a space around the stone, digging out the dirt twice as fast as Watcher could on his own. But even when Glimmer was finally able to grip the stone in her mouth and pull it only moved a little. It would not come out.

The panic rose again in Watcher's chest, that feeling of helplessness. He could hear the growls of Lone Rocks forcing their way into the cave. The dirt walls of the tunnel around him felt like they were closing in to bury them all alive. Then Kicker, a snarl on his lips, shoved them aside.

"Clear out, you pups!" he said. He seized the stone in his teeth and yanked with all his might. Watcher was afraid the little rock would still hold fast, but with one last heave it wrenched free. As Watcher had hoped, the big stone fell along with all the dirt and rocks above it. A small opening formed at the top of the wall, just big enough for Orion to squeeze through. He wasted no time and emerged into the tunnel, covered with dirt. He looked overjoyed to be free, but also famished and exhausted.

There was no time for thanks or celebration. The fighting in the cave had gone suddenly quiet. A loud voice roared through the silence, echoing through the tunnels.

"Gray Woods Wolves! Must another pack fall to the red snow for your father's crimes? Show yourselves and submit to our justice!"

Bone.

Watcher felt his insides turn watery as melting ice. Kicker had been right. They'd rescued Orion only to trap themselves to their deaths. But in the echoes of Bone's pronouncement, Watcher heard a sniffing in the tunnel. It was Windy.

"This way," she whispered. "There may be a chance."

"I thought you couldn't smell beyond the cave," said Kicker, but he and the others were running behind her nonetheless.

"Find the Gray Woods pups! Bring them to me!" Bone's voice raged after them. The pounding paws of heavy hunters and lieutenants charged into the cave, beating in Watcher's ears louder than his own blood. Not even Orion seemed eager to turn and face them, as he had been back in the Gray Woods. Dirt was caked into his fur. He moved slowly and heavily. Watcher could only imagine how hungry and tired he was. All they could do was chase after Windy.

Watcher still had no idea what she could possibly be smelling until he noticed that she paused ever so slightly under each ray of light streaming through the holes in the ceiling. *She's not smelling anything from beyond the cave,* Watcher realized. *She's smelling the edges of the cave itself, where the outside peeked in.*

"Whatever you're smelling for Windy, find it fast," Glimmer whispered. The Lone Rocks were closing in. But Windy said nothing. She was in her trance. She saw only in scent now – the invisible world hidden to other wolves' eyes. She led them down a tunnel that came to an abrupt end, one that seemed to be only half finished. One with no escape.

"I knew it!" yowled Kicker. "She's always followed ghosts, and now she's led us into a trap that will soon flow with our red!"

"Then we'll just have to make sure it also flows with the red of our enemies," said Orion. He shook himself, dirt flying from his fur. From some place deep inside, Watcher knew not where, Orion summoned up some last reserve of strength. His fur bristled and he seemed to grow twice over in size, filling the tunnel.

"Wait," said Glimmer, "look!"

Windy, still in her trance, had walked up to the very end of the tunnel, which ramped toward the ceiling. She dug her nose into a spot of dirt, wound through with ragged roots. The dirt fell away at her lightest touch. A sliver of snow and light fell between her paws.

"It looks like the ghosts save us again," said Orion. He turned back and rammed into Windy with his shoulder, shoving her through the small hole she'd formed with her nose. Kicker and Glimmer needed no such encouragement. They rushed into the cold air, with Watcher just behind.

The litter burst up from the ground like badgers in the summer, appearing at the roots of a great Tree, this one tall among her sisters, with needles still green as the spring. The tunnels must have run for a long way, Watcher thought, for this Tree was on the other side of a round hill, hiding the wolflings from the entrance to the cave on the far side.

At once they began to kick dirt and snow over the hole they'd just formed, masking their exit and their scent. Then, with no time for any rest or a plan, they ran again. They ran for their lives.

17

B one stood in the chamber of the three mounds, staring down at a squirming Crag. Long Claw held the small wolf under one paw, pinning him to the dirt by his throat. Crag was all that remained of the Bramble Woods Pack. The rest of them had fled or lay in the red snow or the red dirt, even Crag's brothers.

Behind Bone stood row upon row of Lone Rock Wolves, all but filling the rest of the cave's tunnels. Their midnight fur still bristled. Their eyes glowed green in the dim light.

"What is your name, whelp?" Bone rumbled.

Crag whimpered the answer, his voice squeezing out from beneath Long Claw's foot.

"And do you know who I am?"

"Bone of the Lone Rocks."

"That's *Lord* Bone to you, worm!" Long Claw lifted his paw from Crag's throat just long enough to rake him across the cheek, leaving three red streaks in his fur and a mewling cry on his tongue.

"L-l-lord Bone, of the Lone Rocks," Crag said again.

"Which one of the defeated behind us was your lord, Crag?" asked Bone.

"We – we had no lord, milord."

"Don't lie to me, runt!" Bone snapped his jaws before Crag's face. Long strands of slather slapped Crag along the snout. "Where has he fled? Where is he hiding?"

"I don't lie, milord! We had no lord. I – I spoke for the pack."

"*You?*" Bone's lips trembled. His snout recoiled as though he'd smelled something rotten. "An insect like you spoke for this pack? Over the three warriors that fought at the entrance to this cave?"

"Those *things* were not warriors," said Dark Fleece, the she-wolf. "They had no life in their eyes."

"They had no fear in them either," said Long Claw.

"They – they were my brothers, Lord Bone," said Crag. "It was I who taught them to have no fear. It was I who made them to be such formidable warriors. I could teach you how to—"

"You can teach me nothing!" Bone roared. Long Claw pushed harder into Crag's throat to strangle any further words silent. "All of this – your cave, your brothers – it is an abomination. No runt has ever been pack lord. No wolves live in holes beneath the earth. Even those who follow the Ancient Laws would have driven you out."

"But I'm like you, milord," Crag managed, his voice clawing from his throat. "I don't heed the Ancient Laws. I sought to make a New Way."

"*You?* Like *me?*" Bone roared again and slashed Crag across the other cheek, matching the red fur left by Long Claw on the other side. "You will never be anything like me. You are a runt. I am a lord. The New *Ways*, the Old *Ways*. All *Ways*. Do you know what Ways are, little runt? They are tricks to protect the weak. To water down our blood until the wolves are as helpless as mice and squirrels. But *strength* – strength needs no way. It needs no protection.

Strength is its own way. It is its own protection. What strength wants, it takes. What strength commands, is done. Look at the wolves behind me. The Lone Rocks are no longer a pack. We are an army! We also have no fear – not of any creature or pack, not even of the Far Runners. We will remind them all of the lesson of strength. Now, you have one chance to save your worthless skin, little Crag. Where are the Gray Woods Wolves?"

"I – I don't know," Crag bellowed. He looked around for mercy on the faces of any of the wolves above him. He found only hard eyes and glistening teeth.

"Were they not here in your cave? Did you not give them shelter under orders from the Council of the Flyers? Where are they? Why was Orion not fighting at the entrance?" Bone leaned in until his fangs all but scraped the top of Crag's snout. Crag tried to wiggle away, but there was nowhere to escape.

"Th-th-they fled, milord. The moment your attack started. I – I didn't trust Orion. I was beginning to – to *train* him as I did my brothers. It was the smallest one, Watcher, who I wanted most to join me."

"Watcher?" Bone sneered. "The cripple?"

"He sees the world like I do. He has owl's eyes. I thought he would understand the New Ways I had begun. I thought—"

"I don't care what you thought, runt. Where have they gone? Answer now or the next thing you shall smell is your own red in the dirt beneath you."

"I cannot say for certain, milord. But Ash, one of our wolves, he told me that when he fetched them from the Council of the Flyers they were asking after some place – some far away valley that an old buck had told them about. But they can't get there, milord! Surely it's too far. It may not exist at all. It is said to lie beyond the borders of the Old Forest itself, past the Fallen Tree Bridge and over the White Mountain."

"Beyond the Fallen Tree Bridge?" said one of Bone's lieutenants, dismayed. "Lord Bone, surely we can't chase them so far." The words hardly left the wolf's tongue before Bone's claw slashed across his face and sent him rolling onto the dirt floor.

"*Can't? Can't?* We are the Lone Rock Pack. We do as *I* command. With strength, there is no *can't.* The Gray Woods Pack did not scar only my face. They scarred the pride of this pack. That scar cannot be healed until all those that carry Gray Woods blood have it spilled onto the snow or the dirt or the grass. Do you understand me?"

"Yes, milord," said the wolf, staggering back to his feet.

"The Lone Rock Pack will run from Great Fields to Haunted Forest. We shall no longer live under any Laws or Way. We are the strongest. Strength shall be our only Law. Do you *all* understand?"

The wolves in the chamber and the tunnel beyond began to bark and howl. They growled and rumbled. They snapped their teeth and slapped their paws upon the dirt.

"I shall have Orion as I had his father and his mother," Bone growled, as much to himself as to Dark Fleece and Long Claw. "He is the only one that could oppose me." Bone looked back down upon Crag. "He and his owl-eyed, crippled little brother. Put this one and his New Ways into the red dirt, Long Claw."

"But you promised me!" Crag shrieked.

"There are no promises between the weak and the strong."

Bone walked away as Long Claw did his bidding, away from the crisscrossing beams of light and into the cave's deepest shadows. Before long, the Lone Rocks ran once more from the hole in the earth, out into the Forgotten Woods, searching the snow and the air for the scent of Anorak's children.

18

The wolflings ran through the thin snows until the ruined land and fading Trees of the Forgotten Woods fell behind them. As the Trees grew greener and the shrubs and bushes thicker, the hills began to fall deeper than they rose, leading the young wolves down into a narrow valley where the air was warmer and grass poked up through the white snow. Whenever they could, the wolves splashed through fast flowing creeks, rolled themselves in fallen nests, or rubbed through burrowed earth to mask their scent and hide their direction from Bone and the Lone Rocks.

As for Watcher, he tried his hardest to keep Orion from having to carry him. His brother was so tired and hungry. But eventually his good leg burned so badly that he fell to limping, like he had been bitten down to the bone. So Orion was forced to scoop him up in his jaws once again.

But after only a short way Watcher told his brother to set him down, to let him run on his own. *I won't be a burden,* he told himself. *I won't.* So even though the pain shot up through his paw with every step, he ran, keeping his eyes on the way ahead. He gave himself only a few quick glances to the right and the left, to see the new

Trees of yet another undiscovered wood, full of strange birds and creatures that made this stretch of the Forest their home.

After a while the litter finally slowed to a trot, unable to keep up the furious pace. Watcher wasn't too far behind, panting hard, his leg aching and throbbing. But before he could push himself even harder to catch up, Orion appeared, having turned back to walk beside him.

"How's your leg, little brother?" he asked.

Oh, how it hurts, Watcher thought. It trembled almost violently. The paw felt ragged, the pads nearly worn to bloody flaps. But Watcher wouldn't let Orion carry him again. For the first time Watcher could remember his brother looked wearier than he did, swaying on his feet as he walked. So Watcher lied.

"It actually barely hurts at all. I think it's getting stronger, really. All this loping has been good for it. It's you who looks tired. You shouldn't have carried me so far."

"Don't worry about me. I can run all day and all night, you know." Orion smiled, but the grin was as faded as his strength.

"You haven't eaten in days and days, not since the Great Crown, have you? You must be starving. You need to eat, Orion. You need to rest."

Orion shook his head. More dirt from his imprisonment in the cave fell from his fur. "I'll hunt for something when we come across some tracks. Then I'll be alright, I promise."

But Watcher wasn't so sure his brother would have the strength when the time came. He was about to say as much when Orion stopped walking altogether. He stood there in the snow under the branches of a pine with his head down, swaying a back and forth on his paws as though thinking very hard.

"Watcher, I want to ask you something. You must promise to tell me the truth."

"I always tell you the truth, Orion," Watcher said. His stomach twisted like a gnarled root, for he had just lied about the raging pain in his good leg.

"Did the Ancient Laws – did our father and mother – or did I ever make you feel like *him*?" Orion's words made Watcher's breath catch. "Did we make you angry, like Crag?"

"No," Watcher said right away, but he knew that he'd said it too quickly for Orion to believe it. To believe that he had thought about it long enough to have told the truth. But Orion waited.

In the place behind his eyes, Watcher saw himself walking behind his mother to the Tree where she'd shown him the seed. He remembered the fear that had stabbed down to his bones, that she might finally have sought to rid herself of him and his burden. He felt the burn on the back of his neck from the clutches of red furs and snout groundings Kicker had given him in the summer, the autumn, and the winter.

"Did you hear Crag talking to me?" Watcher asked after all those images and feelings had floated through his mind, like leaves on a stream.

"No. I didn't know he spoke to you. But I suppose he told you what he told me. He was shouting at me from behind the wall of dirt he let fall on his trap. He said I was just like his brothers. He said I would never know what it was like to always have to bow. To always have to be last. To always have to be afraid." Orion finally looked up from the snow. His yellow eyes were wet and glistening. "When Bone refused to bow to our father, on the hill where I brought down the chieftain, I wanted to fight him right then and there. To the death, if need be. For just that one slight. But in that prison under the Earth, I got to wondering: How many times have you been slighted, Watcher? How many times have I failed to stand up for you?"

Watcher began to tremble again. It made his chest hurt to see so much shame in his brother's eyes. "Other packs wouldn't have even let me live from a pup, Orion. But our mother and father did. I'm just glad to have had a pack at all."

"Any pack would be blessed by the Trees to have you, Watcher. To have your eyes. Any wolf would be blessed to see through them. I wish I could see through them."

"I'm just a three legs, Orion."

"Don't say that!" Orion snapped, a growl in his throat. When he saw that he'd made Watcher flinch, his voice softened again. "Don't ever say that about yourself. You're a Gray Woods Wolf. You're my brother. And if I'd been you, I would have been as angry as Crag for all my life."

"I can't ever be angry with you, Orion. Or with mother or father."

"Why?"

"Crag said you would never know what it was like to have to bow. Maybe he's right about that. But I don't think he'll ever know what it's like to bow when you *don't* have to. I did have to bow, Orion, always. But you always bowed back."

Orion finally came up to Watcher and nuzzled his fur. The tears on his whiskers wet Watcher's face. "You saved me, Watcher. You all saved me."

Watcher turned to find that Glimmer, Windy, and Kicker had all come back for them. His sisters were wagging their tails, running up to Orion to burrow into his big, furry side along with Watcher. All except for Kicker. Watcher caught his eye just before he lowered his head to the snow.

"Yes, *all* of us," Watcher said quickly, trying to cover for his brother. "It was Kicker who pulled out the stone that released you." Still Kicker refused to lift his eyes from between his paws. But Orion didn't seem to notice.

"Now we need to do some hunting," he said. "Kicker and Glimmer, I'll need your help."

Orion seemed so tired that Watcher wasn't sure they would be able to bring anything down, even with three of them. But they had to try. They had to eat.

"We haven't even seen any tracks for stretches and stretches," Kicker grumbled. "Where are we going to find some game?"

"Maybe beyond the river," said Windy, tasting the air with her nose. "There's something there. Some sort of creature, and something in the waters."

"How far is it?" Orion asked.

"Not far," said Glimmer. "I can hear it." She smiled when none of the others said they heard it too. "Maybe my ears make up for my nose."

"Your courage more than makes up for it," said Orion.

"But the ears *are* an added blessing," said Watcher, a laugh forming at the edge of his voice. "I always thought they were a little bigger than everyone else's."

"Now you've done it, Watcher!" Glimmer growled and laughed at the same time. She chased Watcher through the trees, nipping at his heels, running just slow enough not to catch him or make him fall into the snow. The others followed until they all heard the running river ahead. But the closer Watcher came, the louder he heard unusual splashes slapping over the rushing water.

They found the river only a stretch away, making a gentle turn between the Trees as it cascaded down a hill and over rocks, the ice holding no sway in the warmer valley. Watcher skidded to a stop in the thin snow at the riverbank's edge. His big owl eyes went moonround and his nose filled with the most curious scent. He'd never seen or smelled what he was seeing and smelling.

They were fish – clutches and clutches of them – no, packs and packs of them! But they weren't twisting and turning under the river like every other fish Watcher had ever seen. They were leaping! They were leaping above the foaming current like Great Crowns jumping through the Trees.

"Watcher, what are they?" asked Glimmer.

"I've never seen anything like them," he replied. "I don't think Long Tooth ever mentioned them either."

"What I want to know is if we can catch them and eat them," said Orion. He sunk his paws into the shallow river and snapped at the flying fish as they soared past. But he couldn't snag one in his mouth. They were too fast, even for him. Glimmer tried next, wading a little deeper into the river than Orion, but she had no better luck.

"You two are going to get swept away like leaves if you go any deeper," said Kicker, plopping down on his haunches by a Tree, looking as if he could care less about the amazing flying fish his brothers and sisters had just discovered. "We'll never catch those. And besides, we don't even know if we can eat them. They probably taste terrible."

"Well you won't find out back there, *snorter,*" said Glimmer, just before she missed another fish. Watcher thought she and Orion were getting closer to actually grabbing one by the tail, when he felt Windy go rigid beside him.

"Out of the water, both of you! Now!" she snapped, backing away from the bank, taking in deep pulls of river air. "Something's coming!"

"Lone Rocks?" asked Orion.

"No, something else. From the far side of the river. Something big."

No sooner had Windy said the words than the beast appeared. It lumbered from the woods, only a stretch upstream. Watcher's legs went stiff as his bones. If his eyes had gone moonround at the jumping fish, then there was no word in the wolf tongue for how wide they went at the sight of this creature. It was a monster. It walked on all fours and had teeth and claws like a wolf. But it was at least twice the size of a Chieftain of the Great Crowns, with thick fur, long and brown and shaggy.

"Run!" Kicker cried from his Tree. But Watcher couldn't move. Fear had first frozen him to his spot, but something else held him there now, swimming through his blood.

"Wait. I want to see," he said.

"What is it?" asked Glimmer.

"I've never smelled anything like it before," said Windy.

"Watcher," rasped Orion. "Kicker's right. We should go. I'm too tired to fight. I don't know if I could win against such a creature even if I wasn't."

"He's not interested in us," said Watcher, taking another step closer to the water.

"Watcher, you fool!" growled Kicker. "You're going to get us all killed!"

"No," said Windy. "Watcher's right. The thing is not angry or threatened. He's hunting. But he's not hunting us. He's hunting the fish."

Watcher could not tear his eyes from the beast. It waded out into the river, even into the wildest rushes. He may as well have been a big brown boulder, unmoved by the current as though he were a Tree with roots dug deep into the earth. He didn't try to catch the Leaping Fish with his teeth, as Orion and Glimmer had. Instead, he reached back with one of his great paws, nearly as big as Watcher's whole body, and swatted through the air. It took him three tries, but on the third, the monster struck two Fish from the air with a wet smack. They landed on the shore, wriggling and popping on the rocks and the snow. The enormous creature then lumbered out of the water and feasted upon his kill.

The wolflings had never seen a bear before, but Watcher suddenly realized he had heard about them and their name from long ago.

"It is the Uruduk," he whispered, as much to himself as the others. "The monster from the old times. The one from old Long Tooth's stories."

"Those were just made up to scare little pups," said Kicker. But he didn't sound so sure from where he hid behind his Tree.

"Don't you remember? They were some of the creatures made by Father Earth to fight the wolves, in the time of Romulus. They were more powerful than any other thing on the Earth. But as strong as they were, they were slow and dull witted."

"Perhaps we shouldn't test this one's speed or his wits today, Watcher," Orion said. But Watcher was no longer paying attention. He looked further down the river to where a low-lying pine limb hung just over the water, the needles and branches splayed out wide – wide like a big paw. Behind Watcher's eyes he no longer saw a branch. He saw the huge claw of the biggest Uruduk in the woods.

"Come on!" Watcher said, scampering down the bank. He didn't wait for the others, but skirted around the base of the Tree and hopped from the bank onto some rocks that led out beside the branch.

"Watcher, don't you fall in!" Glimmer called after him. But Watcher was too busy with his branch to worry about the frothing white splashes licking at the rocks. He had an idea.

"Watcher, what are you up to?" Orion asked. But Watcher just smiled, a smile like the kind Orion usually gave to him.

"I'm becoming an Uruduk, big brother!" Watcher took a bundle of pine needles in his teeth and pulled back on the branch, bending it like the fat Robin did so many days ago. He walked carefully backwards on the stones until the branch seemed ready to fling him into the river. Then he released it.

The branch snapped over water. It struck a clutch of leaping fish and batted them onto the shore, just like the Uruduk had done with his big paw. Glimmer whooped. She jumped up in the air and kicked her feet, spraying snow all over Windy and Orion. But they only laughed. Watcher pulled his branch back and let it go again, and then once more. By the time he leapt back onto the riverbank, a pile of wriggling fish lay on the tips of grass that peeked through the thin snow.

"Watcher!" Orion shouted. "Watcher, the great Hunter of Fish! Watcher, the Uruduk!"

"Watcher! Watcher!" Windy and Glimmer shouted over and over.

Then Orion finally quieted down his sisters and bowed low to his brother. Windy and Glimmer bowed with him. Watcher felt that trembling again, all over his body, like on the hill where the Chieftain of the Great Crowns had fallen at his paws.

"The first share for the one who made the kill," said Orion. "Say the blessing, Watcher."

Say the Blessing? Watcher's trembling turned to shaking. Only the lord of a pack said the blessing. He'd thought he would never again receive a first share, but he'd known from birth that he would never speak the blessing. He shook his head no to Orion, but his brother and sisters were already bowing their heads to the Fish in the snow with their eyes closed. So Watcher took a deep breath and spoke the words of his father.

"Great Fish, leapers from the water, this day you swam with courage. We take pride in your red snow and the strength it will lend our pack. For it was the Trees who sent us, and to the Trees we shall return."

The first bite of fish was oily and slimy on Watcher's tongue. The scales on its flesh rubbed against the roof of his mouth. But the second bite was flavor like Watcher had never tasted before. It splashed into his mouth, tasting like Watcher thought a living river should taste, cold and fresh and clean.

"Fish tastes good," said Windy with a mouthful of it.

"I can see why the Uruduk like it so much!" Glimmer agreed, laughing and prancing. But Orion was too busy feasting to say anything. Only then did Watcher truly understand how famished his brother had been. How weary from carrying Watcher in his jaws and leading the others. But even with Orion's appetite, there were still two fish left. Two fish meant for Kicker.

Watcher looked past the others and found Kicker still sitting on his haunches by his Tree. He was staring back at Watcher. Behind his eyes lurked a familiar danger. Behind his eyes crept red fur and snout groundings. And perhaps, Watcher thought, perhaps something else. Something worse.

"Don't you want your shares, Kicker?" Watcher offered quietly. Kicker never blinked or looked away.

"I'm not hungry, *Great Hunter*," he said.

19

After gobbling down the fish, the wolflings forded the river and began to lope again on the other side. Orion had yelled at Kicker to eat his shares before they left. But Kicker had ignored him and chased down a little mouse for his own dinner instead. His Fish had not gone to waste, though. Orion ate them both.

Several times Watcher hoped they would stop to rest in a thicket or between clumps of large rocks. His good leg threatened to falter beneath him, its paw raw and searing with every stride. Watcher nearly gave in and called out for Orion to carry him, but even with a belly full of fish, Watcher could see even his brother's strength was beginning to flag.

The litter needed to stop. They needed to rest. But every time they slowed, Windy caught a hint of the *darkness* upon the cold forest air, a hint of Bone. It seemed to hover over the shallow valley like a coming storm. The threat of the Lone Rocks kept them running, but Watcher feared it might soon run them to death.

At last, when Glimmer and Kicker's panting grew so loud that it echoed through the Trees, Orion called a halt. They'd come to the lowest place in the forest, just before the hills began to rise again. A deep mist had settled over the Trees there like a cloud, masking the woods in a gloom.

Watcher could only drag himself along to catch up, so Orion came back for him and snatched him up in his jaws, carrying him to the others where they huddled under a short Tree.

But though the young wolves finally sat or lay in the snow-covered grass, heaving deep breaths over their lolling tongues, sleep would not come. Every time Watcher closed his eyes he saw Bone's lone eye staring back at him in the dark, chasing him awake.

"We'll take turns," Orion said, pushing himself back to his feet with a grunt. "One awake, the rest asleep. Then we'll move on."

"But what about when it's Glimmer's turn?" Kicker snorted into the snow where he lay. "She can't smell, *remember?*"

"But I can hear better than any of you!" Glimmer snapped. She glared at Kicker with angry tears threatening.

"By the time you hear them they'll be right on top of us, *Dull Snout!*"

"That's enough," Orion barked. Glimmer and Kicker went quiet, but Watcher could hear his sister's growl still rumbling in her chest. "Glimmer, I'm sorry, but you'll have to skip your turn. I'll take two turns."

Glimmer hung her head. Watcher saw two tears, one from each eye, drizzle into her white fur. This time she was the one being left behind. Then of course, Kicker made it worse.

"So she'll get more sleep than the rest of us? That's not fair."

"*Fair?*" Orion said, his teeth emerging from behind his lips. "At a time like this you're worried about what's fair?"

A stomach-churning frission rippled through Watcher as Orion stalked toward Kicker. There was no time for fighting. There wasn't even time for stopping or sleeping. *Is there no safe place we can hide?* Watcher thought. He was about to cry out for his brothers to stop, when Windy's sharp whine stilled them all.

"Wolves!" she rasped. "Running into the valley. I – I only just smelled them. They're coming so fast!" The litter jumped to their feet, eyes and ears alert, tails in the air. Somehow Watcher's exhaustion slipped from his body for a moment, replaced by hot sparks racing up and down his legs.

"They've caught us," Kicker mewled, already backing away from the direction Windy's snout pointed. "They've caught us!"

"Quiet," Orion demanded. Then he whispered to Windy: "Is it the Lone Rocks? How much time do we have?"

"I – I don't know if they're Lone Rocks. They are strong and fierce. They are fast and unafraid. We cannot outrun them. They are–" Windy's voice faded into the mist as she fell into her scent trance.

"They're *what*, Windy?" Glimmer hissed, her eyes shifting back and forth across the shrouded forest before her. Watcher was about to repeat her question and try to snap Windy from her trance, when he caught the wolves' scent for himself and suddenly went as still and calm as his sister.

There were many of them. As many of them as Lone Rocks the night they had come to the Gray Woods. Their scent was fearsome, but it was not angry. Proud, but not wicked. The strength of spring was alive in their fur. Of all the scents Watcher knew, this one reminded him of only one other. Of his brother. Of Orion. Watcher then knew who came before their shapes appeared in the mist. The hot sparks in his body kindled into flames.

They glided over the snow, only shadows in the fog at first. They seemed like giants to Watcher. Like bears that could run with the speed of wolves. When they broke through the mist Watcher's breath escaped him like a hummingbird flitting from his chest.

"The Far Runners," Kicker whispered behind him.

He could have shouted it, Watcher thought, for the Far Runners took little notice of the clutch of young wolves they passed. It was not that they did not see or smell them. Of course they did,

Watcher knew. But the Far Runners had no need to fear them – them or anything else in the Old Forest. Each of the Far Runners could have been lord or lady of a pack. They loped in a line longer than Watcher had ever seen, winding like a living river through the Trees, bounding through the lowlands toward the rising hills.

"Come on," Orion whispered. Then he shouted it at the top of his lungs. "Come on!"

Watcher kicked off behind his brother before he could think about what he was doing. His brothers and sisters were beside him and before him, even Windy, awake from her trance. The wonder of the moment gave them strength to power through their weariness. It didn't matter if they couldn't keep up for long; they were going to run as fast as they could for as long as they could. Just to see. Just to know. Just to feel the rush of the wind beside the greatest of all wolves in the Old Forest.

Glimmer and Windy were laughing and shouting at each other. "Come on, Watcher, come on!" they called. He charged forward, ignoring the pain in his leg, his owl eyes fixed on nothing but the great wolves running off to his side. His tongue hung out of the side of his mouth, trailing behind him like Orion's did. And for a moment, one fleeting instant, Watcher kept pace. He flew with the Far Runners. He laughed and laughed with his sisters.

Then, as it was destined to do, Watcher's good leg slipped. He tumbled forward and crashed into the ground, dirt and snow plowing up over his snout and into his open laughing mouth. He had fallen, as he always did. And as always, he slowly picked himself up, watching the Far Runners pass him by.

Just up ahead, he saw Windy slow to a trot, breathing hard not a stretch before him. Glimmer lasted as long as Kicker, the two of them stopping together beyond Windy. The column of Far Runners turned as he watched, curling like a snake through the woods. That was when Watcher saw his brother. Orion. And it was as though he saw him for the first time.

Orion wasn't just keeping pace with the Far Runners. He was passing them. Even now, after all he'd been through, he had strength enough to summon. His body coiled, sprung, and stretched with every stride, dancing over the snow and the grass, as graceful as a Great Crown. No root or fallen tree or bush could slow him down. He leapt over them like the Fish leapt over the Uruduk's River.

The heads of Far Runners began to turn. If they had failed to notice the litter before, Orion spurned them for it. They saw him then. And Watcher knew, even from so far away, for his eyes were like the owl's, they saw the same magnificent wolf Watcher had known from birth. But watching him like this, Watcher suddenly realized that perhaps he'd only known his brother in the part, not in full.

Orion had never run as fast as he could in the Gray Woods. He'd never fought has hard as he could. He'd never done as much as he could. *Perhaps for me,* Watcher thought. *Or perhaps for our father. But he'd held back.* There was no pup in the Forest like Orion, Glimmer had said. There'll be no wolf like him either, Watcher remembered saying. His heart broke when he realized they had both been right.

20

When Watcher at last caught up to the others he all but collapsed between Windy and Glimmer. His sisters and Kicker sat in the snow partway up one of the hills that climbed out of the valley, where the mist had given way to sunlight sneaking through the clouds and the Trees thinned into a clearing at the top.

Watcher could hardly keep from trembling. The scent of the Far Runners cloaked the woods upon the hill. It was a smell like spring, like life fighting its way past winter and up through the hard earth. The great wolves had formed the half circle around the hillcrest, and in the clearing above, Watcher saw the biggest wolf he had ever seen. His coat was golden brown like tall grass in the sunset. A she-wolf sat beside him, as radiant as Watcher's mother had been, with fur as snow white as Glimmer's. Before them stood Orion, bowing his head low to the snow.

"What are they talking about?" Watcher whispered.

"They're speaking very low," said Glimmer, shaking her head. "I could only hear when Orion got angry and yelled something about the Gray Woods to them."

"Orion yelled at the Far Runners?" Watcher said, his voice slipping into a gasp.

"Of course he did," sighed Kicker. "Orion's not afraid of *anything*, is he? Now he's going to get himself killed."

"No," said Windy, her eyes far away and moonround, "there was anger from Orion, but it is passing. Now there is something else on his scent. A choice, I think."

Watcher said nothing. The Far Runners had seen his brother. They'd seen him run. He knew what the choice was, and it made him as afraid as the first time he'd heard of it, back on the hill above the fallen tree when his father had told Orion to ramble and join the greatest pack in the Forest.

A deep voice called out over the hill, echoing over the valley, forcing Watcher to set his worries aside. "Pups of the Gray Woods," the voice said, "Children of Anorak. Come forth."

Watcher swallowed hard. Kicker and Glimmer shifted on their seats and Windy was still testing the air. All the Far Runners had turned their heads and lay their heavy gazes upon the wolflings. *There's no point in making them wait,* Watcher thought to himself. So three legs or not, he went first up the hill. A step or two later his siblings followed him to the clearing to stand before the Lord of the Far Runners and the Lady of the Pack.

"Greetings, young ones," said the lord. Watcher and the others bowed their heads. The great wolf tilted his in return. "I am Great Paw, Lord of the Far Runners. This is Winter Fur, our Lady. I have heard of your troubles and your sorrows. I can see them hiding behind your eyes and weighing heavily upon your shoulders. Word reached us through the birds of what Bone has done, and your brother has reminded us most *forcefully.*" A hint of a growl lit Great Paw's last word. Watcher stole a glance at Orion, just in time to see his brother dip his head a little lower.

"But Bone, craven though he was in committing this dark deed, was no fool," Great Paw continued. "He waited to strike at your pack when there were wars both to the North and the South. When we would have to run farthest and fastest to prevent calamity. Even now we must head south to head off a hardship as great as the one you now face."

"So you're not going to the Gray Woods?" The words leapt from Watcher's mouth before he could stop them. He immediately dipped his snout all the way to the snow, cowering as small as he could before Great Paw. But the big wolf spoke gently again.

"We are the Far Runners, little wolf. Our territory is vast, as is our responsibility. There is still time to prevent the red snow in the South. What happened in the Gray Woods is already done. But do not think Bone will escape justice forever. His time will come."

Watcher could not help a whimper from escaping his snout. Hot tears stung his eyes and a thick heat burned his throat. He heard Windy, Glimmer, and even Kicker, trying to hide their own crying beside him.

"Do not despair, young wolves." The voice that spoke these words so reminded Watcher of his mother's that his tears choked in his throat and he looked up at once from the snow. It was Lady Winter Fur, looking down gently on him and his littermates. The golden sunlight falling into the valley glowed upon her fur. "We must go, but we will not leave you with nothing. You are weary from running. We shall form the circle around you until the evening comes and it is time for us to move on."

"I shall patrol the woods myself, to keep you safe while you rest," said Great Paw. At once he leapt away, followed by a clutch of his lieutenants, racing into the woods. The rest of the Far Runners made a ring of fur and teeth around the Gray Woods litter.

Lady Winter Fur went to each of the wolflings, nuzzling them softly and nudging them down to the ground, even Orion. When she got to Watcher she looked down at his one good leg. The paw was cracked and bleeding. Watcher cast his eyes to the snow, ashamed of the withered leg curled up beneath him.

"Why do you look away, Owl Eyes?" asked the Lady, her voice soft as a breeze through the pine needles.

"I – I'm the runt," said Watcher. "I'm just a three legs."

"Even small things can grow to be great."

"That's what my mother told me," Watcher said, still fighting his tears. "She told me about the seeds, the Children of the Trees."

"Then she was very wise, and you would be wise to remember her words." Lady Winter Fur lay Watcher down and licked the bottom of his paw. Where she did, the raw places tingled and burned. "Go to sleep now, Owl Eyes. The Trees around this hill, the goddesses, are tall and strong. As we guard your bodies they will keep watch over your dreams. Listen to them, and perhaps they will speak to you."

Watcher was about to ask the Lady how the Trees could talk to a wolf, but the moment he closed his eyes, sleep captured him as easily as night catches day, taking him down deep into the dark fields of dreams.

Watcher dreamed. He found himself in a snowy field. At first he thought he was back in the Gray Woods, but the Trees were missing. It was only a vast plain, with the Sky Pack running over the horizon in the golden light of the setting sun.

Watcher heard another wolf's paws crunch behind him in the snow. He turned around and found his mother. He tried to run to her, to nuzzle up against her snout and look into her sunrise eyes. But no matter how far Watcher ran he could not seem to get any closer. She was not running away. She was just standing in the deep snow, so close but forever away. After a while she pointed her gray snout to the ground before Watcher's paw.

"Look," she said.

Watcher did and found a small speck beneath his nose. It was one of the Trees' Children. It was a seed. He looked back up to his mother.

"You must put it in the Earth, Watcher," she said to him, her voice a whisper on the wind. "You must make it grow."

So Watcher dug with his good paw, trying to make a small hole for the seed. But just as he breached the snow and began to burrow into the dark Earth, his claw struck something hard and unyielding, like a rock. Watcher scraped at it, clearing the dirt away from its edges. It was a white stone.

So Watcher began to dig around the stone. But all he did was uncover more and more of them. Yet the more he uncovered the more the stones took a shape. Watcher's paws began to tremble. Before he had finished digging he knew what it was. They were not stones. They were bones.

They were the bones of a wolf – a small wolf. The skull had two large sockets for eyes. Eyes like an owl's. And it had curled up leg tucked against its breast. A lame leg. The bones were Watcher's.

"You must plant the seed," Watcher's mother said again. "You must make it grow!"

Watcher yelped as he woke. His heart still thundered from his dream. But slowly his head cleared and he returned from the field of his vision, where he had been digging up his own skeleton. He was still in the clearing atop the hill. His brothers and sisters were beside him, their chests rising and falling with sleep's deep breaths – all except for Orion.

Watcher bolted to his feet. That old fear he kept hidden down in the dark pools of his chest climbed to the surface again and clawed at the back of his mind. *The Far Runners have left,* he thought, *and they've taken my brother away with them.*

But the great pack still sat in the ring around the wolflings, as though they hadn't moved the entire time, like wolves made of stone.

Evening was coming. Watcher had slept most of the day. From the hilltop he could see a break in the clouds of winter where golden sunlight peeked through. In the gloaming, he saw Orion. He stood off in the Trees, sitting with Great Paw like the way he used to sit with Father.

"You love your brother very much, don't you Owl Eyes?" said a voice. It was Lady Winter Fur. Watcher hadn't even heard her approach, for her steps were quiet like falling snow.

Watcher nodded. His throat was tightening again. He wanted to say: *Please don't take him away from me!* But he couldn't. He wouldn't. His brother belonged among wolves like these. His brother was the greatest wolf. After a moment, he finally managed: "He's saved my life lots of time, milady. He's the strongest wolf I know."

Lady Winter Fur smiled at Watcher. She padded over to him and licked the side of his face, looking at him with those eyes that reminded Watcher of his mother's. "There is more than one kind of strength, Watcher," she said. "And there is more than one way to save a life."

Watcher was going to ask what she meant when Lord Great Paw returned, Orion at his side. Watcher braced himself for the announcement. He readied himself to head on without his brother. He was already hoping that Glimmer would be able to keep him safe from Kicker when Orion trotted past him and began to rouse the others.

"Come on," he said. "It's time to go."

"You're coming with us?" Watcher said, trying to keep the tears from wetting his fur.

"Yes, he is," said Great Paw. The lord's face was a mask, but Watcher thought he heard a disappointed growl in his words. "And I will leave you all with the same warning I left your brother. It will be some time, perhaps a moon or more, before we return from the South. Between now and then you will have to look out for yourselves. If Bone still chases you, then he has skirted around this valley, avoiding a confrontation with us. Your brother says you lope for this Far Valley. Only the Trees know if it is real or not. But either way, you must cross the Fallen Tree Bridge to reach it. Be alert, for Bone may have circled around to cut off your escape. I ask the Trees for your safety, until we return and bring justice with us."

With that, Great Paw kicked off the hill. Snow and dirt flew from under his paws. The Far Runners bayed and howled as they formed the line behind him. The last to leave was Lady Winter Fur. She bowed her head to Orion and the others, but she saved a special bow for Watcher.

"Goodbye, Owl Eyes," she said. "I hope one day to see what wolf grows from the pup." Then she was gone. Watcher and his litter-mates stared after the Far Runners as they tore through the Forest, heading south through the Trees. None of them stared harder or longer than Orion.

After the pack was gone, the Gray Woods litter sat quietly for a while, until Glimmer said: "Windy and I thought you were going with them. With the Far Runners."

"They did ask you, didn't they?" said Kicker, looking down at the snow between his paws.

"It doesn't matter," Orion said. "We have to go. Bone may already be ahead of us. There's no time to waste." He began to trot away, when Watcher called after him.

"Can you come back, though? Can you come back and join them after we're all safe in the Far Valley?"

Orion looked back at Watcher, or perhaps past him, to where the Far Runners still ran. His fiery yellow eyes were so sad. "Come on," was all he said. "It's time to go."

And so they ran, up the hills to the other side of the shallow valley. But as they went, Watcher felt a heavy weight slowing him down, pulling from within his chest. He'd freed Orion from the hole in Crag's Cave. But now he wondered if Orion was still trapped, imprisoned in an invisible hole that followed him wherever he went.

And Watcher wondered if it was he, not Crag, who had put his brother there.

But there was no time for Watcher ask these questions aloud. The wolflings picked up the pace. For soon after the scent of the Far Runners cleared the air and the litter reached the high ground once again, Windy detected faint traces of another pack on the winds. Bone and the Lone Rocks were coming.

21

"Let me carry you a while, Watcher," Orion said as they loped for the Fallen Tree Bridge. He ran beside Watcher and reached with his teeth, but Watcher scampered away.

"No!" he shouted. "I can do it." He didn't look up at Orion. He fixed his eyes before him, gritting his teeth and pushing harder and harder on his good leg. Watcher didn't know if Lady Winter Fur was magical or not, but somehow when she'd cleaned his paw she had also healed it. His good leg still ached, but Watcher wasn't going to let his brother carry him. Not this time.

The litter had long ago left the warmer valley winds behind. The air had become colder again, colder and heavy with the scent of Lone Rocks. The woods the wolflings now ran through were thick with Trees. But the ground had become rockier and more treacherous the farther they went – the closer they drew to the Fallen Tree Bridge.

But that was not all that slowed Watcher's pace. Ever since he'd left the Far Runners his guilt had grown heavier and heavier. He was sure Great Paw had offered Orion a place among his pack – among the Far Runners. But Orion had said no. And Watcher knew why.

It's because of me, he thought. *It's because I can't find a pack of my own. It's because I'm weak.* That knowledge burned Watcher worse than all of Kicker's neck bites and snout groundings ever had. And that burning made Watcher mad.

"Watcher, we need to hurry!" Orion said, again running closer.

"I can run on my own, Orion!"

"The Lone Rocks are moving to cut us off, Watcher!" Orion snapped his teeth by Watcher's ear to make him pay attention. "They're trying to beat us to the bridge. And if they do – if they're waiting for us when we get there – we may not be able to escape again."

"Then run as fast as you can and let them catch me!" Watcher all but screamed. But Orion had heard enough. He snatched Watcher up by his scruff and hoisted him into the air. "Put me down, Orion! Put me down!" Watcher kicked and squirmed in Orion's grasp, but he knew he was fooling himself if thought he could break free. So in the end he just hung there in Orion's teeth and cried. The world turned to water, like he was looking at it from under a river. He couldn't even see Windy or Glimmer's faces when they ran beside him and asked him what was the matter.

"Nothing," he said. But inside, making the burning go hotter and hotter, he thought: *I'm just as bad as Crag. I've put Orion in a trap, one from which he can't break free.*

For a long time after that, none of the litter spoke. They put their heads down and loped for all they were worth, leaping over the rocks that now pushed through the snow. The wind from their speed eventually dried Watcher's teary eyes. But when they had been running for stretches and stretches and the moon had risen blue and white over the Forest, Windy let out a startled yelp.

"The Lone Rocks," she said. "I can smell them again. The Far Runners were right. They must have skirted around the hills instead of following us down. But they haven't just circled from one direction. They're coming from both sides. And they're coming fast!"

"They're going to catch us," Kicker cried, panic leaping into his voice. "All this way and they're going to catch us in the end!"

Orion, his mouth still full of Watcher's scruff, turned to growl at Kicker to take hold of himself. And almost ran them all to their doom.

Both the woods and the rocky ground came to an end before them. Orion dug his heels into the snow, skidding to a halt. Kicker and Glimmer plowed into his back, shoving him forward – to the very edge of a sheer cliff.

Watcher swung out in the grip of Orion's teeth. For a breath he hung over nothing but air, the Earth falling away beneath him, into blackness like the chasm from his nightmares that was Bone's empty eye. But Orion bit down hard to keep Watcher from falling to his death, stinging the back of his neck with hot pain.

Orion backed up from the cliff, setting Watcher down to catch his breath. "That was close," he panted. "Watcher, are you alright? I bit down so hard. I'm sorry."

Watcher wanted to shout that he was fine, that his neck had grown tough from clutches and clutches of Kicker's bitings. But he saw the way Orion looked at him. He heard how sorry he really was. Watcher took a deep breath. *They were my brothers,* Crag had said to him in the caves. So much anger in his voice. In his big eyes. Eyes like Watcher's own. *I don't want to be like Crag,* thought Watcher. *I won't be like him.*

"I'm fine," he said at last. "Really, I'm fine."

"What is this?" Kicker said, staring down into the canyon's depths. None of them, not even Watcher, could see to the bottom. And none of them, not even Orion, could possibly jump to the other side.

"It's the Crack in the Earth," said Watcher, remembering back to Long Tooth's tales. "It was another one of the ways Father Earth tried to kill Romulus. By swallowing him whole."

Watcher had never seen anything as deep and wide as the Crack before. Not even the Wide River. Tall Trees, old goddesses from when the world was young, lined either side. Blue moonlight glowed through their needles like frosty breaths on a winter morning. Their branches drooped toward the Crack, as though it was an open mouth trying to drink them down like rainwater.

"How do we get across? We're trapped!" Kicker's voice was climbing higher and higher, flying with fear. "They're going to get us!"

"Shut up, Kicker!" Orion snapped. "The Fallen Tree Bridge is the only way to the other side."

"I can smell it, I think," said Windy, breathing deeply of the air. "It's not far. But we need to hurry. The Lone Rocks are closing in from both directions. Long Claw is before us. Bone and Dark Fleece are at our backs."

The clutch of them set off again, but fortunately Windy was right, they didn't have far to run. The Fallen Tree Bridge appeared before them.

The bridge's end on the litter's side clung to the cliff's edge with roots like eagle's talons. They curved into the rocks like two knuckled fingers, spread open in an entryway onto the bridge. The gnarled pathway stretched across the deep chasm to a yawning black mouth in the Trees on the other side, tunneling into thick woods. Looming over those Trees was the White Mountain, it's snowy peak awash in blue moonlight.

"We have to cross *that?*" Kicker said, stealing a glance from the thin bridge down into the black depths. "There must be another way."

"Even if there is we'd never reach it," said Windy, turning a small circle as she sniffed the air. "The Lone Rocks are almost on top of us. We must cross here. We must cross now!"

"But what's to stop the Lone Rocks from chasing us across to the other side?" Kicker mewled, backing away from the bridge. "We can't outrun them forever. At least not *all* of us."

"Say that one more time and I'll leave you on this side to slow the Lone Rocks down!" growled Orion.

"Maybe," said Glimmer, "if they don't see us go across, and all they see is this bridge and the dark forest on the other side, they'll question themselves and Bone. Maybe they'll also be too afraid to cross."

"I'm not too afraid!" Kicker snarled. But Watcher could hear it in his brother's voice and could see it in his eyes, sneaking wary glances to the cliff's edge.

"There's no time to argue! We must go now!" Without waiting for Orion to give the word, Windy stepped onto the tree bridge and started her way across. Glimmer came next, and after, Kicker.

"I'll never hear the end about the girls going first," he whined as he slowly stepped through he roots.

Watcher swallowed hard. He almost asked Orion to carry him across in the safety of his jaws. But he wouldn't. He had to do this on his own. He crept up onto the bridge and inched himself through the root entrance. Even beneath Watcher's small body, the tree bridge groaned like a tired old wolf. The Crack seemed to breathe beneath him, blowing up a cold wind, trying to knock him off the bridge. Trying to swallow him whole.

Watcher was half way across when Orion stepped on behind him. The bridge shuddered. Its clawing grasp on the ledge behind Watcher seemed to slip. The bridge rocked back and forth. The wind over the canyon began to gust. It yanked at Watcher's fur, grabbing at his good leg. He stumbled and fell to his chest. Only the claws on his hind legs, digging deep into the bark, kept him from falling. Behind him, Orion called his name. It sounded so far away. All Watcher could see was the blackness below. All he could hear was the howl of the wind.

Watcher closed his eyes. He remembered what old Gold Hoof had said to him. That the journey would be hard. *That one of you may fall before the end.* Watcher wondered if this was the moment. Would he be the one to fall? The wind in the Crack blew again. It was as though Watcher caught a whisper at its edges, speaking to him.

Come on, said the wind, *just let go. It will be so easy once you're falling. It will be better for the rest of them if you do.* Watcher opened his eyes and looked down into the Crack. *It would be so easy,* he thought. But then he heard another voice from the far side of the bridge, shouting over the gusts.

"Watcher, look at me! Don't look down! Look at me!" It was Glimmer. Her eyes were fixed on him – eyes like his mother's. She stood on the far end of the Bridge. Watcher could tell she wasn't going anywhere without him. It was as though she was reaching out to him with her voice, trying to pull him closer.

"Yes, Watcher," said Orion behind him. "Look at Glimmer. Follow her voice. I'm right behind you! We can make it!"

"Please, Watcher, one step at a time!" Glimmer seemed almost ready to come back out on the bridge and grab him. But Watcher couldn't let her do that. *We* can make it, Orion had said. *We.* Watcher summoned all his courage and forced himself back onto his leg. One hobbling step at a time he willed himself across. Twice more the bridge shuddered. The wind from the Crack whirled and ripped. But at last Watcher made it between the branch doorway at the other side and stepped onto firm land.

"You made it!" Glimmer yapped. She and Windy jumped around Watcher, licking his face and nuzzling his fur. And when Orion made it to their side he jumped down and joined them.

"You did it, Watcher," he said. "*You* did it."

"No," Wathcer said, only barely catching his breath. "*We* did."

"We made it over the bridge, but we haven't escaped yet," said Kicker. His eyes were moonround and staring back across the Crack. Watcher followed his gaze. What he saw made his skin crawl like worms beneath his fur.

Glowing green orbs danced along the ledge, bounding closer and closer from the North and from the South. Baying, barking, and ragged breathing preceded the bobbing lights. They were eyes. The eyes of the Lone Rock Pack.

22

"Into the woods!" Orion rasped. "Hide in the shadows, quick! We can't let them see us, so don't run. Stay still. We'll find out if Glimmer's hope holds true."

Watcher scrambled into the black, tumbling over the roots of an old pine to crouch in the dark. The ancient goddess behind which he hid was one of those teetering on the very edge of the canyon, all but falling in. Her roots just clung to the Earth as though she might topple over at any moment.

Across from Watcher, on the other side of the entryway into the woods, Windy and Glimmer huddled together, squeezed behind a prickly bush. Kicker had run farther than Watcher wished he would, disappearing behind another pine at only the last moment. And above Watcher stood Orion with his heartbeat pumping so hard that it drowned out the rapid patter of Watcher's own.

The floating green orbs reached the far side of the Fallen Tree Bridge. In twos and threes the bodies that held the glowing eyes stepped into the blue moonlight, midnight-furred and sharp-toothed Lone Rocks. *So many,* Watcher thought, his paws shuddering beneath him. *Almost as many as the Far Runners. And all nearly as big.*

Before the army of dark wolves stood Bone. Even from so far away, Watcher could see the black pit in his head where Anorak had torn the eye away so long ago.

"Were they here?" cried Bone, ragged breaths chasing his words. The long chase had exhausted the Lone Rocks – even their lord. "Dark Fleece, have they already come this way? Are we too late?"

The she-wolf stepped through the ranks, holding her snout to the air to sample the scents upon the wind. But Watcher could tell that her nose was not nearly as sharp as Windy's. The canyon's gusts that so nearly dragged Watcher to his doom now aided him by confusing her smell.

"They have already been here, milord. But I cannot smell them on the other side. For all I know they could have come this way a day ago, or fallen off the bridge to their doom. We are too late." She inched away from Bone even as she spoke, for his fur bristled and a growl erupted from behind his gleaming teeth.

"Curse those Gray Woods curs. Curse those Children of Anorak. I want their red. I want it! I want to see it spilled on the snow or the dirt or the rocks. I demand it! I must have it!"

As Bone raged, Watcher heard Orion's breaths go deep. He heard a growl fighting to break free from his brother's chest. But Orion had been born a hunter. He knew how to keep quiet, even when his blood burned. Watcher knew Orion would keep from betraying their hiding place.

But there was another sound on Watcher's side of the bridge. He heard it once, then twice. He stole a glance to Glimmer. From her wide eyes, he saw that she heard it too.

Scratch, scratch, scratch, went the noise.

Watcher peered over his shoulder and saw a shadow flicker amongst the Trees. Kicker was still moving. He was still stealing through the woods, trying to go deeper in. Trying to get as far away from Bone as he could.

Scratch, scratch, scratch, he went, over the dirt and snow.

Watcher wanted to scream. *Stop, Kicker! Stop, you fool!* But to even whisper would give them all away. So Watcher held his breath and prayed to the Trees that his brother would not be seen.

"I will have them, I swear it!" Bone continued to boil like a storm cloud on the other side of the canyon. "I won't rest until every Gray Woods Wolf in the world is dead."

"But milord," said one of his lieutenants, looking timidly to the other exhausted Lone Rocks for support. "Anorak is dead. The Far Runners have done nothing to halt your taking of the Gray Woods. You've driven Orion and the others from these lands. This is a victory wolves will speak of to pups for moons and moons. Is that not as good their deaths?"

"It is a hollow victory," rumbled Bone. "As hollow as the cave in my skull, from where Anorak stole the eye that once saw the world."

"But surely they must have fallen, milord?" said another, peering over the canyon's ledge. "The winds alone would have pulled them down. And even if not, this bridge would not hold us all across, would it?"

Scratch, scratch, scratch, Watcher heard again over the sound of the Lone Rocks' voices. The more he heard them, the louder Kicker's footsteps sounded in the night. *What is he thinking? Why won't he be still?*

"If I hear one more wolf speak a word that even resembles fear," Bone warned," I shall have him thrown into the Crack in the Earth! We are Lone Rocks. Strength knows no fear!"

"But milord," said Dark Fleece, "how will the other creatures and wolves of our new lands learn of our strength if we are not there to show it to them? We have been gone many days. The Gray Woods Wolves who did not fall the first night are now dead or in exile. Let them stay that way. We must be ready to face the Far Runners should they come for us."

Bone finally stopped shouting, cursing, and pacing. He paused at the foot of the bridge, seeming to consider this counsel. Watcher's stomach twisted up like a tangle of weeds as he watched Bone think and think.

"So be it," Bone finally said, shaking his huge head and snapping his teeth at the ground. "So be it! We shall leave a single wolf here on watch, who shall report to me if the Gray Woods Wolves dare show their faces again. For on that day, all the red that flows through their bodies shall be mine! Lone Rocks, with—"

Scratch, scratch, scratch.

Watcher froze. Orion went rigid above him. But this time, another wolf also grew still. Still and watchful.

Bone stared across the ravine with his one good eye. His mouth hung open, unspeaking. The woods on both sides of the Crack in the Earth went silent as snowfall. Then Bone's mouth curved into a toothy smile. Watcher's hope melted into terror.

"I see them!" Bone cried. "They are just over the Bridge! They are still there. Across! Across with me, Lone Rocks! Let us finish this and go home!"

Bone took the first step onto the Fallen Tree Bridge.

"Curse Kicker and his cowardice!" Orion growled. He leapt from his hiding place into the opening of the dark woods. Watcher ran out after him, meeting Glimmer and Windy in the middle.

"We have to run," Watcher cried. "We have to run now!" He was about to charge into the forest, his sisters beside him, when he realized that Orion had not moved.

"Orion, come on!" Glimmer shouted. But Orion still faced the Fallen Tree Bridge. Without a word or look, Watcher knew what his brother was going to do.

"No, Orion, you can't!" He ran back to block Orion's way, but it was already too late. Orion stepped onto the bridge, his eyes locked with Bone's.

"This is the only way, Watcher. The bridge is narrow. I can fight them one or two at a time. I can hold them off long enough for you and the others to get away. I will avenge our father and mother before I fall."

"I don't care about revenge, Orion. I care about you!" But it was as though Orion could no longer hear him. He stalked forward. Fur bristling. Mouth growling. Teeth glinting.

"Bone!" Orion shouted. "It was not you who so longed to meet with me. It is I who have longed to meet with you! And it is your red that shall be mine."

"You shall fall like your father, Orion."

Watcher's eyes were frozen on his brother as he walked slowly and shakily to meet Bone at the Bridge's center. Watcher's head grew light, as though the whole world had become as delicately balanced as the Tree Bridge, tilting beneath him and threatening to throw him down.

"Come on, Watcher," said Glimmer, her voice cracking and thick with tears. "We have to go. We have to run. We have to leave him behind."

But as Watcher turned, as he felt the dizzy weight of sorrow threaten to tug him to the ground once again, he had a thought. He looked to the old Trees, those leaning toward the canyon. He looked at them with his owl eyes and remembered how the bridge had shuddered beneath Orion's weight, as though it would break. As though it might break and *fall*. *The* Fallen *Tree Bridge*, he said to himself. *How did it get that name in the first place?* Once again he remembered the fat sparrow on the branch, the way it had made the branch bend and lean.

Then Watcher did run. But he did not flee. He charged the Tree behind which he had hidden.

"Watcher, what are you doing?" Glimmer screamed, but she and Windy were just behind him anyway.

"Hoping that something small *can* knock down something *big!*" Watcher shouted back.

He threw himself at the Tree, so precariously leaned on the edge of the Crack. He heard the pine groan, its roots clawing at the Earth.

"Great Tree," Watcher cried as he leapt at it over and over, kicking off of it with his hind legs each time. "Forgive me. You have stood tall over this forest for moons and moons. You have given shelter to the creatures of the world. But give aid to me and my brother now. For we came from the Trees, and to the Trees we shall return!" Each time Watcher struck the Tree, she groaned a little louder.

"I see, Watcher!" shouted Glimmer. "I see!" She joined him, and they took turns slamming against the Tree, kicking it toward the canyon and the place where the Fallen Tree Bridge now stretched. Windy also helped, but she paused to shout to Orion.

"Orion, stay close to this side! Stay close!"

Watcher couldn't be sure if Orion heard her or not. He and Bone had met each other on the bridge. Their meeting was violence. Their growls and snarls echoed down the canyon. The shuddering bridge swayed, unsteady beneath their paws, but still they swung their claws and snapped their teeth.

Orion looked to be gaining the advantage, Watcher thought, until he saw the Lone Rocks sneaking in attacks from beside their lord. It would not be long before one of them would trip Orion, and down he would fall into the Crack in the Earth.

Go down! Watcher thought, urging the Tree in his mind. *Fall!* But though the old Tree groaned as Watcher and his sisters pushed against it over and over again, it was not falling fast enough.

"Kicker!" Watcher screamed into the woods. "Kicker we need you, please!" Glimmer and Windy took up Watcher's call as well. The three of them cried and cried for their brother.

The growls on the bridge grew louder. The bays from the Lone Rocks rose in the dark. They backed Orion up on the Tree Bridge, surging at him like a river washing over a rock.

"Kicker!" Watcher screamed once more. Just when he was about to give up hope, two miracles happened at once.

Bounding through the trees came Kicker. Watcher could see the tears gleaming in his glowing eyes.

"Get out of the way!" he yelled.

Watcher and his sisters tumbled aside. But as Kicker approached, another great commotion descended from above. Watcher looked up to see a column of swirling specks twisting before the moon like a curling vine, accompanied by a screeching war cry. It was Lady Frost Feather, with nearly half the Council of Flyers behind her.

The birds rushed down onto the Tree, pulling hard on its branches just as Kicker leapt against it. The old goddess gave a final moan as her roots cracked. Then she fell. She tumbled over, arching across the Fallen Tree Bridge.

"Orion!" Watcher screamed.

At the final moment his brother heard his call and saw the falling Tree. He shoved Bone with all his might and slashed him across the side of his face, leaving three long streaks of bright red fur across from his empty eye. Then he leapt back to the canyon's ledge.

Yet Orion's final blow may also have saved Bone's life. He too saw the Tree crashing down on top of him and charged back to the far side of the bridge, knocking his own wolves out of the way and down into the canyon as he ran.

The Tree crashed into the bridge with a clap like thunder. Both trunks snapped like twigs. They cascaded into the Crack in the Earth, taking a clutch of Lone Rocks with them, howling as they fell.

Watcher ran to Orion. His brother was heaving deep gasps on the canyon's ledge, his body atremble. Glimmer, Windy, and

Kicker came too, laughing and crying all at once. Even the Flyers were squawking excitedly as they landed beside the wolflings. But across the ravine, Bone howled into the night.

"You are cursed forever, Gray Woods Wolves! You, Orion, Son of Anorak, and you, Watcher of the Owl Eyes! I shall have your red and spill it all. This Crack in the Earth does not go on forever. There are other ways around it. I was going to let you live in exile, but now I shall harry and pursue you to the ends of the world, I swear it!"

23

After the Lone Rocks had run off along the edge of the deep canyon, Lady Frost Feather sent the rest of the birds back to the other packs of the Old Forest to tell them what had happened. But the old owl herself stayed for a while to talk with the Gray Woods litter.

"The Birds of the Forest will be squawking and chirping about this night for moons and moons to come, I'll tell you that, young ones," she hooted, flapping from one branch to the next above the young wolves' heads as they trotted down the path that led deeper into the woods. "The Battle of Fallen Tree Bridge they'll call it. I have no doubt!"

"We'll be in a story, Lady Frost Feather?" asked Glimmer. "They'll talk about what we all did?"

"Oh, of course, my dear, of course!" said the owl. "That's what birds do. We birds have the best memories, which is why we are the Keepers of the Ancient Laws, after all. And of all the birds, owls have the deepest memories of the lot. If any of those silly wrens or sparrows forgets your names, you can trust that I'll be there to remind them. But how any of them could forget watching Orion battle an entire pack on the bridge is beyond me. And Watcher? To use a Tree as your weapon? This will make you nearly as famous as your brother, I'd warrant!"

"Yes, it will," said Orion. The edge on his voice stung Watcher and snatched the smile from his face, and Glimmer's as well. "Did you hear Bone shouting your name over the Bridge, Watcher? Did you hear him promising to kill you?"

"It was Watcher's idea to knock the Tree over, Orion," said Glimmer. "He saved you."

"I know he did!" Orion came to a stop on the path. Sadness slipped alongside the anger in his voice. "Now Bone knows he did too! Bone was shouting curses down on him for it. Of all of us, I knew that Bone wanted me dead most of all. I held out some hope that if he finally did manage to kill me, he might not care if the rest of you escaped. But not now. Now if they catch us, we're *all* dead. You should have let me fight to the finish, Watcher. You should have run. You should have let me go!"

Watcher hung his head. His eyes and nose stung. Even when he tried to help his brother, he only managed to dump more weight on his shoulders. He wanted to apologize. He wanted to tell Orion that it was impossible for him to just watch him die, when Kicker spoke up and made everything worse.

"So, is even the mighty Orion jealous now?" he said. "Not feeling so gracious when a runt takes even a little of your glory? Don't want the birds remembering that without us, the Battle of Fallen Tree Bridge would have ended with you at the bottom of a canyon?"

Orion leapt on Kicker, barking and snapping, pinning him to the ground. Orion's hair was still matted and sweaty from the fight. Red fur glistened from his wounds in the moonlight. Kicker's ears went flat against his skull. He whimpered and moaned beneath his brother's bared teeth.

"There wouldn't have even been a battle if it wasn't for you, *coward*." Orion spat.

Watcher saw Kicker flinch beneath that word. It struck him as hard as if Orion had slashed him. It burned him worse than a snout grounding or red fur on the back of his neck.

"But he came back, Orion," Watcher said quietly. "We wouldn't have been able to knock the Tree over if it hadn't for Kicker." For a breath, Watcher thought Orion was going to scar Kicker anyway, but he finally shook his great head and let Kicker up with a snort.

"Why do you always do that, Watcher?" Orion sighed. "Why do you always stand up for him, even when you know he hates you?"

"Just stop this all of you!" Glimmer shouted, growling at all three of her brothers, even Watcher. "We're alive, aren't we? We just survived a battle with an army. Doesn't that mean anything to any of you? Bone's pack killed our family. Then they killed all of the Bramble Woods Pack, too, if you don't remember. But *we're* alive. We've made it farther than I ever thought we could. But how hard do you think Bone would be laughing now if he saw this? How big do you think he'd smile if he knew he didn't even need to chase us any farther? If he knew that he could just let us fight amongst ourselves to finish what he started back in the Gray Woods?"

Any fight left in Orion's eyes went out like the moon behind the clouds and he hung his head. Watcher's chest began to ache all over again. Kicker got up and refused to look at any of the others.

They might have stood there in silence beneath the moonlit shadows of the Trees for the rest of the night if Lady Frost Feather had not flapped down onto a nearby root and spoke for them.

"Don't be so hard on yourselves, young ones, or on each other." She patted Watcher and Orion on the shoulders with her wings. "Glimmer is right. You should be thankful to be alive. Don't waste precious energy arguing when you must prepare yourselves for the challenges yet to come. Your journey is not yet over."

Lady Frost Feather waved the litter closer with her wings, looking them all in the faces with her enormous eyes. "You cannot stop here in the woods that lead to the foothills of the White Mountain. Believe it or not, these are the most ancient lands in the Old Forest, perhaps even the lands where Romulus himself sacrificed his own life to restore balance to the world. Some say that the spirits of the First Wolves still run the trails here, loping in the shadows between the Trees. The ghosts of those that did not travel to the Endless Fields in the Sky. These are the Haunted Woods."

A wind howled through the Trees then, like a wolf's howl, as if to say: *It's true! We're here. We're waiting for you.*

Watcher shivered, but he didn't let himself crawl to Orion's side like usual. *I am a Gray Woods Wolf,* he tried to tell himself. *I can be brave on my own.*

"Some dangerous and wild creatures make these woods their home, along with the ghosts. But that is the least of your worries. Bone was right. The Crack in the Earth does not go on forever. Many stretches from here, both to the North and the South, it becomes passable ground once again. Bone will find those flat lands. He will not turn back for home. You have scarred the other half of his ruined face, Orion. He hates you now more than ever. All of you." The owl's eyes fell on Watcher. He forced himself to swallow down a whimper in his throat.

"There aren't any wolf packs in the Haunted Woods to help us, are there, Lady Frost Feather?" asked Windy. She stood close to Watcher, almost leaning against him as she tested the air with her uncanny snout. "I smell traces of them on the ground and in the Trees. But their scent is like leaves that have long since blown away in the wind."

"You are right, Windy," said Frost Feather. "No wolves make these ancient grounds their home. Not many creatures do at all, save for a few Great Crowns, some mice, and perhaps even the Uruduks."

Watcher gritted his teeth. He remembered the huge beast by the river, as big as a boulder and swatting Leaping Fish from the air with its enormous paws. *Is there no safe place left in the world?* He wondered. *Is there nowhere like the Gray Woods?*

"Make your way quickly through the woods," Frost Feather continued. "Don't wander away from the clear paths between the Trees. If the old goddesses are merciful, you will pass from these woods and reach the White Mountain. Beyond that peak, even my eyes have not seen. Nor do I know of any who have crossed and then returned. Storms fall heavy on the Mountain. The snows and the rocks are treacherous on her slopes. But if the legends are true, and if old Gold Hoof was right, perhaps there is a place beyond it. A Far Valley you might again call home."

"Won't you come with us?" Watcher asked, trying not to sound as afraid as he felt.

"No, dear Watcher, I cannot. My place is here, in the Old Forest. When the Far Runners return from the South I will need to tell them all that I have seen. But I will watch you from the skies with my far-seeing eyes for as long as I can."

Another howling gust of wind – or at least that's what Watcher hoped it was – poured through the Trees, followed only by silence. Watcher snuck a glance back down the path to the Crack in the Earth. Even if he wanted to turn back now he couldn't. The only bridge lay at the bottom of the canyon, broken in half.

"Come on," Orion said softly after a while. "No point in wasting any more time." He too was looking back across the canyon, toward lands he would never see again. His gaze was so heavy, Watcher thought, and he wondered what pained his brother most to leave behind. But Orion eventually turned and started again into the Haunted Woods. Glimmer and Windy followed. Then came Kicker, both his snout and his tail all but dragging on the ground.

"Watcher," Lady Frost Feather said before he could join them. She hopped down from her root to the ground and put her wings on the sides of his face. "You've done so well. Your father and mother would have been proud. *I'm* proud of you."

Watcher wanted to say something, but at her words all he could see was the sunrise that used to warm him from his mother's eyes. Tears blurred Lady Frost Feather from his vision.

"It will be all right," said the owl softly. "One day it will be all right. Just keep your eyes open, Watcher. Keep watch over the others. Keep watch for the *right* way."

"I'll try," Watcher managed. Before Lady Frost Feather could say anything else or his tears overtook him, he ran down the path, following his brothers and sisters into the darkness of the Haunted Woods, under the shadow of the White Mountain.

24

All night the young wolves loped through the Haunted Woods, until blue moonlight gave way to a dim yellow, slipping through the pine branches. Though Watcher had already come so far and faced so many trials, over the ice of the Wide River, through the Forgotten Forest, to Crag's caves, and the Fallen Tree Bridge, these woods unsettled him most of all. They unsettled him like the screams of unseen animals in the dark.

The Trees were tall and far-reaching. But they did not seem to look down with kindness as the goddesses from the Gray Woods had. These loomed like giants and blotted out the Sky with their branches, keeping their secrets in the dark. Even the snow had hardly broken through. Only a carpet of dry needles crunched beneath Watcher's paws. Moss hung from the branches and clung to the pine trunks like green webs. Thin creeks trickled about the gnarled roots that crawled through the dirt.

Yet the sounds of woodland creatures that should have echoed through the Trees were quiet, Watcher thought, as though all the animals snuck from place to place. Even so, the woods did not seem still. They did not seem tame. *Something* moved among them. But it was not wolves. At least not any living ones, that was.

Windy had been right about them. There had been none here for a very long time. There were faint markers on the Trees, the only marks that had ever touched them. They were so faint Watcher had to press his nose to the bark just know they were there. But the wolves that had left them were long gone.

Worse than the quiet amongst the Trees was the quiet between the litter. It made Watcher ache inside. Sometimes Glimmer and Windy whispered to each other, but never very loudly and never for very long. Orion scouted up ahead, out of sight and all but out of smell. Watcher kept hoping his brother would burst through an old thicket to run beside him, just like before. But he didn't. Instead Watcher was left to fret over Kicker.

Kicker walked between his sisters and Orion. His eyes burrowed into the ground and his tail dragged between his legs. Everything about Kicker seemed to droop like the moss on the Trees. All except for the black patch of fur on his back. Every so often a bristling would travel over his shoulders like a ripple on a pond. Something was brewing inside him, Watcher thought, the way dark clouds gathered on the horizon before a storm. It made Watcher afraid.

After he'd trekked this way for some time and his good leg had gone weary and numb, Watcher came through a pair of trees to find Orion sitting atop a hill, waiting for him. Glimmer and Windy were already curled up beside each other at the foot of the rise and were falling asleep. Kicker had thrown himself on the ground beside a Tree with a twisted trunk, facing away from the others as he so often did.

Watcher thought about going straight to his sisters and falling right to sleep beside them. He'd never been so afraid to talk to

Orion before, never so unsure of what they might talk about. But he took a deep breath and climbed the hill anyway.

Orion sat facing the way they had come. He peered through a break in the branches where a sliver of golden sunlight snuck through to softly touch his yellow eyes. Watcher sat beside him on the dry needles. For a few long breaths they were quiet. Watcher wished he could think of something to say that would make Orion smile that old smile, or laugh that old laugh. But nothing came. The silence persisted until he was about to give up and go down to his sisters, when Orion spoke.

"It doesn't feel like winter in these woods, does it, Watcher?" he said. "It feels more like—"

"Like the day *before* winter," Watcher finished. "Like the cold is just sitting there on the other side of the night, waiting to come in the morning."

Orion sighed and nodded. "Yes. That's how it feels. Just that way. You always know the right words for such things, Watcher. You always know the right names." A faint trace of Orion's smile touched the corner of his mouth. "It's almost worse this way, though, isn't? To feel like the day before winter? I don't mind the cold. I don't fear the dark. But I just want it to *be* here, you know? If something is going to happen, even if it's bad, I just want it to happen already. If I'm going to fight, I just want to get on with it."

Haven't enough hard things already happened? Thought Watcher. *I'm not ready for any more.* That ache within him thrummed again. It was like he needed to wretch, but his stomach was empty. Then Orion spoke again.

"I miss father," he said. "I miss mother."

That was it. The sour thing in Watcher's stomach that he needed to spit up. Warmth filled his big owl eyes. "I do too. I miss the Gray Woods. I miss the birds there and the bugs. I miss our creek and our river. I miss the Trees and the hills where I could look from one end of the world to the other. But mostly I miss Mother. I miss the way she waited for me after the long lopes."

The tears slipped down Watcher's fur and fell onto the needles. He watched them land in little dark spot until he felt his brother's snout nuzzle against his own.

"I'm sorry I yelled you, Watcher."

"I'm sorry, too. About before, on the other side of the bridge. I should have let you carry me."

"No, you were right. You're right about more than you know, Watcher. I can't carry you forever. You are a Gray Woods Wolf. You can make your own mind."

Watcher looked up to find his brother again staring back the way they had come, back through the golden lit break in the trees. His tears had washed some of the clinging sadness away. But looking at his brother's far-away eyes he knew there was still more to come.

"We need to eat," Orion said after a while. "Come on." Watcher followed Orion down the hill, where he gathered up Glimmer and Windy. "There haven't been many tracks," he said, "not of Great Crowns anyway. But I think I've smelled some badgers and some mice. What about you, Windy?"

"Yes," she said, lifting her snout. "And there are *some* Great Crowns out there. Not many though. They're keeping well hidden. But I can find them if we look long enough. Some stretches up that way." She nodded ahead, through the thick Trees.

"Alright then. Glimmer, you can help. Kicker, are you ready to hunt?" Orion turned over his shoulder to where Kicker lay beside the twisted Tree. But silence was his only answer. A low growl boiled in Orion's throat. "I asked you a question, Kicker."

"Oh, I'm sorry, my coward ears must not be working so well," Kicker finally said. But he didn't get up and he didn't turn around. "What can I do to serve the *great* Orion? How could I possibly be of use to the wise and all-knowing Watcher of the Owl Eyes?"

"Now is *not* the time to test me." The growl thickened in Orion's chest. His tail rose up behind him. Finally, Kicker got up as well. His own fur bristled. He peeled his lips back from his fangs.

"But that's what you really want, isn't it? Admit it! You want me to challenge you so you can be rid of me once and for all."

"Kicker, no!" Glimmer shouted. But Kicker just barked at her, snapping his teeth.

"Yes, a challenge," he continued, "that way you can do what you *really* want to do, eh, Orion? You don't want to hunt *with* me. You want to *hunt me.* You want to scar me, just like you said back in the Gray Woods."

"Just say the word, *coward,*" said Orion.

"Stop it!" Glimmer tried again. "What would Father say? What would Mother?"

Glimmer's words slapped both Orion and Kicker on their noses. But though their growls went quiet the fur on their backs still threatened. Watcher could feel the itch for a fight steaming off them. But at last Orion barked loudly and took off in the direction of the Great Crowns.

"Stay here then and watch over the others," he snarled as he ran past Kicker. "Glimmer come on!" Glimmer trotted a few steps after Orion, who had already disappeared through the Trees. But she stopped beside Kicker, who was still breathing hard and glaring hotly at the ground before him.

"Did Mother ever tell you why she named you Kicker?" she asked. Kicker pretended he wasn't listening. But Watcher saw his ears prick. Watcher realized he didn't know that story either. "You were born smiling, she told me. The moment you crawled from her and touched the spring grass you made a sound like a laugh and started kicking in the air, as though just the touch of the world was all the joy you needed. And for the rest of the spring and even most of the summer you were that way. Then autumn came and you changed. What happened to you, Kicker? What happened?"

"Glimmer, come on!" Orion called through the Trees again. Glimmer lingered for another moment, then she too sprang through the brush and disappeared.

Watcher couldn't take his eyes off Kicker. His brother's face twisted and quivered. He legs trembled. At last he unleashed a loud howl, as though crying out to the moon, and ran off through the Trees in the other direction.

"Kicker!" Watcher called after him, but Windy stopped him before he could give chase.

"Let him go," she said. "Let him be alone. I'll keep track of him from here." Then she sat down. Watcher sat beside her. That feeling of winter creeping in at the edges of this strange wood crawled beneath his fur. Like Orion, he felt that something bad was going to happen. And like Orion, he now wished it would just happen already.

25

By the time the sunset's light was crisscrossing in thin orange streams into the woods, Watcher worried that Kicker might not return. Night was coming. He didn't want any of his brothers and sisters, not even Kicker, alone in these woods after dark.

"Stop worrying, Watcher," Windy said sleepily, her eyes half closed. "He's not far off." She nodded her nose past the hill, off to the east from where she lay in the crunchy pine needles. "That way. And besides, Orion and Glimmer will be back soon."

"I know his *body* is close, Windy," said Watcher. "But I think his heart is getting farther and farther away."

Windy said nothing to this. After another moment or two her soft breathing went deep and steady and she fell asleep. Watcher thought about making a bed on the needles beside her. He was so tired. It felt like he and the others had been running for their whole lives. He couldn't remember lying still anymore. And he was hungry. But Kicker's howl still echoed in his ears. How anguished it had been. How full of hurt.

I have to find him, Watcher decided. *I have to tell him we want him to come back.* Watcher was sure Windy would not have gone to sleep had she smelled even a hint of danger, so he left her where she was and set off into the Haunted Woods.

There are so few birds, Watcher thought to himself as he picked his way through the mossy Trees. *Almost no sign of Forest Folk at all.* But Watcher could smell the faint traces of at least a few other creatures in the air. Much of the scent was Kicker's, from somewhere just up ahead. But some of it was from other, less familiar animals.

Soon Watcher had gone far enough that he could barely see the hill behind him in the darkening evening. He could only just smell Windy sleeping at its foot. He was thinking that perhaps he should turn back when he caught a glimpse of his brother in a small clearing up ahead.

Kicker sat still on the pine needles. His ears lay flat. His eyes were to the ground. His slender shoulders shook. *He's crying*, thought Watcher. Even after all the neck bitings and snout groundings from the Gray Woods, Watcher's throat ached for his brother.

He hesitated at the clearing's edge, deciding whether to reveal himself to Kicker or to leave him be. But before he could decide Kicker spoke into the silence. "It's hard to sneak up on someone with all these dry needles everywhere, isn't it, Watcher?" his voice was thick and husky.

"I wasn't sneaking, Kicker. I was just coming to get you. Orion and Glimmer will be back soon. There'll be food to eat."

"So now you think you can boss me around too, do you? Now that you're as famous as our perfect big brother?"

This is all going wrong, thought Watcher. *I'm just making it worse, as usual.* "You know I don't think that."

"Then leave me alone."

Kicker got up and walked further into the woods. Watcher thought about letting him go. He thought maybe it would be best if he did turn back for the hill where Windy slept. But something inside him pulled him again, as strong as that tug that made him need to see all the creatures of the Forest with his own eyes. He followed Kicker deeper into the woods.

"You're not a very good hunter, Watcher," said Kicker's voice. But Watcher could not see him in the Trees. The shadows were deepening in the evening light.

"I'm not hunting. You're my brother. Don't you remember that? We're all that's left of the Gray Woods Pack. We have to stick together. Please come back with me."

"*The Gray Woods Pack*," Kicker's disembodied voice snorted. "What's that supposed to mean to me anymore?" The angry words stung Watcher, but he kept on following them anyway.

"It means that we're family," he called. "The only one we've got. We're *your* pack. A wolf doesn't have a hole or a nest. The pack is his only home. Don't you remember?"

"Now you're throwing around father's words, are you? Think you see the world like he did, don't you?"

"No," Watcher said.

He came upon Kicker in another clearing. This one was marked with rocks and caves – black holes into the Earth. A cold shiver ran beneath Watcher's fur. *Nothing good has come from caves so far,* he thought. Two stared out from the side of a hill, just beyond Kicker, like eyes in a skull. Another yawned from the ground like a mouth.

"It's so easy for you to talk about the pack, isn't it, Watcher? You were lucky to have one at all, weren't you?"

Those words bit Watcher like teeth. But what could he say? It was true, wasn't it? He'd often thought those very words to himself. It just hurt worse to hear them spoken from another's lips.

"Yes," he said. "If I'd been born to another pack maybe I wouldn't even be alive. Maybe they would have made sure of it. But I wasn't. I was born to the Gray Woods, to Mother and Father. And so were you." Watcher crept closer and closer to his brother. But this time Kicker didn't run away. He snorted and shook his head.

"Mother and father cared more for a three legged cripple and a dull snout than they did for me, didn't they?"

"That's not true, Kicker. I think that if Orion went to join the Far Runners, Father was going to bring you up to be his successor. If—"

"*If?*" Kicker snarled. "*If?*"

He rose up and turned on Watcher. His fangs were bared. His growl shook. Watcher took two steps back. He suddenly wondered how wise it had been to come after Kicker at all.

"Don't you get tired of it, Watcher? Having an *if* attached to every one of your hopes? To every one of your dreams? Having an *if* attached to your very existence? *If Orion this. If Orion that.* What about me, Watcher? Does it even matter what I do or don't do? What I want or don't want? Maybe if I'd been a cripple, Mother would have waited for *me* sometimes after the long lopes. But she only ever waited for *you.* Maybe if I'd been born a little bigger, just a little stronger, Father would have waited for *me* at the top of the hill to talk sometimes, not just *Orion.*" Kicker's growling voice cracked. Watcher heard the pain of invisible neck bitings and snout groundings seep out through it.

"They loved you, Kicker."

The look on his brother's face told Watcher that those words meant nothing. Kicker stalked forward, circling, trapping Watcher in the clearing, backing him toward the dark caves. Slather began to glisten at his jaws. His yellow eyes burned.

"No, Watcher, you poor, stupid wolf. They loved Orion. They worshipped him. They cherished Glimmer too, for her beautiful coat and her happy smile, even though she was a dull snout. They knew they could trick some other lord into taking her for a she-wolf, didn't they? And Windy, seeing all those ghosts with her snout. She was a treasure of the pack. And you, Watcher. You they pitied. They all pitied you! I might have even taken some pity, if Mother and Father had left anything at all for me."

All the hurt within Kicker turned to fiery rage. *He's going to bite me!* Watcher thought. Not for a bit of snout grounding either. He was going to bite for the red. His muscles tensed and his tail rose. Watcher trembled, wondering how far he could get if he tried to run. But the answer was *not far enough.*

It was the roar that saved Watcher. But not one from a wolf or the woods. This roar came from the cave.

All the fury in Kicker's face melted away. He yelped and scampered backwards into the clearing. Watcher should have run with him. But as always, he had to see. Without thinking he turned around.

He saw the eyes first. They were red as the falling sun, burning in the cave's black depths. Then came the rest into the light. It was brown and huge and lumbering.

An Uruduk.

The caves were the bear's home, and Watcher and Kicker had disturbed its slumber. It emerged on two legs, tall as a Tree. When it fell down on all fours it shook the ground beneath its enormous paws. Then it charged.

Watcher cried out. He reeled back, trying to run. But his good paw slipped on the pine needles blanketing the forest floor. He tumbled to the ground in a tangle of churning limbs that could not find purchase enough to escape.

The Uruduk came upon him fast. It rose up again, paw pulled back in the air and tipped with four claws that could cut Watcher's little body in half. Watcher wanted to close his eyes. But as with the Great Crown upon the hill, he couldn't tear them away. He would keep them open until the end.

"Watcher! Get away!" Kicker's teeth suddenly sank into their usual place on Watcher's scruff. But the bite was not meant to hurt. It was meant to save Watcher's life.

Watcher flew through the air, tossed head over heels by Kicker. He landed in a cloud of needles and dirt. When he looked back, he saw what would have happened to him. It happened to Kicker instead.

Kicker was a moment too slow to dodge the blow. The Uruduk's claw caught him across the flank. It threw him through the air like one of the fish from the river. A trail of red sprinkled the ground and Watcher's fur, spurting behind him as he spun over Watcher's head and landed with a thud in the dirt.

"Kicker!" Watcher screamed. His feet finally found the ground again and he ran to his brother. Kicker's eyes were blinking open and closed. Four slashes, so red they were almost black, ran down his side.

"Run, Watcher," he said quietly. His tongue hung from his mouth onto the ground. "Run."

The Uruduk pounded the earth, once more on all fours and coming to finish Kicker off. Watcher spun about. He wagged his tail and jumped as high as he could, trying to get the Uruduk's attention. He began to howl at the top of his lungs.

"Over here! Over here!" he cried, circling away from where Kicker lay on the ground. The Uruduk possessed size and strength like no other creature alive, but speed and agility still belonged to the wolves – even one with three legs. Watcher sprang right and left. He kept just out of the Uruduk's reach. He led him away from Kicker's body. But he could not keep this up forever. He grew quickly exhausted. The Uruduk was slowly blocking his turns. Slowly backing him into the caves. Watcher knew he was cornered. When he heard another wolf's howl finally answer his own.

Orion.

Watcher's brother and sisters leapt into the clearing, barking and baying. Windy stopped by Kicker's still form, licking at his wounds and nuzzling into his fur. Orion and Glimmer came to either side of the Uruduk, fur bristling and teeth snapping. Orion drew himself up to his full size with tail and ears high in the air. His rumbling barks gave even the giant Uruduk pause.

Now surrounded, the great beast began to swing wildly. He nearly caught Orion on the snout. He almost cleaved Glimmer down the side. Watcher was momentarily forgotten. He looked around the clearing. There was no Tree Bridge or icy river to allow their escape. Four of them could flee and easily outrun the Uruduk. But that would leave Kicker to die.

Think, Watcher, think! He screamed inside his head. But *there is no bridge* and *there is no ice* were the only answers he heard back from the voice behind his eyes. Then Watcher saw the cave on the ground, the one that looked like a mouth. If there was no ice, he thought, he was going to have to make his own. He was going to have to trust that bears were as dim as Long Tooth had told in his stories.

"Windy! I need your help!" he called. Windy bounded across the clearing, just staying wide of the fighting. "Find fallen pine branches, brittle ones that still have brown needles. Drag them here. Drag them over the hole. We have to cover it." Windy gave him a nod and then she and Watcher were off. In the old, unkempt forest, fallen branches were blessedly everywhere. Watcher and Windy dragged them across the cave opening.

"Watcher!" Orion called, "whatever you and Windy are doing, hurry!" His voice was growing thick and ragged. He and Glimmer were tiring. Though they clawed and bit at the Uruduk's back every time it turned to chase one of them or the other, such wounds were nothing to the monster. Its claws came closer and closer to the wolves' flesh with each swing.

"Lead the Uruduk this way, Orion," Watcher said as Windy put the last branch in place. "Try to get him to step on these branches!"

"Glimmer, act like you're running away," Orion shouted. "Let's give him one wolf to chase."

Glimmer gave a false yelp and loped away. With only Orion before him, the monster stalked ahead, raging and roaring. Back and forth he swung his massive paws. Orion just ducked the swings. He stayed so close to the Uruduk that it made Watcher's insides twist to watch. Orion backed up until his paws touched the edge of the branches.

"Careful!" Watcher cried. But Orion did not retreat another step. He stood his ground, baring his fangs and unleashing his fiercest growl. The Uruduk pulled itself up to its full height and raised both paws as though he meant to fall on the pesky wolf and crush him into the dirt. It brought down the blow with all its strength. But Orion leapt to the side at just the last moment. The Uruduk struck the branches and crashed straight through, tumbling into the hole. *Just like the Lone Rocks on the ice,* Watcher thought to himself.

Thick quiet settled with the dust after the fight. Watcher limped to the edge of the hole to look down into the darkness. The Uruduk lay amongst the shattered remains of the branches. A groan escaped his throat. It stirred slightly where it lay.

"He won't be that way for long," Orion said, drawing great gasps. "And something tells me he'll be able to climb out when he wakes up. We need to be going."

Watcher and Orion ran from the hole. Glimmer and Windy were already standing over Kicker's still form. Watcher felt his throat constrict as he drew close. Kicker's eyes were closed. He was no longer speaking.

26

"He's still alive," said Windy. Her voice broke as she sniffed at Kicker's face. "But he's at the Edge of the Woods, so close to leaving."

Without another word she bounded away, following her nose from Tree to Tree in the woods surrounding the Uruduk's caves. Watcher could barely see what she was doing behind the wall of water over his eyes. But she soon returned with a few leaves in her mouth, chewing them into a mush and spitting them onto Kicker's red wounds. She shoved them deep into the gashes with her snout.

Glimmer set off behind her as she went back for more, then Watcher and Orion joined them as well. Soon Kicker's wounds were stoppered with the green, its sharp smell dulling the heavy scent of red in the clearing.

A low moan rose up from the cave in the ground. The Uruduk stirred in the trap. "We need to get Kicker away from here," said Windy. "We'll have to be careful. We'll have to go slow."

Orion and Glimmer did most of the work, pushing, dragging, and lifting. Watcher helped whenever he could. It took the litter almost all night to move Kicker back to the hill. Every time Kicker groaned, Watcher felt a stinging tingle along his own side, where he should have been cut. His tears started again.

"He saved me," Watcher whispered, as much to the woods as the others. "I thought he was going to kill me. But when the Uruduk came, he saved me." If his brother and sisters heard him, Watcher couldn't tell. They were too exhausted for talk.

At long last they reached the hill, just as gray morning came again. The shares from the small Great Crown that Orion and Glimmer had hunted the day before still lay in the needles, for not even scavengers seemed to live in the Haunted Woods. The wolflings fell on the food and devoured it at once. Orion and Glimmer collapsed from having pulled their brother so far.

"Go ahead and sleep," Watcher said. "I'll stay awake with Kicker."

"Talk to him, Watcher," said Windy as she lay down between Orion and Glimmer. "He won't answer. But if his spirit is still in the woods, it will hear you. Perhaps it will linger beneath his fur for a while longer."

Even though it was morning the woods grew quiet after the other wolflings fell asleep. Watcher wished there were birds singing or bugs buzzing among the moss laden Trees. He could tell Kicker about them. He and Kicker had never spoken very much, especially not after the summer. That was when Kicker at last understood that he would never grow half as big or run half as fast as Orion. The longest the two had talked since then was when Kicker had pinned Watcher down to redden his neck or ground his snout. So when Watcher couldn't think of anything else to say, he began to tell a story.

All through the day, as morning gray became afternoon yellow and then evening gold, Watcher recounted old Long Tooth's tales. He told them as if Kicker was truly listening, saying "and remember when this happened," or "don't forget about this!"

But eventually Watcher began telling stories of his own. They were like Long Tooth's in a way, but these stories were about Orion, running with the Far Runners and doing great deeds. Watcher put Kicker into the tales as well. He told how the two of them dueled the fearsome Uruduk together and returned to the Gray Woods to bring justice to Bone. It wasn't hard for Watcher to invent these adventures. Orion had long been the hero of old Long Tooth's stories too, when Watcher had listened to them in the Gray Woods and made pictures of them behind his owl eyes.

For two days Kicker's eyes refused to open. Sometimes his breathing grew so quiet and so scarce that Watcher feared it had stopped altogether. Each night and each morning he pled with the Trees to spare his brother. To keep his spirit from leaving the woods.

On the morning of the third day, Watcher sat beside Kicker, telling him the story of how Romulus, the Lord of the Wolves, gave himself up for the good of the Forest and ascended to the Endless Fields in the Sky. He had just gotten to the part when Romulus refused to howl when a croaking voice interrupted him:

"I've heard this one already, Watcher. Tell me something new."

It was Kicker. Watcher nearly fell over. Then he erupted in laughter, shouting and hollering. "He wants another story! He wants a new one!"

Glimmer, Windy, and Orion joined Watcher, prancing around Kicker, yapping and barking to the Trees.

"We thought we'd lost you, little brother," said Orion, nuzzling into the fur on Kicker's face.

Kicker tried to smile and say something back, but all he could manage was: "thirsty."

The littermates took turns running to the closest stream. They held the cold water carefully in their mouths and carried it back to their brother a few swallows at a time. Orion went searching for food and caught a small mouse in a nearby thicket, chewing it up and feeding it to Kicker in small bites. After having eaten and drunk, Kicker fell back to sleep.

It went on like this for some days more. One of the wolflings would stay by Kicker's side, waiting for him to wake up so he could eat and drink, always a little at a time. For Watcher these were good days. Kicker slowly regained his strength. No trace of the Lone Rock Pack's scent had yet drifted into the still air. And the Haunted Woods, for all her shadows and secrets, still felt mysteriously warmer than the other stretches of the Forest, still strangely out of winter's grasp. So Watcher got back to doing what he did best: wandering, exploring, and watching.

Sometimes his sisters came with him, but Watcher liked it best when it was him and Orion. For a few days it felt like summer again, back in the Gray Woods. Though the Trees were dark and stern and there weren't many bugs or creatures to chase and follow, there was time to talk and even a little to laugh. To remember better days.

But each night, when Watcher and Orion got back from their walkabouts and Watcher would sit down in the pine needles to tell Kicker another story, Orion would climb the hill that had become their camp and would look back longingly through the break in the Trees until it was dark.

"Kicker told me about some of your stories," Orion said to Watcher one afternoon while the two of them sat on the banks of the winding stream, watching the only fish they'd seen for days swim lazy circles beneath the rippling water. "He said you might even be a better storyteller than old Long Tooth was."

"I don't know about that. Old Long Tooth knew more stories than any wolf in the Old Forest. Even Father said so."

"I'd say you've been *living* plenty of stories yourself this last moon or so, haven't you? And inventing new ones. Kicker says his favorite is when me and him go back and give that Uruduk a beating he won't forget."

Watcher laughed, still following the fish as it turned slow revolutions in the water. "It's not a bad one. But I'm thinking of changing the ending. You end up making friends with the Uruduk, and then he goes back with you to the Gray Woods to teach Bone a lesson. The Uruduk's name is Brown Bottom."

Orion and Watcher laughed together. But Orion's smile lasted only a breath or two. His yellow eyes held fast to Watcher's face, like they would when the two of them used to talk in the Gray Woods.

"Why do you always make me the hero of your stories, Watcher?"

"Because that's who you are, Orion. You've always been the hero. Not just in the stories. You really are the hero. My hero." Watcher wasn't expecting it, but his throat went tight and his eyes grew warm when he told Orion that.

"What about you, Watcher? Who do you think you are?"

Watcher thought about it for a moment. He looked into nowhere and everywhere until he saw a picture of a day many moon's hence, when his teeth were long and his fur patchy and dull. He lay amongst Orion's pups, making them laugh and telling them of the legend of their father. "I'm the one who gets to see it all happen. I'm the one who gets to tell others, so they never forget. Like the owls."

Orion finally tore his eyes from Watcher's face, letting them fall back to the stream. Watcher could see that his brother was no longer following the fish. He was looking at his reflection in the water. Watcher thought it was as if he was holding a silent conversation with the rippling version of himself on the current.

Orion was quiet the rest of the afternoon, until he said, "it's time to go back." When he got to the hill, he climbed it once more and stood there, gazing through the branches until the blue moonlight replaced the orange sunset.

Watcher realized then that like Kicker, Orion too had *ifs* attached to his hopes and dreams. Dreams of being a Far Runner and getting justice for father and mother. And Watcher felt like

Crag again then, like he was his brother's *ifs*. Only Orion didn't shout them out to the world like Kicker had. He shared them with only his reflection in the stream.

The next morning, Watcher woke to find a wolf looking down on him. He was about to ask Orion what he wanted when he realized it wasn't Orion at all. It was Kicker. He was smiling. Watcher couldn't remember the last time he'd seen Kicker smile.

"You're up!" he said, jumping to his feet, suddenly wide awake. He was about to rouse the others when Kicker motioned for him to wait with a shake of his head.

"I thought I might go get my own drink this morning, Watcher," he whispered. "No offense, but secondhand water from all your mouths tastes terrible." Kicker and Watcher laughed a little. "Will you go with me?"

Watcher nodded. Together the two of them made their way down to the stream. The woods were still dark in the morning gray. The moss so green it was nearly black. For the first time in his life Watcher was the one who had to go slowly, so his brother could keep up. "We can rest if you need to," he said. "There's no hurry."

"No, I'm fine. Besides, I need to get used to this again. We can't stay here forever. Too many Uruduks and not enough Forest Folk. We'll need to get to loping again if we're ever going to make it over the White Mountain." Kicker smiled at Watcher again, a smile that hoped and believed.

They made it to the stream and sat down on the bank to drink. While Kicker was sipping from the current, he caught sight of his flank in the reflection – scarred forever with four white slashes.

"They're not ugly," Watcher said when he saw what Kicker was looking at. "They make you look like a warrior. Like one from the old stories."

Kicker finally looked up from the water and said: "I heard your stories, Watcher. The whole time I was away."

"Away?"

"When the Uruduk hit me and I closed my eyes, I saw the Edge of the Woods. I saw light streaming in from the clearing beyond, from where there is no returning. Mother and father were there. I could see them, just past the Trees. Mother was waiting for me, Watcher. She was waiting for *me*." Kicker's voice cracked and he had to take another sip of water before going on.

"I thought about going to her. But then I heard your voice. You were telling a story. It was about me and Orion. So I stayed to hear the end. Then you told another, and another. Each one was better than the last. That was when I knew. I had to know how *our* story ended. I had to see *our* pack – my brothers and sisters – make it to the end of the journey."

Kicker tried to look Watcher in the face, but his eyes clouded with tears and he dropped his snout to the ground. "Watcher, I – I'm sorry. I'm sorry for everything. I – I –" Kicker's voice failed him, but Watcher wouldn't leave him in silence.

"Kicker, do you remember what you said to me, just before the Uruduk came? About the *ifs*? How you didn't want them in your life? I've been thinking about that. And, I don't know, but maybe not all *ifs* are bad. Like this one: *If* it weren't for you, I wouldn't be alive. I'm glad for that one at least. Thank you, Kicker. You would have made Father proud. You *have* made him proud."

The warm water flooded Watcher's eyes as well. He nuzzled up against his brother and Kicker nuzzled him back. He never thought there would have been a day when Kicker's gaze held something more for him than neck biting and snout grounding. But it had come after all.

27

Kicker's strength returned quickly, and before long he was running again. After days and days of rest, for the first time in his life, he and Orion hunted together. When they returned with shares from a fallen Great Crown Orion proclaimed that Kicker's scars were those of a great hunter, one who had faced an Uruduk for his brother. At those words Kicker did that for which he had been named. He leapt up in the air and kicked for joy. Watcher couldn't help but fall over on his side in the pine needles, laughing.

Stomachs filled and hope renewed, the Gray Woods wolves set out once more on their journey for the Far Valley. They took their time through the narrow pathways of the Haunted Woods, for there was still no scent of Bone and his Lone Rocks nearby. They talked and joked, and Watcher discovered that Kicker loved to laugh more than he'd ever let on. He also seemed to love listening to Watcher's stories, over and over.

"Tell another!" he said, leaping between the Trees. "But not any of Long Tooth's boring stuff. Tell me the new stories, Watcher. Of the mighty Kicker and his faithful sidekick, Orion."

Watcher laughed and so did his sisters, and even Orion. But every once in a while, whenever they crested another hill or came to a place where the Trees grew thin, Watcher caught Orion looking over his shoulder, searching back through the woods for some place he couldn't quite see. The farther away they went, Watcher thought, the greater the pull on Orion was becoming. The greater that invisible weight seemed to press down on his shoulders.

But toward the end of the first day, when Watcher's good leg was aching and he was beginning to fall behind again, he came upon Windy, stopped on a large stone at the bank of a stream, where a bit more light filtered down through the branches. She held her nose to the air, sniffing at some scent that seemed to flutter around her face like a bug trying to elude her.

"What is it, Windy?" Watcher said when he caught up. "What do you smell?"

"I smell –" she sniffed again, as if making sure, "I don't know how, but I think I smell the Spring."

"We didn't stay at the hill that long," said Watcher, laughing a little. "It wasn't even an entire moon. Spring can't possibly be coming."

"No, you don't understand. I don't smell the coming of Spring. I smell a piece of it already here. It's like a marker left by a wolf on a Tree. The wolf is gone but the scent remains."

Watcher followed Windy's eyes. The Forest before her seemed blacker than usual between the Trees, as though the woods themselves sought to hide whatever this was that she had discovered. But shadows or no, Windy could not seem to resist the pull and she wandered into the darkness.

"Orion! Glimmer! Kicker!" Watcher called at the top of his lungs. It was only a moment or two before they sprang back into view.

"What's wrong?" said Orion. "Where's Windy?"

"She's gone in there," said Watcher, nodding toward the shadowy place. "She said she smelled the Spring."

To this, neither Orion nor Glimmer said a word. They stared into the darkness, which seemed to defy the afternoon sun. But then Kicker said: "If Windy smells it, it must be real. Even if it's ghosts." Before anyone else could say anything, he followed her trail into the shadows with Watcher and the others just behind.

The darkness hung thick as the moss from the branches. Watcher thought the shadows seemed to cling to him like dirt or snow caught in his fur. Orion, Kicker, and Glimmer tread slowly before him. When they looked back, even the yellow glow of their eyes was dim.

Watcher shivered. If Windy had smelled the Spring it was surrounded by Winter. The mysterious warmth that had laid over the Haunted Woods evaporated. The wind moaned and howled through the Trees. Frost lay over the pine needles on the Forest floor.

What was it Lady Frost Feather said about these woods? Watcher asked himself. *Some say the spirits of the First Wolves still dwell here,* she had said. *That the Trees still hide them.* Watcher was suddenly sure that it was true, that these dark Trees were hiding great wolves who waited to leap out and take the unsuspecting litter by surprise.

Soon though, the wolflings came into a clearing. The now gray, wintery sky peered down on them through a ring in the bony branches. The cold wind was beginning to bite through Watcher's fur. There seemed to be nothing alive in the clearing at all. The ground was only a patch of dirt, covered in frost, devoid even of pine needles. Sharp rocks pierced the Earth like teeth. At the far edge of the clearing stood a great Tree. She was tall and old. Old and all but dead. Her bark was silver gray like the hair of the oldest wolves. At the base of the Tree, entwined in her roots, was a black hole.

"There's nothing here, Windy," said Watcher. "Maybe we should go."

But Windy said nothing. She sat just beyond the hole that was wrapped in the roots, staring up at the Tree's branches.

"Windy," whispered Orion. "What do you smell?" His hair bristled on his back. His eyes and ears were alert and shifting.

"Spring," she said in her far away voice.

"Look!" said Kicker, following her eyes. "Look at the Tree branches." Watcher did, and he had to catch a startled breath. At the dead branches' tips small buds grew full and round – buds like those that came in springtime. *How?* Watcher wondered. *It's Winter, and this Tree is nearly dead.*

"They look as though they could bloom any moment," said Glimmer.

"It's the Tree," said Windy, still staring at it. Still breathing it in.

"*The* Tree?" asked Watcher. Cold prickles dimpled the skin beneath his fur.

"The First Tree. The Tree that brought forth Romulus and the First Wolves. Can't you smell his scent on her branches? It's like the smell of a pup on his mother's fur. She's waited moons upon moons to see any of her children again. No wolves have come to this place for a long, long time."

Watcher felt a buzz beneath his skin, like dragonflies in his bones. *The First Tree?* He and the others stood still, hardly breathing. The only sound in the clearing was the wind curling through the branches. The old Trees moaned in the cold. Then Watcher's eyes fell to the hole. His body shivered. His stomach curled up inside him. *There's something down there,* he thought. He had to see what it was.

"Watcher, what are you doing?" said Kicker, fear flickering in his voice as Watcher hopped closer to the Tree. But he did not try to stop him and he did not run away.

Watcher stepped to the very lip of the hole, his good leg on the gnarled root circled around it. Another paw appeared across from his. It was Orion. His jaw was set and his teeth were clenched, ready for whatever might leap from the dark. They both leaned their heads toward the black.

Watcher saw something white protruding from the dirt just inside the hole. It was a stone, he thought. Then he saw another and another.

Watcher's tongue went dry and sticky. The buzzing dragonflies in his bones went frozen and still. They were not stones. They were bones. *Like in my dream!* He thought. But these were no bones of a lame runt. These were the bones of a giant wolf.

"What is that?" said Orion.

"It's a skeleton," said Watcher. But as their voices echoed down into the dark and their frosty breath touched the white bones, the darkness in the hole fled from a blinding blue light.

Watcher yelped and fell back from the Tree. He heard Orion tumble backward as well. His vision was all spots and flashes, like lightning behind a cloud. When he blinked them away he saw the wolf.

It was more the shape of a wolf than a wolf itself. Like a shadow that had stepped off the ground. Its body was made of something like moonlight. *Like moonlight in a mist,* thought Watcher. The litter scrambled into a tight knot in the middle of the clearing, Kicker pulling Windy back by the scruff of her neck. None of them dared speak.

The Blue Wolf stood on the roots about the dark hole and stared at the wolflings for a long moment. Then he bowed to them. As terrified as they were the litter bowed back. The wolf threw his back his head as though to unleash a mighty howl, but the howl was silent. Then he lost his shape, streaming up into the air before the ancient Tree like a wintry breath until he became a wolf's head in a blue cloud. *Like the Sky Pack!* Watcher thought.

Glimmering streaks then poured down from the cloud, falling like fluttering fireflies from the summer, like glowing rain. Where the light touched the ground the frost faded away. Green grass sprung up through the rocky dirt. Leaves exploded from the First Tree's branches. Her buds burst into blossoms of pink and white. From the hole in her roots a spring bubbled up, pouring out into the clearing and running in a stream through its center. The cold winter wind became warm again.

"Like Spring," said Watcher. He laughed. He couldn't help himself. He laughed and his brothers and sisters laughed with him. They began to jump and run around in the clearing, rolling in the soft grass, drinking from the delicious water.

But just when Watcher thought: *We could stay here. We could stay here forever,* the Blue Wolf returned. He stood at the edge of the clearing that was now a small bubble of Spring in the Haunted Woods. He flicked his head over his shoulder toward the Trees. Then he ran.

"Come on!" Watcher shouted all of a sudden. "He wants us to follow him. Come on!" The Gray Woods litter raced after the Blue Wolf. He was fast, even faster than Orion it seemed, flashing from Tree to Tree. But he was so bright that Watcher could see him from afar, even as he fell behind.

Into the darkest tangles of the Haunted Forest the Blue Wolf led, where the winter wind returned and only dim gray fought through the pine branches. As suddenly as he had set off the Blue Wolf then stopped. He stood beside a thicket, nodding his head for the wolflings to come closer.

What's back there? Watcher wondered. *More ghosts?* But when he and the others peered into the thicket they found the bodies of a clutch of small wolves. At first Watcher feared they were all dead. Their fur was bedraggled and matted. Many of them bore marks of red. But as he listened in the quiet woods he heard the faint sounds of their breathing.

"Who are they?" Watcher asked. He turned his head, as though expecting an answer from the Blue Wolf. But the glowing creature had disappeared.

28

Watcher's brothers and sisters were as wide-eyed and breathless as he was. It was as though they were afraid to speak, to say out loud what they had just seen. *Had it been Romulus, returned from the Sky Pack?* Watcher wondered. *Had it been just a dream?*

But Windy, who had been smelling ghosts all of her life, shook free of her wonder and began to sniff at the wolves in the thicket.

"These aren't from any one pack," she said, grabbing the others' attention, "but from many. They've come a long way. They're all soaked in the smell of fear."

"Ramblers?" Kicker asked. "All the way out here? But how did they get past the Crack in the Earth with no bridge?"

"They went around," said Watcher. His chest went tight and heavy as the sound of Bone's threat across the canyon echoed in his ears. "They must have gone the way Bone said he was going."

"Then the Lone Rocks could be close behind as well," said Orion. "Or maybe already ahead, blocking the way." His ears perked up and his tail rose, as though Bone could be just behind the Trees, waiting for him.

"Orion, there's something else," Windy whispered. She sniffed at one of the wolves, who somehow had not yet woken. "Some of these wolves are from the caves. Some of them are from the Bramble Woods."

"What?" Orion unleashed a rolling growl. His fur bristled to join his ears and his tail.

At Orion's raised voice the fainted wolves finally woke. But when they found themselves surrounded by the Gray Woods wolves, they panicked and wailed, falling into a frightened clump in the thicket. Only one of them managed to stand tall, even on his shaking, exhausted legs. Watcher knew that wolf's face. It made his skin crawl. It was Ash. It was the very wolf who had led them into Crag's caves.

"Deceiver!" Orion roared, his yellow eyes lighting afire. "Trickster and coward! I should tear you apart!" Orion stalked into the thicket as though intending to do just that. But before he could do anything rash, Watcher hopped into the thicket as well, coming between the two wolves.

"Orion, wait!" he said. "Look at them. Look how frightened they are. Look at their wounds. We need to know what happened and why they're here. Let him have a say."

"Did I have a say when I was trapped beneath the earth?" Orion roared. "When they buried me alive and nearly turned me into one of those *creatures*?"

"No, you didn't," Watcher whispered, coming closer and nuzzling his brother's snout. "But the Blue Wolf led us here for a reason. And I don't think it was to kill, do you?"

Orion shook his head. After a few long breaths, his fur lay flat again and he hid his fangs. But he still glared mistrustfully at Ash from over Watcher's head.

"What are you doing out here, Ash?" he growled. "Who are all these others?"

"We were looking for you," Ash replied. He shook from ear to paw, just like the rest of the wolves. They were all but pressed together, whining and crying.

"Why would you come looking for us?" asked Glimmer. "Why would you come looking so far?"

Ash all but collapsed to a seat in the thicket, as though he had no strength to stand. Gone was that sleepy smile he wore back in the Bramble Woods Cave. His lips trembled. Distress flooded his eyes. "It was Bone," he began. "When the Lone Rocks destroyed the Bramble Woods Pack only a few of us managed to escape. We rambled and went looking for another pack. But the Lone Rocks were everywhere, patrolling the borders of the Gray Woods and the Bramble Woods as well. They challenged any ramblers trying to cross through. The strong wolves were given no choice. They were forced to join the Lone Rocks. To join Bone's army. But the weak wolves, they weren't given a choice either. Only they didn't let them go. They – they –" Ash's voice failed him. Water filled his eyes until it trickled onto his fur.

"They put them into the red snow?" Watcher's chest emptied. That night in the Gray Woods flashed behind his eyes. He saw the red snow under the hill by the fallen tree again. *They're like us,* Watcher thought. *Wolves without a home. Wolves without a pack.*

"We heard that the Far Runners had gone into the South," Ash continued. "The birds we met along the way told us to be patient, that there would be justice when they returned. But when will that be? Justice then won't keep us alive now, will it? We almost gave up hope. But then I remembered. I remembered something you asked the Council of the Flyers when you stood before them. You asked about a place over the White Mountain. The Far Valley you called it. And I remembered your brother." Ash snuck a fearful glance at Orion, whose yellow eyes still burned.

"I thought: if there was any wolf who could challenge Bone, who could offer protection, it would be him. And if this Far Valley was a real place, then we would try to go there too. I know we don't have a right," Ash hung his head, "I know *I* don't have a right. Not after what we did to you. But at least help the others. At least help them, please."

Watcher looked up from Ash to the other ramblers. They were mostly small – none any bigger than Kicker or Glimmer – none much bigger than Watcher himself.

"When was the last time any of you ate something?" asked Glimmer. Any anger or mistrust she might have held for Ash was gone. She looked like Watcher's mother again. Eyes like the sunrise.

"I don't remember," said Ash. He was crying again. "We've been loping and loping. We never stopped to eat we were so afraid."

Glimmer turned her sunrise eyes to Orion, asking a question with no words. Orion sighed. His flaming yellow eyes finally cooled and his shoulders dropped, as though even more weight had fallen down from the Trees and landed on his shoulders.

"Watcher, you and Windy stay here with the Ramblers," he said. "We'll see if we can find anything." Then he and Kicker and Glimmer took off into the thick, mossy woods.

They were gone for a long while, for the Haunted Woods held so little life, but Watcher and Windy spent that time calming the ramblers down and assuring them they would not be harmed. Soon enough Orion and the others returned, carrying only mice and a few small burrowers, but enough of a dinner for the smallish ramblers.

While the frightened wolves ate, tearing into the food as though they hadn't seen any for moons and moons, the litter whispered amongst themselves.

"They're small," said Orion, shaking his head. "Hardly one of them could be hunters or warriors. None of them could go into battle against the Lone Rocks and live, that's for sure."

"And don't forget the White Mountain," said Kicker. "We still have to cross that too."

"We can't leave them here," Watcher said. "I think that's why the Blue Wolf led us to them. We're supposed to take them with us. We're supposed to take them to the Far Valley."

180

"Watcher's right," said Glimmer. "We can't leave them out here." Windy nodded with her sister and Kicker's newfound smile finally climbed back onto his face again as he too agreed.

"Alright," Orion finally conceded. "Alright."

When Watcher told the ramblers they howled and cheered. With their bellies full and strength returning, some of them leapt and kicked. Ash cried. He wept huge tears and kept thanking Orion over and over again.

For the first time since the Gray Woods, Watcher and his family formed a line with a pack's worth of wolves and began to lope through the woods. They went slow so everyone could keep up, but as it happened, the thicket where the ramblers had collapsed was not far from the edge of the Haunted Woods.

The gray light grew brighter. The Trees grew further apart. The pine needles gave way to patches of grass and a thin layer of snow. Then the Forest came to an end.

The wolves stopped at the Treeline, quiet amongst themselves. Rolling hills stretched out before them, covered in snow and dotted here and there with shrubs and bushes. And beyond the hills, looming so high that it seemed to scrape against the Fields of the Sky, stood the White Mountain. It took Watcher's breath away to think they would have to cross such a thing. But on the other side, *Watcher knew,* the Far Valley waited.

As the wolves began to trot from the Trees Orion came to stand by Watcher. He wasn't looking with the others, out toward the Mountain. He was looking back, forever back, toward the woods.

"So," he said quietly, almost a whisper, "this is the end of the Old Forest."

Watcher had never thought of it that way. But it was true, wasn't it? He'd always thought of the Gray Woods as home, but as long as they had been in the Old Forest they had still been connected to the place where they'd all been born.

"I guess it is," Watcher said after a while.

"Watcher, do you think the Blue Wolf was something real? Or was it just a dream?"

"I don't know for sure." Watcher thought about it for another moment. "Maybe it was the First Tree trying to tell us something."

"What?"

Watcher thought for a moment, back to his dream and how his mother had told him to plant the seed where his skeleton was buried. A skeleton like the Blue Wolf's. But it still didn't make sense. "I'm not sure," he said.

Orion nodded and, after one last look back into the Woods, trotted from the Old Forest. But Watcher saw that he ran as though he was pulling something behind him. Something heavy. Another pang of guilt gnawed Watcher from within. He'd figured out what the weight was, and it wasn't really him or his siblings, or even these new ramblers. It was the weight of Orion's dreams, pulling him back to the Old Forest. The farther away they loped the heavier those dreams became, and it was taking all of Orion's great strength just to keep moving forward.

29

Back in the Old Forest, at the far northern edge of the Crack in the Earth, there was a stretch of land called the Wastes. It had not rained there for seasons and seasons. The Trees no longer greened in the spring. The rivers and streams were nothing but sickly trickles. Their beds were only cracked earth.

There was no pack that marked the Territory of the Wastes. But as the moon rose over that barren land a wolf howled into the night.

It was Bone, urging forth his warriors. It had taken them longer than he'd thought to come around the Crack in the Earth. But they had done it. Now they pointed their snouts once more for the White Mountain. Once more they closed in on their prey, on Bone's enemies.

Bone would not make the same mistake as Anorak, who let Bone live after defeating him in battle. He would not allow the Gray Woods wolves to form a new pack. He would not stop until the Children of Anorak, *all of them,* lay beneath his feet in the red snow.

30

Watcher stood beneath the hard glare of the White Mountain, shivering in the cold winds that swept down its snowy face. From far away, on the hill in the Gray Woods, the mountain had looked big enough. Watcher had often imagined what it would be like to stand on top of it and see the whole world. But imagining and doing were two different things. Standing at its foot the White Mountain looked more like a White Monster.

The ice and snow hung like impenetrable fur from the mountain's peak. The shadows in the crevices stared like dark eyes. The sharp rocks stabbed from the white snow like biting teeth and tearing claws.

"One last hill to go, right Watcher?" said a voice. "Then we're home." It was Kicker. He seemed as nervous as Watcher felt, his fur whipping in the wind. Watcher saw some of his brother's old fear still lurking behind his eyes. But he had found his smile again in the Haunted Woods, along with the new scars upon his side, and he forced it onto his lips.

"Then we're home," Watcher repeated. It felt good to say it aloud. Watcher made himself think of the Far Valley. In his mind it looked like the Gray Woods, filled with little rivers and green glens. Full of plenty of animals to follow and plenty of birds to watch.

"Then we're home," said Windy, squeezing up against Kicker's fur.

"Then we're home," said Glimmer. After they'd all said it they found themselves smiling at each other and ready to climb. All except for Orion. He stood at the front of the line, standing tall on the first slopes, as though preparing to fight the mountain one against one in a challenge to the death.

After a moment he trotted over to his brothers and sisters, gathering them close. "Keep the line tight together," he said. "The winds are strong already and we're only at the foot of the mountain. I think they'll get stronger the higher we climb. The footing will become less sure."

Watcher saw worry for him swimming in Orion's eyes. *Orion has enough to worry about,* he thought. *He's pulling all of us and those heavy dreams behind him. He doesn't need to worry any more about me. I am a Gray Woods Wolf. I will climb for myself.*

"The thicker the snow the better," Watcher made himself say. "If it's up to my chest it'll be like having a fourth leg I can just lean on whenever I get tired." Kicker and Glimmer laughed. Even Orion managed a smile. But the next gust of wind blew it away. It was cold and unforgiving.

"Okay then. But we also have to keep a close eye on the others. Ash and one or two more seem strong enough, but most of the others – I'm not sure they're as strong as us. I'm not sure they're as strong as *you*, Watcher."

Watcher stole a glance past Orion to where the ramblers stared up the mountain. By the looks in their eyes Watcher was sure they saw the same monstrous face in the mountainside that he had. *But did they have the courage to face it?*

Most of them weren't but a season older than Watcher. They had runt names like Twig, Root, Shrub, and Rocky. Then there was

Little Paw, Moon Tail, Puddle Jumper, and Silence. Silence was the biggest of them all, with shaggy black fur. She never spoke a word louder than a whisper to anyone.

"They all have four legs anyway," Watcher said. "So they should be at least one leg stronger than me." When Watcher looked back to Orion he saw that a ghost of the old smile had returned once more. His brother's yellow eyes looking deep into his own.

"There are many kinds of strength, little brother. Not all of them can be counted in legs or measured in size. That's the strength they need. That's the strength you can share." And with that Orion turned away and called for the wolves to begin their ascent.

Climbing was hard for Watcher. The snow indeed lay thicker the higher they went. The ice grew hard and slick. His good paw often caught in the drifts. But though he fell he never stayed down for long. He hopped right back up and pushed ahead, straining with his back legs. He didn't want to become a distraction. He didn't want Orion to have to carry him again. Orion was busy enough carrying several of the others.

Watcher began to lose track of how many times he saw a wolf lose purchase and tumble past him in a cloud of white dust, wailing for help. And every time Orion bounded down the mountain after, pulling the wolf up in his teeth and carrying him back to the group. *The mountain might be easier for Orion to climb,* Watcher thought. *But if he kept that up he would be climbing two mountains instead of one.*

So Watcher, Kicker, and Glimmer began to help. Watcher wasn't strong enough to pull another wolf up the Mountain. But when he saw one falling he would hop in his path and hunker down in the snow, keeping him from falling too far down. It was bruising, exhausting work for him. But when his brother said "thank you, Watcher!" when he didn't have to go so far to pick up a fallen comrade, Watcher felt his strength redouble.

By the time they were halfway up the afternoon sun was just dipping past the mountaintop. Watcher let a little of the dragonfly buzzing back into his bones. The Peak looked so close. He felt he could stretch up and touch it with his nose. And the Far Valley was just on the other side, waiting for him. Just thinking about it made Watcher smile. But when he looked over to Windy, to ask if she had started smelling the Trees, the smile slipped from his face.

She had stopped climbing, standing still in the snow as though she was made of ice. She held her snout to the mountain air. Her eyes had gone moonround, the way they had when she had first smelled the darkness in the Gray Woods.

"What's wrong, Windy?" he asked. "What do you smell?" Windy blinked out of her trance, looking back and forth between Watcher and the mountain peak. Not even the ice stuck in her fur could mask her dread.

"It's a storm. A storm is coming, Watcher. And it is angry."

They were too far up the mountain to turn back, but not close enough to cross the peak. Dark clouds spilled over the highest lip of rocks and poured down the slope. The wind batted Watcher and the other small wolves back and forth like mice under a wolf's paws. The cold cut through their fur like teeth. And the snow, both that which the clouds hurled down and that which the wind kicked up, swirled thick as a white fog.

Watcher fell and fell and fell again. Three legs were hardly strong enough to climb a mountain, much less stand against this storm. He couldn't see Orion for the blinding snow. But as he had always done, Watcher refused to stay down. He quickly taught himself not to fight the wind, but to use it. When it blew to the right, he went up and to the right. When it blew to the left, back that way he came. When it blew to his back, he charged straight up the mountain. Back and forth, stop and start, he forged his way behind the pack.

He only fell once more, when his good paw tripped on something in the snow. Watcher thought it was a stone at first, until the stone called his name.

"Watcher!" It was Rocky, one of the littlest wolves from the ramblers. She clung to the mountainside, cowering against the wind and shivering with cold. Watcher took her by scruff of her neck and, using all his might, pulled her back to her feet.

"We have to keep moving!" he yelled to her. "We can't stay here. Use the wind! Lean into when it hits your face and walk with it when it hits your tail."

Rocky tried again, and again she stumbled. Watcher tried to catch her, but her weight and the wind together yanked them both into the snow. Panic surged into his chest. He felt himself slipping with Rocky down the mountain.

"Watcher! Hang on!" Orion's dark shape suddenly appeared above him. His fur whipped all about his body, but his legs were like Trees rooted into the ground. He plucked Rocky up from the snow as if she weighed nothing and then pulled up Watcher. He carried Rocky by her scruff and walked before Watcher, shielding him from the wind until they made it back to the pack. The rest of the wolves huddled close together, inching their way up the mountain. Orion set Rocky down beside Windy and Glimmer before shouting over the storm.

"Kicker, keep moving up! One paw in front of the other. Go slow so the small ones can keep up!" Kicker was barely a shadow at the front of the ragged line of wolves, but Watcher saw him turn his head and nod back to Orion.

Then Orion put his snout to Watcher's ear to speak, still shouting so he could hear. "Another wolf has fallen down the slope. It's Ash."

Watcher gave his brother a startled look. *What will you do, Orion? Will you leave him? Will you find him in the storm and take your revenge for the cave?* But Orion seemed to hear what Watcher was thinking.

"Don't worry, little brother," he said. "I'll bring him back up. But you need to keep close to Glimmer! The storm has shaken her. She needs your courage. I'll be back soon. Don't wait for me." Then Orion was gone again, bounding down the mountain like a buck in the forest.

"Where's Orion going?" a voice quailed beside Watcher. It was Glimmer. Her eyes were moonround and she was trembling from snout to tail. Her white fur had gone all but invisible against the snow. "Why is he going back down the mountain?"

"He's going back for Ash, Glimmer. Ash fell down and Orion is going to get him." Glimmer nodded. But she didn't move. She seemed frozen in place, as though waiting for Orion to come back.

Watcher understood her fear. Storms in the Gray Woods had always frightened him. The way the wind howled through the Trees. The way the mighty branches bent and broke. The way all the other creatures he so loved to watch would disappear in the gathering dark. But if there was one other pup who had been more afraid of storms than Watcher, it was Glimmer. For in blinding rain, or beneath black clouds, while Watcher could still smell his family close by, Glimmer's dull snout could not. In a storm she was completely blind.

"Don't worry, Glimmer," Watcher said. "Stay next to me. One paw in front of the other. If a three legs can get through this, so can you." He tried to smile, even as the cold bit his face and the wind ripped at his fur.

"Just stay close to me, Watcher," she said. "Stay close enough for me to see and to touch."

So Watcher wedged himself between Glimmer and Rocky, with Windy just in front. Together they fought their way up the hill, the pack walking in nearly a single clump. So close together, Watcher could hear the frightened whimpers and cries of the ramblers between the gusts of wind. Some of them looked ready to surrender to the storm and let it blow them away.

"Don't give up!" he shouted over the wind. "We're getting closer and closer with every step. I know some of you are runts, like me. For us every lope is hard. Every lope is a challenge. This is just another lope! We can make it. I bet the storm is easier on the other side of the mountain. We're on the hard side now. But once we cross over, I know we'll be all right.

"I can already picture the Far Valley. It's waiting for us. There'll be more game than we can hunt. More creatures than we could ever count. Soft grass and cool water. There'll be a warm sunrise, just waiting for us." *Like my mother used to wait for me,* Watcher thought.

Soon the whining and crying faded away. It was replaced by wolves shouting back to Watcher. "Just over the peak," they would say, or, "one paw in front of the other!" And so they pressed on. A soft snout nuzzled the fur on Watcher's face as they went.

"I think only a three legs could have done that," she said. It was Glimmer. She was smiling. Her red tongue and shining yellow eyes were nearly all Watcher could see in the storm. "Only a three legs knows how to find hope when there's none to be seen or smelled."

Watcher was just about to smile back when a sharp crack snapped above the wind, like teeth snapping together in a great mouth. The echo cascaded down the mountainside. The wolves stopped in their tracks. Ears perked up and fur bristled.

"Was that thunder?" asked Glimmer. Fear haunted her voice.

"No," said Watcher, thinking and remembering. "I've heard a sound like that before. On the Wide River. When the ice broke."

Then came the rumbling. It was a roar. It was as though the monster Watcher had seen in the mountain had finally woken and found intruders daring to climb his body. Now he was roaring in anger. Watcher looked up and saw how the monster would brush these insects away. A wall of moving white rushed through the blinding snow. It rushed for the wolves.

"Run!" Kicker screamed above the din. "Run for the rock!" Watcher saw the dark shadow of his brother leap along the mountainside, moving toward a vague shape in the white. It was a tall, jagged outcropping that tore up from the snow. If they could make it, Watcher thought, it could be their shield.

The wolves ran. Watcher leapt as hard as he could with his two back legs, using his front foot only to catch himself for the next spring. Rocky and Windy had jumped just ahead of him. Glimmer was to his side. Together they closed in on the rock. *We can make it,* Watcher thought. *We can make it!*

But that which Watcher had always dreaded on the long lopes happened again. A paw slipped on the snow and a wolf fell. Only this time, it wasn't him.

Glimmer had let her eyes drift to the rushing avalanche. Not watching her way, she'd tripped and fallen a full length back, tumbling into the snow. Watcher turned back for her, but it was too late. Her bright yellow eyes went wide and she shouted something just before the wall of noise deafened him. The white flood swept her away and the world went dark.

31

Watcher poked his nose through the ice above his head. He sucked in a greedy breath. His head was light and spinning for lack of air. Squirming and kicking, he scrambled to break free of the snow that buried him, but he only managed to slip himself deeper into the hole. It was still hard to breath. He could hardly see. Panic threatened. The snow was swallowing him whole.

Watcher gave one last jump with his hind legs. His good paw caught the edge of the hole – but the powder crumbled under his claw. Down he went again. Watcher cried out for the Trees to help him, but it was teeth that came to his rescue. He felt them catch the back of the neck and fling him into the light.

"Are you alright?" Orion looked down on him with wide eyes. "Watcher, are you alright?"

Watcher spit and coughed up all the snow he'd swallowed trying to escape, but he managed to nod that he would live.

He saw Ash just up ahead of Orion, sniffing frantically at the snow. "Here, Orion, here!" he said. "I think this is Windy, and Rocky right next to her."

Orion covered the distance in a single leap, plunging his head into the white. Up he came with Windy first, her legs churning in the air, hacking out huge puffs of snow. Then came Rocky. Then Orion was off after Ash, who had already found the next two buried wolves.

Watcher looked around as his senses returned. The worst of the storm had passed. The dark clouds rolled over the foothills below, lashing the base of the mountain with snow and lightning. But evening light had returned to the sky above the peak. Kicker's rock had saved them, Watcher thought. They'd still been buried, but they hadn't been swept away. Only the tip of the jagged stone was visible above the avalanche.

I just made it to the edge, Watcher thought, looking back at the hole from which Orion had saved him. *One step slower and I would have been—*

Watcher's next breath froze in his lungs. *Glimmer!* She'd been last in line. She'd been just behind him. She'd fallen just a few steps away. He remembered the way her eyes had gone wide. The way the flood of snow had struck her.

"Orion!" Watcher screamed. "Where's Glimmer? Where's Glimmer?" Watcher didn't wait for his brother or Ash. He leapt down the hill, the snow and ice so much thicker than before. Windy came just behind him. "Sniff here, Windy," he said. "All along here. Maybe she wasn't taken too far down."

Orion seemed to fly down the mountainside to Watcher's side. "What's wrong, Watcher? What do you mean about Glimmer?"

"The rock, she didn't make it behind the rock!" Watcher's voice turned hot and thick. Tears stung his big eyes. He couldn't smell her. He shoved his nose into the snow and tracked back and forth, but he could not smell her. *Stay beside me, Watcher,* she had said. *Stay beside me.*

Watcher looked to Windy. She stood frozen in place, drawing deep breaths of cold mountain air with her almost magical nose.

But when she looked back to Watcher, he saw the answer in her moist eyes before she spoke.

"I can't smell her."

Watcher refused to believe it. "We have to find her, Orion!" he pled. They were already moving down the mountain when a timid voice caught them from behind.

"There are still more buried in the snow here, Lord Orion." It was Ash. He cowered on the mountainside, quivering where he stood, head down – bowing – refusing to lift his eyes from the snow. "I'm not big or strong enough to pull them out. They'll die if we leave them here much longer. Then we must get clear of the mountain. The smallest among us will not survive another storm."

Watcher saw that invisible weight fall down on his brother's shoulders, like an avalanche falling from a mountain all his own. His neck and his back bowed beneath it. His eyes went far away. Then they closed as he spoke.

"Ash, find the rest of the pack. I will dig them up."

"But what about Glimmer?" said Watcher. His lips trembled.

"Windy will keep sniffing for her," said Orion. "If she finds her, I'll pull her up. But once the pack is free from the snow, we have to cross over the mountain."

Watcher barely breathed as Orion dug out the rest of the pack, one by one. Not even when Kicker appeared, digging himself out and climbing up beside the rock, heaving in gasps of air. Watcher couldn't take his eyes off Windy. She kept working her way farther and farther down the slope, her nose to the snow and then to the air, then back again. Every once in a while she would pause or take a step back. Hope would jump in Watcher's chest. But each time she shook her head and moved on. Glimmer was gone without a trace.

No one said a word when Windy finally rejoined the pack by the rock. The rest of the wolves were safe. Orion and Ash had found them all. All except for Glimmer. *I fear one of you may fall before the end,* old Gold Hoof had said to Watcher in the Forgotten Forest. But Watcher never thought it would be Glimmer.

Why couldn't it have been me? he wondered. *I wish it would have been me.*

When it was time to leave Watcher found himself still sitting on the snow that had nearly buried him alive, staring back down the mountain. He kept thinking that if he watched long enough, if he held out hope long enough, he would catch her running up the Mountain. But she never did.

Orion padded up in the snow beside him. "It's time to go," he said. His voice was as heavy as Watcher's chest felt. But together they waited silently for a moment, looking back over the Forest that had once been their home.

The black storm clouds had rolled further on. The two of them could see everything from the mountainside. The barren foothills, the Haunted Woods, the Crack in the Earth, the Forgotten Forest, and beyond that, the Gray Woods.

"I don't know why, Orion," said Watcher, "but I thought everything would be better if we could just make it to the Far Valley. When I pictured it behind my eyes, it was like – like I could run on all my legs. And Glimmer could smell as far as she could hear. I thought it could be like Mother and Father had never died."

Orion didn't say anything for a moment. He kept looking back, the way he had ever since the Haunted Woods. Then he leaned over and picked Watcher up to his feet by the scruff of his neck.

"Dreams are fast, Watcher," he whispered. "Sometimes too fast for anyone to catch. Even me."

As he watched his brother trot back up the mountain, Watcher understood what Orion meant. All of Watcher's dreams had lain over the White Mountain. But Orion's were back in the Old Forest. Now he was leaving them behind again to lie beneath the snow with Glimmer.

The pack set off to the mountain's peak. For the rest of the climb Watcher said nothing. He was too busy thinking. An idea had sprouted in his mind – a frightening idea – but one that had taken hold and sent its roots down deep. Maybe he couldn't save Glimmer, Watcher thought. But it wasn't too late to save Orion. It wasn't too late to save his dreams. But that would mean Watcher would have to fight something even greater than the White Mountain. He would have to fight his brother. He would have to fight Orion.

32

When the wolves crossed to the far side of the mountain, the land stretched as far as Watcher's owl eyes could see, all the way to the horizon. The evening sun hung over the lip of the world, painting the Treeless stretches crimson. On this far side of the White Mountain the slopes were marred by a craggy ravine, seemingly as deep as the Crack in the Earth and lined with boulders, ice, and snow at the edges. But as the crevice reached the foothills it opened up and became the gateway into an endless green valley.

The ramblers barked and laughed. They wagged their tails and howled as they started down the mountainside. *It was there,* Watcher thought, *just like Gold Hoof said it would be.* The Far Valley. But as Watcher looked to Kicker and Windy, who were still sitting on the mountain beside him, he knew that much of their joy had been left on the other side of the mountain.

"Glimmer would have been happiest of all," said Windy.

"She'd be halfway down the mountain by now, just running for that valley." Kicker tried to laugh, but it ended in a shuddering sniff. "What if we get to the Far Valley and there are already wolves there?" he said all of a sudden, tears in his voice. The smile he tried to keep in place fell. "What if the Valley can't be our home?"

Watcher let his eyes drift to the place where the red sun now sank out of sight, to the place no wolf had ever seen before. Then he looked back at Windy and Kicker and found their smiles for them.

"Then we'll keep going. We'll lope all the way to the End of the World. Glimmer would have wanted that. To never give up. It would be the most magnificent story any wolf ever told, wouldn't it?"

"Yes, it would," said Kicker. He smiled back, even through his tears. Windy came between them and nuzzled each of them under their snouts.

"Then it looks like it's time for us to find out once and for all," said Orion, speaking for the first time since he and Watcher and talked on the other side. Watcher swallowed hard. *If it was going to happen, it had to happen now.*

"Time for us, yes," Watcher said. "But not time for you, Orion." Watcher trembled. His throat ached. He had to clench his teeth to quiet the voice behind his eyes, screaming to take those words back.

Both Kicker and Windy went still and quiet, looking back and forth between Watcher and Orion. Orion's eyes were latched onto Watcher's face, yellow and moonround.

"Watcher, don't be ridiculous. We've come all this way together. Now the Far Valley is right there and you want me to leave?"

Watcher trotted over to stand before Orion, the snow beneath their feet red as though on fire. He felt Kicker and Windy's gazes heavy upon him, but they said nothing.

"I don't want you to leave, Orion. I want you to be where you're meant to be. I want to take the weight off your shoulders. I've seen it growing heavier and heavier ever since we crossed the Fallen

Tree Bridge. I want to release you from it. I want you to be happy. To be free."

"Watcher, I, I am. I–" Orion's gaze dropped to the snow. "I'm with you. With Kicker and Windy. I am where I'm supposed to be."

"Don't lie to me, Orion," said Watcher. "And don't lie to yourself. We all saw you. We all saw you that day when you ran beside the Far Runners. You were free then. You were who you were born to be. Our dreams are down this mountain, in that Valley. But yours are back there with the Far Runners. You're fast enough to catch your dreams, Orion. I know it."

Orion stood silent before Watcher, his fur blowing in the wind. He looked to Kicker and Windy, shaking his head as if they might agree with him and talk Watcher out of this madness. But Kicker and Windy still said nothing. They were crying. Especially Kicker. He was sobbing, but he wouldn't say a word.

Orion clamped his teeth together. He raised his head and his tail, the way he did when he became that immoveable force, the invincible wolf.

"No," he growled. He loomed over Watcher and showed his teeth, his shadow growing dark on the mountain snow in the deepening evening. "I'm not leaving. This is where I belong."

Watcher stood his ground. As he'd climbed the mountain, after the avalanche that had taken Glimmer away, he'd remembered something Windy had said to him back in Crag's cave. *There's always a challenge, Watcher.* But Watcher couldn't be the same as Crag. He wouldn't do what Crag had done to his brothers. He was a Gray Woods Wolf. He would challenge the way his Father would.

"I – I challenge you for leadership of the pack." Watcher said. It came out like a whisper. It was as though his body fought to keep the words inside. Orion's set jaw fell open.

"Watcher, what in the name of the Trees do you think you're doing?" he hissed.

Watcher choked down all the fear and tears surging up his throat. He stood as tall as he could on his three legs. For the first time in his life he let his fur bristle and found the growl in his throat. "I challenge you for leadership of the pack!"

"Watcher, this is madness!" Orion's yellow eyes blazed. He snapped his teeth and slather slung from his lips. "We're not even a pack anymore. Besides, you can't challenge me. You would die!"

"We *are* a pack, Orion!" Watcher came even closer to Orion and shoved his little snout into his brother's big one. "Don't you remember Father's words? *I* am a Gray Woods Wolf. *I* make my own mind! This is *my* right, by the Ancient Laws. So I challenge *you*. Now fight me or yield."

Orion roared. It terrified Watcher down to his paws. For a moment he thought Orion was going to take him into his jaws and shake this challenge from him. But still Watcher refused to back down.

"You can't do this, Watcher!" Orion screamed.

"Can't what, Orion? Can't run? Can't hunt? Can't fight? You said not to call myself just a three legs. Or is that only true when you're there to make it true? Do you really believe in me or not?"

"How will you hunt?" Orion snapped his teeth again. "How will you live?"

"With the invisible strength, remember? With owl's eyes and the gifts that the Trees gave me."

"And what about Bone?" Orion's voice cracked. His growl weakened as Watcher drew even closer.

"I don't need to be afraid of Bone, Orion!"

"Why?" Orion asked. His voice finally fell into a husky whisper. "How can you say that?"

"Because my brother and the Far Runners will stop him."

Orion went silent. For the first time in his life, Watcher saw his brother tremble. Tremble the way he did. The fire in his yellow eyes cooled. It was replaced by tears. As the sun finally slipped below the world and the burning red snow turned back to cool white, Orion bowed first to Watcher. He bowed until his nose touched the ground.

"I yield," he whispered. They were words Watcher thought his brother would never say. But he did. To him. "The challenge is yours."

Watcher rushed forward and nuzzled his brother's fur. Then came Kicker and Windy, falling together and saying their good-byes. Then, as though afraid he could not go if he did not run, Orion turned and stretched his legs for the mountain top. Watcher looked after him until the tears blurred him in with the mountainside.

I love you, Orion, he said to himself.

There was a crunching in the snow behind them. Watcher realized that the ramblers had come back up the mountain.

"Where's Orion going?" asked Ash. "Why is he leaving?"

"He's going to join the Far Runners," said Watcher. "He's going to go stop Bone."

"Then who will lead us into the Far Valley?"

Watcher was about to say that Kicker would, when his brother spoke before he had the chance.

"Haven't you all heard the legend of Watcher of the Owl Eyes?" he said. "The one who brought down the Tree at the Crack in the Earth? The only one to ever challenge Orion and win? He will see the way for us."

Watcher wanted to shake his head, to say *No! I'm just a three legs and a runt!* But his brother just gave him that smile, the one from the Haunted Woods, and sprang forward, running a circle around the pack, rallying them back to their feet.

"Come on, you wolves! We have a valley to explore! Off this Tree-forsaken mountain we go. Now let's get on with it!"

He began down the slope, with the ramblers – the pack – following behind him. Windy paused before following, to nuzzle

Watcher once more on the face. "You were the only one, Watcher," she said, "you were the only one who could ever challenge Orion and win. Because your heart was the only heart as strong as his." Then she followed the others. But Watcher stayed for another moment, looking back to see Orion cross the peak.

"Won't you howl for your brother?"

It was Rocky. She'd stayed behind, standing beside Watcher in the snow. Watcher shook his head no. The howl was there, screaming in his chest to break free, but he trapped it. For he knew if he howled Orion would turn around and come back. So like Romulus, the First Wolf, the greatest wolf, Watcher refused to howl. He wept in silence as night came. Great tears streamed down his fur and dropped onto the snow as his brother ran over the mountain and disappeared.

33

Watcher and the small pack reached the ravine just as the moon came over the Mountain, shining down on them with her bright blue light. But her comfort did not remain with them long. The night grew black and the silence thick as they descended into the narrow ravine. If there had been another way, the pack would have taken it. But as far as they could see, the crevice was the only way in or out of the Far Valley.

Rocky precipices loomed high on either side, falling steeply down to a narrow pass. The stony walls blocked out the cold winter winds, but also stifled the moonlight and any sound from the world above. The further the pack traveled into the canyon, the more fear began to replace their momentary exuberance. Before long their whimpers echoed off the stony walls.

"Don't stop now," Watcher called out. He could only see them for the dim glow of their yellow eyes. "We crossed the entire Old Forest and the White Mountain to get this far. We can't let some shadows stop us when we're so close."

"What if there's something down here in the dark?" whined one of the ramblers. "Something waiting for us?"

"Then it'll be sorry it got in the way of us and our valley," said Kicker, even though he had to take a few deep breaths before stepping forward again. "Now come on. Let's go!" Kicker barked the last, perhaps as much for his own courage as for the others. As the echoes of his call sailed up the ravine walls, dread prickled over Watcher's skin. Pebbles and ice clattered down the rocks. He feared another avalanche had come to bury the rest of them. But the mountain soon stilled.

"Everyone quiet," Watcher whispered harshly. "Wait here for a moment." The yellow eyes stopped bobbing in the black, staring at Watcher. "Kicker," he rasped. "Bark again. Bark loud."

Kicker unleashed his loudest bay. More pebbles, ice, and snow tumbled into the ravine as Watcher observed with his owl eyes.

"What is it, Watcher?" asked Windy.

"The avalanche on the mountain," he said, thinking hard. "I think it may have been the thunder, not the mountain, that made it fall. We need to be quiet as we go through this stretch in the ravine. The snow and rocks here are precariously perched."

So the wolves ceased even their whimpering as they followed Watcher through the narrowest part of the canyon. They climbed over rocks and boulders that had fallen long ago. They used their noses to see each other when the light grew too dim. But before long, the ravine walls began to slope more broadly. The path at the bottom grew wider. The moonlight crept back down into the depths. A warmer breeze by far than the cold winds on the mountain touched the wolves' fur.

With every step Watcher took, the smell of Trees grew heavier and richer in his nose. Hope began to bloom like a spring flower. He turned a sharp corner in the crags and suddenly found himself standing before a wall of green.

The goddesses grew tall and strong, as if from a time when the world was young. Their branches stretched all the way up to the tops of the canyon walls. The trunks were so thick and close together that even the smallest wolf would struggle to squeeze between them. But in one place the ravine cut through the woods, forging a path through the forest like a Tunnel of Trees.

Watcher could hardly hear or smell or even think over the humming in his body. How far had they come to get here? How much had they fought and lost along the way? Would it really be worth it in the end? But in only the few breaths it took for him to tread through the Tunnel of Trees and emerge into the Far Valley, he knew the answer was *yes*.

The Trees and hills in the lowlands glowed blue in the moonlight. Forest and field stretched farther than Watcher could see or smell, nestled between tall ridges that shielded the Valley from the harsh winter winds and any intruder. Sparkling streams wound around little hills. The grass in the glens rustled under a warm breeze. At the wolves' arrival, flocks of birds lifted up from the Treetops, singing their nighttime song. Watcher caught the glimmering eyes of Great Crowns leaping through the clearings.

"We're here," he said. "We're home." The ramblers who had come timidly behind him now spilled past, running and jumping down the gentle slope that opened into the Valley, howling and laughing, tumbling each other over in the grass.

Watcher smiled, but he didn't run or jump himself. Instead he sat down at the Valley's edge where Kicker and Windy came to sit beside him. They smiled and nuzzled one another's fur in silence, as overcome by the sights and sounds of a new Forest as they were by the absence of Glimmer's laugh and Orion's smile.

34

As the ramblers played in the grass, frolicking to the edges of the undiscovered forest in the valley beyond, Kicker and Windy finally ran off to join them. But Watcher settled himself down to rest. His leg ached from climbing down the mountain and winding through the crevice to the Tunnel of Trees.

The goddesses of these woods are tall and green, he thought as he settled himself down. Their evergreen scent flooded the warmer winds that blew over the land. The smell made Watcher drowsy. His body grew heavy.

He rested his head on a tuft of soft grass and closed his eyes. What was it Lady Winter Fur had said about Trees such as these, which were so old and grew so tall and straight? *They can speak to you*, she said, *if you listen.* Sleep snuck up on Watcher and captured him as easily as Orion once lifted him up by the scruff of his neck.

Watcher stood atop the White Mountain. The moon was full and vast. She stretched across the sky like a great eye, peering down upon the earth. Her children, the stars, twinkled all about her.

Beneath her blue light Watcher straddled the mountaintop, standing tall on all four legs.

I'm dreaming again, he thought to himself. He was just wondering if it was the Trees trying to talk to him when he looked down the mountain and saw a trail of footprints in the snow, leading back to the foothills and the Haunted Forest beyond. He followed the tracks with his owl eyes and found Orion walking toward the base of the mountain.

"Orion!" Watcher called. Though his brother didn't seem to hear him, Watcher's voice echoed off the mountain louder than a runt's voice should. He looked down at his four legs and realized that in this place – this dream – he wasn't a runt anymore. He was a full-grown wolf, big and strong enough to have made his father proud.

A laugh tumbled over his teeth as he launched himself down the mountainside, springing like a buck over his brother's tracks, bounding over the ice and snow.

"Orion, it's me!" He shouted again when he caught his brother – faster than he'd ever run in his waking life. "Can't you hear me? Can't you see me? Look how big I am! Look how strong! It's me, it's Watcher."

But Orion still trudged through the snow in silence. His tail dragged behind him. His eyes were cast down to his paws, as though he were all alone. *He can't hear me or see me,* Watcher thought. *I'm like a ghost.*

But still Watcher followed his brother, invisible though he seemed to be, and watched him. Watcher had thought Orion would be running as fast as he could back to the Old Forest. Perhaps heading a little south while he was at it – racing to find the Far Runners. But his brother still struggled with every step, as though that weight still crushed him to the snow.

"What's wrong, Orion?" Watcher asked aloud. "What is this weight you still carry? Can't you see that you're free?" But Orion looked like he was still trapped in Crag's prison, only without any dirt or stones to hold him in. Then, as though Orion was asking the very questions that Watcher posed, he reared back and howled to the great moon above the mountain.

A wolf answered his call.

This wolf did not howl in return, nor did he bark or bay. He did not come racing from the Treeline to give Orion aid. He simply appeared on the first foothill beneath the mountain, with no tracks leading to or from the place where he stood.

It was the Blue Wolf.

He had returned, glowing bright as the moon herself on the snowy ground. Orion stood frozen at the base of the mountain. Even Watcher, safe though he thought he would be in the folds of his dream, went still and quiet.

The Blue Wolf never spoke. He pawed at the snow. Waiting. When Orion did or said nothing the Blue Wolf stamped his foot and shook his head. His mist of a tail stood tall behind him and his ears perked upright.

He wants to run with Orion, Watcher thought. *No, more than that. He wants to race.*

Even in the dream Watcher's heart thumped so hard it shook his bones. Orion seemed to understand in the same breath. Without a second thought he sprang down the mountain. And Watcher chased with him.

There were no ramblers to hold Orion back. There was no little brother to carry in his jaws. Watcher saw him put all his strength and will into every stride. The rocks and the snow blurred beside him and beneath him. But more joyful still, Watcher wasn't left behind. He raced just after Orion, close enough to reach out and bite his tail. When Orion laughed for joy Watcher laughed with him.

The Blue Wolf seemed to spring from foothill to foothill in single strides. His body flashed like a blinking star. He was fast as the moonlight itself. But Orion would not let him escape. Watcher's brother dug his heels into the snow, down to the hard dirt underneath. His tongue trailed out the side of his mouth. The moon was no longer just in his eyes or in his blood. Like the wolf he chased Orion had *become* the moonlight.

Soon Orion and the Blue Wolf ran side by side. Glowing blue embers trailed into Watcher's eyes as he followed them. The Blue Wolf tried to spring away once more, but Orion found some reserve of strength he kept secreted away. His paws seemed to leave the earth and dance over the snow. The Blue Wolf could not elude him. And Orion and Watcher laughed louder and higher still.

Finally, when Orion could run no more and was gasping for air, he slowed to a trot. The Blue Wolf slowed with him. Watcher's dream blood raced within him, but he felt no pain, nor did his legs burn like they did in the real world. He watched as Orion bowed to the Blue Wolf. The Blue Wolf bowed in return.

As the three of them stood there, Watcher, Orion, and the Blue Wolf, the ground beneath their feet shifted and took new shape. Watcher sprung back, leaping from foothill to foothill in single jumps. When he was far enough away to see what had changed beneath his paws he had to blink twice, for he did not trust his owl eyes. The snow-covered hills had taken the shape of a white wolf. Of Glimmer. It looked to Watcher as though she were asleep, her eyes closed forever by the avalanche from the White Mountain.

As Watcher stared in disbelief the Blue Wolf leapt up into the sky. As he had done in the clearing of the First Tree, he lost his shape and became a glowing cloud. But this time Orion went with him. He too turned into a wolf's-head cloud, bright as the Blue Wolf's but the color of summer gold.

Together they rained embers down on the snowy hills. Grass and flowers sprang up through the white powder. The giant Glimmer in the ground opened her eyes.

There was little chance for Watcher to revel in the moment. The ground shifted again, and this time Watcher found himself turned away from the White Mountain and facing the Treeline of the Haunted Forest.

Green lights spilled from the woods like a swarm of glowing bugs. At the head of the lights led a lone green orb, carried on a midnight-furred body.

Bone.

Watcher's blood went both cold and hot. The glowing eyes swirled off the ground as though they had wings. They spun together until they formed a single orb, as bright and massive as the moon in the sky. All the lightless bodies came together and formed a cloud of their own, a cloud as dark as a thunderhead in the shape of wolf's body. But this wolf cloud did not rain life down on the world. It flashed lightning and rumbled threats. The shadow stretched across the sky, blotting out the moon and the stars.

The enormous one-eyed shadow wolf reached for the White Mountain, crested the peak, and spilled down the other side in a lightless flood.

"No!" Watcher screamed. He looked around for the Blue Wolf or Orion, but neither of them could be found. Watcher cast his eyes to his paws and found that he now stood over the shape of his skeleton again. But this time, sprouting from the eye in the skull was a single green stalk, reaching up in a curling tendril for the sky.

The lightning blazed and the thunder clapped again as the shadow wolf's tail crossed the mountain. "Bone!" Watcher screamed. "No!"

35

Watcher yelped as he snapped awake. His ears and his tail stood straight. His blood pounded. He looked all around for the giant shadow of Bone, half expecting it to be lurking right over his shoulder to devour him.

But the valley was at peace. The moon shone on the soft grass, rippling in the breeze. Watcher could still hear the other wolves yapping and playing. He had only been asleep for a moment. Another sound trickled into his ears over the barking and baying. It was the flapping of wings.

A feathery shape fell from the sky. It tried to land on a nearby Tree branch, but it toppled from its perch and tumbled down to the grassy ground not far from where Watcher sat. It only took Watcher a single deep breath of his nose to recognize the bird's scent, touched by a taste of the Old Forest and the Gray Woods.

"Lady Frost Feather!" Watcher shouted, running to her side. The old owl was just picking herself up. Her feathers were mussed and wind-shorn. She gasped for breath, looking as though she might collapse dead into the grass at any moment. "Lady Frost

Feather, I can't believe you came here. Look! We made it! It's the Far Valley."

But when Watcher finally met Frost Feather's eyes his happy smile dropped away. There was no joy on her feathered face. Only warning.

"I wasn't sure I would make it in time," the old owl gasped. She hardly had the strength to speak. "I thought the winds over the White Mountain would be the death of me. No owl has ever flown so high or so fast. But I had to try. I had to find you. I had to warn you."

Watcher's insides went cold. He already knew what she was going to say. His dream had not been a dream at all. It had been the Trees speaking to him. Warning him.

"Bone is coming, isn't he?" Watcher finally managed.

"Yes," said the owl, "with his Army still behind him. Where is your brother, Watcher? Where is Orion?"

"He's gone," Watcher said with a thick voice. "He's gone to join the Far Runners. Glimmer is gone, too. An avalanche on the White Mountain carried her away."

Frost Feather said nothing for a long breath. Then she finally managed to climb up onto her clawed feet and put her feathery wing tips to the sides of Watcher's downcast face. "Then it will be up to you, young one. So call your remaining brother and sister and come with me."

Watcher yelled for Kicker and Windy. When they joined him, Frost Feather rode on Kicker's back, for she was still too tired to fly any further. Together they travelled back through the Tunnel of Trees and along the black ravine until the White Mountain's moonlit peak came back into view.

Tingling fear rose up in Watcher's chest. A wave of glowing green flames poured over the peak. Black shadows crawled down the mountainside like a column of ants. Watcher knew who they were, but he still asked Windy and prayed to the Trees that perhaps he was wrong.

"It's Bone," Windy whispered. "He didn't stop at the Wide River. He didn't stop at the Fallen Tree Bridge. Why did we think he wouldn't cross the White Mountain?"

"It's like Long Tooth said," Kicker said softly, shaking his head in disbelief. "There's a black hole inside of Bone, as deep and as empty as the one that once held his eye. He'll never stop chasing us. He won't stop until he puts us all in the red snow."

"We need to warn the pack," said Windy. "If we start running now we might still escape."

Watcher suddenly felt so heavy, like he was made of stone and sinking into the dirt on the ravine floor. *We've come so far,* he thought, *just to find just this place.* Now that they were finally here, he realized that to drag himself from the Far Valley would be the death of him. It would be the death of his brother and his sister and all the ramblers as well. After they fled this valley, would Bone stop chasing them then? *No,* thought Watcher. *He'll chase us from the next, and the next, and the next. He thinks he's the fire, like Gold Hoof said. He won't stop until he's burned everything to ash.*

"It won't do any good to run," he finally said. "Bone will chase us to the End of the World and then push us over the edge."

There was a commotion behind them on the ravine path. Watcher turned to find the ramblers had come up behind. Their eyes too were fixed on the mountainside, where the glowing eyes and dark bodies of the Lone Rock Pack descended upon them.

"It's Bone!" cried Ash. Terror flooded his voice. The other ramblers began to whimper and pace in frightened circles. "We have to flee!"

"No!" Watcher shouted. "No more running." His voice silenced the ramblers as it echoed down the ravine. Pebbles and ice clattered down the rocky walls to mark the quiet that followed.

"Then what should we do, Watcher?" Kicker asked. "Orion is gone. The Far Runners are too far away to help. Bone is coming with an army. We're a pack of runts and ramblers. What can we possibly do?"

Watcher said nothing for a long breath. Most of the ramblers hung their heads and mewled softly. The rest of them, Ash, Rocky, and even Kicker and Windy, stared at him. More than ever before Watcher understood the weight that had so burdened his brother, Orion. He felt it now, like the entire White Mountain had fallen in an avalanche on his shoulders.

The avalanche.

Watcher swept his eyes up the rocky slopes of the ravine. His owl eyes beheld the large boulders topped with ice and snow looming upon the edges. He thought of how the sound of his voice brought the smaller rocks tumbling down. And he wondered: *Is it possible?*

"We could fight," he finally said.

Any rambler not looking at Watcher before snapped their eyes to him then. Their gazes were full of disbelief. They shook their heads and murmured amongst themselves.

"Fight?" Kicker howled. "Look at us. We're small. We can't fight *them!*" He cast his eyes to the mountainside, where the black shadows and green eyes drew closer and closer.

"But we've already *been* fighting," said Watcher. He spoke not just to Kicker, but to all the wolves with him. "Can't you see? At first, we never thought we would escape the Gray Woods. But we did. We used the ice on the Wide River to help us. Crag said we would never escape his cave. But we broke through. The Council of the Flyers said the Far Valley was a myth. But we crossed the Fallen Tree Bridge and even the White Mountain to get here. Would you have thought that a small wolf could do all those things, Kicker? Would you have thought a *three legs* could?" Then suddenly, as he spoke, Watcher understood his dream.

"We have to bury the idea that we're runts who can't do anything," he said. "We have to bury it like a seed, like one of the Children of the Trees. Only then can something better – something stronger – grow in its place."

"I wish I could believe you, Watcher," said Ash. "But none of what you say changes the truth that we can't fight Bone and his army and win."

"Maybe not if we fight the way *they* fight, Ash. But Orion once told me that there was more than one kind of strength." Watcher stood as tall as he could on his good leg to look Ash and the others in the eye. "Lady Winter Fur of the Far Runners said the same thing. I think one kind of strength is the strength that can find help when there seems to be none. A kind of strength that can use a voice instead of teeth."

"Who can help us now, Watcher?" asked Windy. "We're alone."

"The Mountain will help us, Windy," he said. "The same Mountain that tried to kill us will be our ally." Then Watcher reared back and howled as loud as he could. His call reverberated through the ravine. More than just pebbles fell this time. Larger rocks and great chunks of ice crashed to the ravine floor. The ramblers backed away in startled awe.

"Young wolf," said Frost Feather, cackling with her owlish voice as the rumbling of rocks and ice had subsided, "this is a mad plan indeed. But if it works, it will go down in the legends of wolves for all time. I will stay with you, my wolf-son. I will stay with you and see this through to whatever end."

Kicker flicked his eyes back and forth between the freshly fallen stones before him and the coming Lone Rocks on the mountainside. He took a long, deep breath and, from somewhere inside him, summoned a smile that would have made Orion proud. "I always thought you'd be the death of me, Watcher. I just never thought I'd be so proud to do it. I'm with you to the end."

"And me," said Windy, nuzzling up beside him. "We won't fight with the Mountain alone, either. I think the sky is coming to help us, too. Another storm is on the way. It's coming fast and strong." She pointed her nose to the sky, where indeed the first tendrils of black clouds were reaching for the moon.

"And us," said Ash, speaking for the ramblers. "We are a pack now. We fight together. So tell us what to do."

All the wolves gathered close around Watcher as he whispered his plan. There was little time for planning and little hope if their machinations failed. For Windy was right. A storm was coming. But not just one of cloud and lightning. The real storm ran at the head of an army, with one good eye full of hate and revenge.

36

Thunder rumbled in the deepening dark. As black as it had been the first time the wolves had traversed the canyon, it grew blacker still beneath the cover of storm clouds. Only the flicker of lightning lit the path before Watcher and the others. Together they formed the half circle between the high reaching rock walls, only a stretch or two before the Tunnel of Trees.

"It sounds like a big storm," said Kicker, sitting beside Watcher in front of the others. He spoke through clenched teeth. His eyes were fixed ahead, his ears up and alert. *He's afraid,* Watcher thought. *We all are.*

"Yes," Watcher finally agreed, trying not to think of the black pit in Bone's face. "One way or another it will be the last storm."

More thunder pealed, echoing off the mountain. Watcher hoped that perhaps the storm's loud claps would do the pack's work for them and bring down the rocks above the canyon. But though some ice and stones tumbled down, the big boulders re-mained atop the precipice.

Watcher swallowed hard. A lump of doubt welled up in his throat. What if he was wrong? What if this wasn't going to work? But it was too late for that. There was no running now. Another rumble now followed that of the thunder. *Paw steps.* Watcher's heartbeat quickened. *An army of paw steps.*

The ramblers shifted and whimpered behind Watcher. "Steady," he said, "steady." He hardly felt steady himself. His good leg shook like a reed in the wind beneath him. But he could not give in to panic, not if the plan was going to work.

It would be enough to block the Lone Rocks' way into the Valley with the boulders. But not enough for Bone. No matter how long it took, Watcher knew the Lord of the Lone Rocks would find another way. He would never stop hunting the Gray Woods wolves. Bone had to be under the rocks when they fell. So the pack had to hold their ground and bring the Lone Rocks' charge to a halt. They had to lure them in slow and close.

For this they had planned a trick, one Watcher had wished to play himself. But Kicker had insisted. He would be the one. Watcher hoped he was ready. The time had come.

Bone and the dark-furred Lone Rocks rounded the bend between the canyon walls. They loped for Watcher and the ramblers. Their green eyes burned and danced in the black. Their bared fangs glistened and their snarls carried over the storm.

"Are you ready?" Watcher whispered. Kicker nodded.

"Give the signal as soon as you can, Watcher. Even if I'm buried beneath the rocks with Bone, don't let them get past. Don't let them get into the Far Valley."

Watcher wanted to tell his brother that he wouldn't let that happen, but the Lone Rocks were suddenly close enough for Watcher to smell the hate on Bone's breath. To see the black hole in his face.

Kicker charged forward. Watcher's fear curdled beneath his skin. Over the rising winds Kicker called out his challenge.

"Bone of the Lone Rocks! You come uninvited to our territory! Leave now or face our challenge!"

Watcher's leaping heart nearly stumbled to a cold stop. He thought Bone and his pack would not even pause, that their light-less fur, white teeth, and reddened claws would wipe him and the ramblers away without even a fight. Kicker must have though the same thing, because he howled again, even louder. More rocks and snow rained down the ravine in the echoes. But the boulders still held firm.

"Bone, you murderer! You betrayer! Aren't you wolf enough to face a challenge? Or are you still a coward, like you were with my father?"

At this Bone finally skidded to a halt – yet not quite close enough to spring the trap. He was still short of the biggest boulders. Kicker would have to bring him closer.

The Lone Rocks drew up behind their lord, packing the canyon side to side. Their eyes were wild. They snapped their teeth and lashed their tongues. From their ranks Bone strode forward, sneering down on Kicker.

"Who is this runt?" he rasped, still breathing hard from his long run over the mountain. "Who is this rambling whelp that dares challenge Bone, Lord of the Old Forest? Where is Orion? It is he who is the coward if he will not face me. And where is Watcher of the Owl Eyes? Where is that wretched three legs?"

"I'm here," said Watcher. His voice cracked like a puddle of ice. *If you can't be brave, Watcher,* he told himself, *at least pretend to be!* So he said it again, this time adding his fiercest growl, the one he'd used against Orion. "I'm right here! And if you manage to get past us, you'll see my brother eventually. He's gone to join the Far Runners."

A troubled murmur passed over the Lone Rocks. But Bone just laughed. "If we manage? *If?* Little cripple, we could find more challenge from a pack of mice than from you."

Bone sauntered closer to Kicker, and Kicker gave way. The Lone Rocks inched nearer behind, itching to fight. *Just a little closer,* Watcher thought. *Just a little.*

"Your challenge means less than nothing to me, little wolves," Bone continued. "I should have my army march over you right here and now, and claim this Far Valley for our own."

"Then even they would know you are a craven dog, Bone of the Lone Rocks." Right on time, Lady Frost Feather descended from the stormy sky, circling down to land beside Kicker. "How long do you think your soldiers will tolerate a coward for a lord?"

"Can I not be free of you infernal birds and your squawking anywhere in the world?" Bone raged. He snapped his jaws and sent slather flying.

"You cannot be free of the Ancient Laws, Bone, if that is what you mean," said Frost Feather.

"Strength is its own law, bird," Bone growled. "As it seems I must prove again and again!"

"Of course you must continue to prove it," said Frost Feather, calm as ever. "That's the problem with strength. You must always keep proving it. Time is always causing your brand of strength to rise and fall. And here you are, bragging about how strong you are with an army at your back. But what does that really prove about *you?* That's why the Ancient Laws call for the challenge. To settle such disputes wolf against wolf. And I see a young wolf that has made challenge to you." She nodded to Kicker. "If strength is your law, Bone, then let your own be tested."

"By *this?*" Bone laughed. "Challenges are to be fought by equals, bird. There is no challenge here." The Lone Rocks laughed with their lord. But Kicker had felt wounded pride before and knew how to prick it further.

"Your laughter sounds like whimpering to me, Bone," he chortled. "I am Kicker, once of the Gray Woods, now of the Far Valley! Bone claims to be the strongest, but how many of you were there when he killed my father? How many of you helped because he couldn't do it on his own?"

Bone's teeth emerged from behind his quivering lips. Yet a whispering murmur passed over his pack. So Kicker went on, goading the soldiers further.

"When was the last time you actually saw Bone prove his strength without your help? When was the last time he fought alone? If you want proof of *my* courage, here it is! I have faced an Uruduk and lived!" Kicker turned his side to the Lone Rocks. At the sight of his scar, the Lone Rock Wolves went quiet again. Their glowing green eyes shifted from the young upstart back to Bone. "A storm's coming, Bone," Kicker railed on, prowling back and forth, trying to look as fierce as possible. "We don't have all night."

"What are your terms, little worm?" Bone snarled, half a smile still on his quivering lips.

"If I beat you, you and your pack must respect our territory and go back to the Old Forest. If you win, the Far Valley is yours."

"When I win, little mouse, I will bathe this valley in your red, as I did the snows in the Gray Woods with the red of your father and mother."

Bone stalked forward. His fur bristled high on his back and his tail stood tall. He suddenly looked like a giant with teeth that could tear another wolf to pieces.

Watcher felt himself go faint with fear for Kicker, but his brother didn't run. He bristled his own fur and growled. But he did not come forward. He made Bone come all the way to him, to a narrow place between the canyon walls where boulders and ice sat on the cliffs above. The Lone Rocks, eager for the action, pressed in close behind.

Now! Watcher thought. *Now!*

"Now!" he shouted aloud. He charged forward to stand by Kicker. He reached deep within himself for all the sound he could muster. He unleashed it, along with Kicker and all the other ramblers.

Their howls carried high above the storm's winds and the Lone Rocks' growls. They shook the fragile crust at the ravine's edges. A rumbling filled the narrow canyon as stones and snow and ice began to fall.

Large rocks struck down several of Bone's soldiers. The Lone Rocks began to whine and panic. Some even ran away. "The Mountain fights for the Owl Eyes!" they cried. "The Earth threatens to swallow us whole for what we've done!"

Even Bone's one good eye went moonround and filled with fear. But for only a breath.

For that one moment Watcher thought they had won. So many of his plans had worked thus far. The ice. The Tree Bridge. The hole in the Uruduk's clearing. But just when he thought the big boulders would fall and end Bone's war, all went still again.

Watcher's howl faded. The avalanche he had trusted to save them all had not come. The boulders had refused to fall. The fear in Bone's eye slowly faded away. Slowly turned back to hate. He began to laugh.

"Clever Owl Eyes, you nearly had me in your trap. But now it is you who has no escape. I shall accept your challenge and make you watch your brother die."

Then Bone sprang forward and fell on Kicker with biting teeth and slashing claws.

37

The whole world seemed to spin around Watcher. He lost his breath like falling into an icy river. Kicker stole a single glance at him. There was no blame in his eyes. Only sadness. He would have to fight Bone – to the death.

Bone fell on Kicker, snarling and growling. Kicker did his best. He flitted this way and that on the canyon path, avoiding the fatal blow. But his courageous dance lasted only a moment. Bone caught him with a swiping claw. He ran it down Kicker's flank, turning his fur deep red. Though Kicker staggered and nearly fell he still did not run. He got back up, gulping huge tired gasps.

"Would that your brother was here, little wolf," Bone said with a laugh. "At least he would have put up a decent fight."

Kicker roared and charged, swinging his claw with all of his strength. His blow never landed. Bone was too fast. He slashed Kicker again, sending him tumbling to the ground.

Tears flooded Watcher's eyes. He could not stand by and watch his brother die. Not when it was his plan that had doomed him. He took a deep breath and charged. He launched himself forward, barking and howling like a mad wolf. He sprang for Bone, swinging his one good claw. It never struck.

Bone swatted Watcher aside with the back of a paw. Watcher felt it whip across his face and the world spun again. He landed hard on the ground. The ramblers behind him fell to whimpering and crying once more.

As Watcher lay in an agonizing heap, a bolt of lightning streaked through the air and struck the Tunnel of Trees at the end of the canyon. Hot wind blew over Watcher's back. The flash had sparked a fire.

Orange flames leapt up and crackled madly. In their light Watcher could see that Kicker had no more fight left in him. He did not have the strength to stand.

The firelight glowed red in Bone's eye and painted the canyon walls with crimson. He laughed again, howling with glee. "It's a sign," he cried. "I am destined to wipe away all traces of the old ways: Anorak and the Gray Woods Pack, The Ancient Laws, The Far Runners, the Territories. We shall return to an even older rule: The Rule of Strength. Of Tooth and Claw. I am not a Child of the Trees. I am a Child of the Fire! The first thing I shall consume will be the last of the Children of Anorak." Bone stood over Kicker's fallen body. He opened his jaws above Kicker's head.

"Stop!"

A voice rang out over the thunder, the wind, and the fire. It called to Bone. It stopped his jaws from closing in death around Kicker's throat. It put fear back into his lone eye.

"They are not the last!"

Watcher thought he was dreaming, or maybe seeing one of Windy's ghosts. He knew that voice. He knew that face.

Orion had returned.

All the wolves in the canyon went quiet. Even the storm and the fire seemed to still. Watcher lifted his head from the rocky ground and looked through his tears. Every wolf stared with him, as though Romulus himself had returned.

The Lone Rock line parted down the middle. Some of them growled and snapped their teeth. Others bowed their heads in respect. But walking through, like a Chieftain of the Great Crowns striding through tall grass, was Orion.

Watcher thought this dream could be no more miraculous, but when Orion stepped free of the Lone Rock's line, out from behind him scampered a white wolf with sunrise eyes. It was Glimmer. Alive!

The dream was not a dream then, thought Watcher. *It was the Trees. They were showing me!*

Yet not even Watcher's eyes had gone as round as Bone's. He stared at Orion, slack-jawed. He shook his head as though he too thought he was dreaming. He slowly backed away from Kicker and Watcher's fallen forms, his proud tail dipping.

"I heard you were looking for me, Bone," Orion growled. He circled to stand between the Far Valley Wolves and the Lone Rock Army. "I heard you wished I was here. I heard you longed for a *real* challenge." He let his teeth gleam in the firelight.

Bone turned to his pack, silently begging them to surge forth and fight Orion for him. Though Lady Night Fleece and Long Claw bristled and growled at Orion, none of the other wolves moved. *This was the fight they truly wanted to see,* thought Watcher.

Orion took the moment to turn back to Watcher and the others. He dipped his head and nudged Kicker with his snout. Kicker looked up, his fur matted, red, and ragged. But still that smile on his face. "I – I didn't run, Orion," he said. "Not like at the Bridge. I stood my ground."

"I know, Kicker. I know you did."

Watcher scrambled to his feet as Orion turned to him. For a moment, Orion let a smile replace his snarl, that same one as when he'd brought down a Great Crown like it was nothing. The smile of a wolf with no fear.

"I – I saw you, Orion," Watcher said. "I saw you in my dream. I saw you with the Blue Wolf."

"He saved me, Watcher," said Glimmer, her yellow eyes aglow. "He pulled me out of the avalanche's snow. So I could come back."

"Did he send you back too, Orion?" asked Watcher. "Did he send you back to save us?" But Orion only shook his head.

"The Blue Wolf didn't send me anywhere, Watcher. Do you remember when you said that I was the hero in Long Tooth's stories? What I never told you was that you were the hero of mine. I came back because it was you who saved me, so many times. I love you, little brother. Until the Trees take us back, I do."

Then Orion nuzzled both Watcher and Glimmer once more, before turning back to face Bone. Embers from the fire drifted down about him like a rain of Fireflies. He raised his tail and bristled his fur. When he spoke his voice shook the air like thunder.

"So you believe in the rule of strength, do you, Bone? Let us put it to the test!"

Orion and Bone circled each other only once. With a guttural chorus of snarls and bays they set upon each other. The Lone Rocks and the ramblers watched under the light of the fire, in the whirling winds and beneath the crashing thunder of the storm.

Bone reared up and tried to rake his claws down Orion's shoulders and face. He underestimated Orion's speed. And his power. Orion bolted under Bone's swipes and rammed him in the stomach, bowling him over. Then he fell on him biting and clawing.

Bone only just managed to skitter away and avoid death. But there was no overcoming Orion. He fought as though he could not grow tired. He fought as though he was still the moonlight, unstoppable as the Blue Wolf.

"Why?" Bone finally demanded, staggering once more to his feet after another of Orion's onslaughts. His fur was streaked and wet with the red. The fire's embers blew all about him, taunting him. "Why did you come back? You're not one of *them*." Bone glared with his good eye at the ramblers. "You are strong. They are weak. You could have joined us. You could have joined the Far Runners. You could have ruled the Old Forest as a god among wolves. But even if you beat me my army will still put you into the red. And for what? Runts and ramblers?"

"You don't see, do you, Bone?" said Orion. "There is more than one kind of strength. More than one kind of wolf. They can *all* be great, if only given the chance to grow. To be great is to help them grow, like the rain in spring!"

"I will never let this seed grow!" Bone spat. "The line of the Gray Woods shall end!" He gathered up the last of his strength and hurled himself at Orion. Orion met him in midair. He caught Bone by the throat and bit down hard to the sound of Bone's lifebreath catching in his neck. When they landed, Orion shook Bone's body in his jaws. Then he tossed him against the canyon wall where the fire's smoke hid his body from sight.

"Curse you and your Gray Woods' blood!" Lady Dark Fleece howled into the storm sodden sky. She and Long Claw stepped to the front of the Lone Rock Army to take command.

Though some of the Lone Rocks bowed their heads to Orion or even turned and ran back for home, the rest of their eyes fell heavy upon him. Their fur bristled. Their lips peeled back from their fangs. They crouched and readied to spring. Watcher could see that they would not honor the terms of the challenge. They were going to kill them all anyway.

In that moment all seemed to go still and quiet. Orion turned over his shoulder and looked back at Watcher. Their eyes met. That smile split his face.

"Goodbye, Watcher," he said. Then Orion gathered himself before the Lone Rocks. He did not wait for their attack. He charged them.

"No, Orion!" Watcher shouted. But he had seen his brother's smile and had known what it meant.

Orion met the tide of midnight-furred wolves head on. He bored into them. He tossed some into the rocky walls. He trampled over others. He brought them down with his claws and teeth. The Lone Rocks surged up around him like ants trying to climb a hill. But in the midst of it all, there was Orion, tall and glorious with a smile upon his lips. When he reached the middle he looked up into the sky and howled. A howl like from the First Wolves. Like one from Romulus.

"Watcher!" Windy screamed from beside him. "Howl! We must howl!"

Watcher leapt to the front of the Ramblers and once more reached down inside himself, somehow deeper than even before. And he howled with his brother. The ramblers, his brothers and his sisters, *his pack,* howled with him.

This time it was a howl powerful enough. A roar like an army of Uruduk's rumbled over the ravine. The boulders and ice that had refused to give way before now came crashing down.

Fear once more took the Lone Rocks army. This time they did not simply whimper or whine. They fled back down the ravine for the White Mountain. All except for Long Claw and Dark Fleece. There was no time for them.

The avalanche fell upon them like a stone maw, clamping down on them with a great commotion. Dust and snow billowed up in the air to join the smoke and embers from the fire. Then all went quiet again.

38

Watcher emerged from the cloud of smoke and dust, staring at the pile of stone and ice that now blocked the way to the Far Valley. It was impassable, the way closed by the mountain for all time.

Windy and Glimmer put Kicker between them, helping him forward as ramblers followed.

"Now that is something that I have never seen before," said Lady Frost Feather, sailing down from the dark sky. "Nor has any other bird that has ever lived, I think."

But Watcher barely heard her. He felt empty inside. Hollow like a dead Tree. He said nothing and trotted to the rocks. They climbed as high as the canyon's walls. He sniffed at the rubble and then cried out with a loud voice.

"Orion!" he screamed. "Orion, can you hear me?" His voice alone echoed back to him. His nose smelled only the smoke on the wind. The crackling fire was now the only sound in the ravine.

"Watcher," squawked Lady Frost Feather, flapping down beside him. "You did it. Bless the Trees and your Owl Eyes, you did it."

"But Orion." Watcher's voice trembled with his lips. "He's gone. Even if he wasn't buried he can never come to the Far Valley now. He's gone from me forever."

"He left with a smile on his face and love in his heart, Watcher. He is a Gray Woods wolf, and he made his own mind. There truly was no pup like Orion, was there?" she said softly.

Watcher nodded. He could hardly see for the smoke and his tears. His throat ached and his snout stung. "There was no wolf like him either."

"And yet he has failed," a ragged voice called over the rocks, preceding a shadow that crawled from the smoke.

Watcher's eyes went wide. His bones went cold. The wolf was covered in red fur, tattered and shorn. In his face only one eye burned with hate in the light of the flames.

"Bone," Watcher said, trembling once again.

"Yes, little Owl Eyes. I yet cling to life." Bone emerged from the smoke as Watcher backed away from the wall. The Lord of the Lone Rocks staggered as he walked, life oozing from his wounds. But strong enough still, Watcher knew, to make one last kill.

"Your army is broken, Bone!" said Watcher, backing down the canyon path as Bone drew closer and closer. "The Lone Rocks have fled. The Far Runners still wait for them in the Old Forest. There's no point to all this. Just go! Go to the other side of the Far Valley and take your life with you, for what it's worth."

"How dare you give commands to me, runt! Cripple! Three legs!" Bone roared. "How dare you even look at me with your arrogant, freakish eyes. How dare you not bow them to the ground before your superior."

"You don't know what the bow is for, Bone. Even my brother, who beat you, bowed back to me."

"He was a fool, little runt. And though I have lost everything I shall at least leave the woods knowing you and the other Gray Woods' worms will leave with me!"

Glimmer growled from behind Watcher and leapt over his shoulder, trying to take Bone by surprise. He swatted her aside with a paw. He did the same for Windy, who followed. Even Ash came streaking forward, but Bone caught him by the scruff of his neck in his teeth and flung him into the canyon wall. They all lay still and wounded on the ground.

"No one left to defend you, little runt," Bone taunted. He was laughing now, a coughing, wet laugh, full of death. The embers from the fire lit upon his fur and began to smoke. He suddenly seemed no longer a wolf, but a living flame, come to burn everything before him to the ground.

All Watcher could do was retreat. The ramblers whimpered and whined, pressing themselves against the rocky walls. Kicker tried to lift himself up to fight, but he was too weak. Watcher fell back through them all, until the flames whipping over the Tunnel of Trees threatened to singe his own fur.

"No more trees to shove down on me, little cripple," Bone continued, slather dangling from his jaws. "No rocks to drop on my head. No more tricks to save you." Bone was taking his time. Watcher could see he wanted to savor this moment, to enjoy it, for it was all he had left. Watcher envisioned Bone's teeth slicing through his fur and his flesh.

"Now you shall see the truth of what I told your father, your mother, and your brother, Watcher of the Owl Eyes," said Bone. "In the end, the only real law is strength. Those who have it will always rule those who do not."

Watcher had no choice. He sprang backwards into the Tunnel of Trees, still engulfed in ravenous flames. The heat was almost unbearable. It singed his fur. The smoke choked him. Sparks and embers rained down upon his back.

Bone hesitated at the Tunnel entrance, looking with fear on the fire he had worshipped only moments ago.

An ear popping snap cracked in the Trees to Watcher's side. The fire had become too much for even some of the old goddesses. One broke near the base and toppled into her sisters in an explosion of fire and embers.

Bone took a step back from the Tunnel. But as more and more Trees groaned and swayed under the flames, Watcher wanted Bone to come *closer.* He wanted him to follow him deeper into the fire. He prayed that the Trees might help him again – one last time.

"What's the matter, Bone?" Watcher shouted over the crackling tongues of fire and the bursting wood of exploding trunks. "Found something stronger than you? Found something you fear? Tell me, is it the fire, or is it my owl eyes?"

Bone's lone eye turned from the flames back to Watcher. Malice black as the pit on the other side of his face consumed it.

"I fear nothing!" he roared. Into the Tunnel he charged. He lunged at Watcher. But Watcher was not a still target. He rolled to the side as Bone sailed over him. Bone's claw caught his shoulder, cutting deep through his fur and into his flesh.

Watcher cried out in pain. But he did not stay down. As he'd forced himself to his feet on a hundred lopes, so he did again. Another Tree crumbled as he stood, falling partway across the path that led to the Far Valley.

"You see, little cripple," said Bone, his voice coming in halting rasps. "Even as the red flows from my body, I am still too strong and too fast. I am still the lord. You are still the runt."

He swung again for Watcher. His claws nipped the fur on Watcher's snout. But the young wolf ducked just in time and squeezed past Bone. Another Tree fell, this one coming from the other side of the Tunnel and crashing across the path, sealing it completely. The only way out of the tunnel was back toward the canyon. But between Watcher and escape stood Bone.

Bone smiled his last smile. He swayed on his paws. Ready to end this game once and for all. His focus was completely upon Watcher.

What was it Orion and Kicker had said to him? Watcher thought to himself. Then he remembered, all the way back to that night in the Gray Woods, before the Lone Rocks had come. Watcher looked at the Trees. He felt the heat of the fire. He listened to the old goddesses groan. He waited.

"You should thank me, Watcher of the Owl Eyes," Bone said, red dripping from his mouth. "You hate me for taking your father and mother from you. Well now you can thank me for sending you to join them again. Goodbye, little cripple."

Bone leapt in the air, jaws open to bite Watcher on the throat. Watcher waited until the last possible moment, until Bone was nearly on top of him. Then he shot underneath, pushing with his back legs as hard as he could.

Bone sailed overtop and landed hard on the path. Had he not been so injured by Orion, the Lord of the Lone Rocks might have spun quickly enough to seize Watcher by the tail and drag him to his death. But he was wounded and a moment too slow.

Watcher had not merely been dodging Bone. He'd also been dodging the Tree that now fell across the path back to the canyon. The flaming trunk nearly smashed Watcher to the earth. But he rolled beneath it and came up standing on the other side.

Watcher turned around just in time to see Bone realize the trap into which he had fallen. The big wolf looked for a way out, but the fallen Trees and the fire had blocked him in and sealed his fate.

"Curse you, Watcher!" he roared as the smoke began to hide him from Watcher's eyes. "Curse you and your infernal traps and schemes!"

"I didn't trap you, Bone," said Watcher. "You were too focused on a creature weaker than you and didn't mind your surroundings!"

The fire rose higher and the smoke grew thicker. It drowned out Bone's roaring voice and blinded Watcher to the Lord of the Lone Rock's end.

Watcher collapsed in an exhausted heap, silent save for his gasping breaths. As he lay there amongst the burning Trees, his body aching and his shoulder burning, a cool kiss touched the back of his neck. It landed just on the place where all the scars from a puphood of neck bitings and snout groundings hid beneath his fur. Then came another, and another.

It was the rain. The storm that had brought the lightning, the wind, the thunder, and the fire, now brought the rain to put out the flames. To wash the land clean and make things grow again. Like the rain of the Blue Wolf.

39

Some Seasons Later...

"Stop biting me, Sharp Tooth, you *scat sniffer!*" said Summer, squirming beneath her brother's weight in the soft grass. He wasn't biting hard, but he knew she *hated* when he pinned her.

"You gotta get away, *tiny*," Sharp Tooth replied with a laugh, putting his paws down and holding her fast. "Won't let you go til you make me."

"But I'm smaller than you."

"Not my problem."

"It's about to be!" The sound of their mother's voice stole the smile from Sharp Tooth's face and put it back on Summer's. "What did I tell you two just this morning?"

You two? Thought Summer. Her face twisted up to match her brother's. She scrambled to her feet as her brother leapt off, only to find her mother glaring down with disapproval.

"Mother, what did I do? You saw! Sharp Tooth had me pinned!"

"She started it!" Sharp Tooth shouted. "She told Rose and Thorn that my tail looked like a badger's butt!"

Summer giggled. She stole a glance at her brother's short little tail, wagging hilariously behind him, and giggled even harder. *Well, it does,* she thought.

"Well then," said her mother, shaking her head. "If you two won't listen to me, perhaps you'll listen to your father."

"But I—" said Summer.

"But I—" said Sharp Tooth.

"But nothing!" It was too late for either of them. Heads down and tails dragging they followed their mother through the long grass toward the Tree Tunnel and the hill where Summer's father liked to sit in the evenings.

Along the way they passed Silence, one of the Huntresses, teaching a few of the other pups some tricks. She nodded when they got it right and shook her head when they got it wrong. They also saw their aunt Glimmer and Uncle Ash, trying to corral their small army of pups.

They were just summer pups, Summer thought proudly, even though she and Sharp Tooth, Rose and Thorn, were only spring pups themselves. It was just turning autumn and she and her brother's soft fur was still puffy and thick.

The leaves in the Far Valley were beginning to turn colors and the winds were growing cool, but it was still a bright and warm day. The birds were still in the Trees and the bugs zipped over the grass.

The Great Crowns would be moving on soon, her father had told her a few nights before. The pack would have to lope after them. Summer wondered how her father *knew* things like that. How could he possibly know all the names of all the different types of bugs and birds and burrowers that lived in the Far Valley? It was like he knew *everything* about the whole world.

Summer's mother led them past the Tree Tunnel. So many of the Trees there were just baby Trees, not yet full grown goddesses. Mother had said that was because of a fire that had happened a long time ago, but Father hadn't told them that story yet. Besides knowing all the creatures and ways of the Far Valley, Summer's father knew *all* the best stories.

They finally reached the hill and found Father, sitting as he always did, his head up and his big eyes facing the setting sun. Father's short leg was tucked up under his side like a bird's wing. He was talking with the old owl, Lady Frost Feather, who Sharp Tooth said must have been as old as the Far Valley itself.

Before Mother could say a word to Father, Summer and Sharp Tooth were suddenly tumbled over by a laughing ball of fur. It was Uncle Kicker. Soon they were all laughing. The pups never got in as much trouble when Uncle Kicker was around.

"Hello there, little pups!" Kicker shouted, nuzzling them hard with his snout and turning them over every time they tried to get up. "Been out in the world hunting, exploring, and fighting today?"

"That's why they're here, Kicker," said Mother, giving him that she-wolf look with her fierce eyes. "For fighting and teasing."

"No surprise there. They're related to me!" Kicker winked at them. "A little tumble now and again is good for a pup." He finally let Summer and Sharp Tooth go, standing with a small limp. Mother had told Summer it was rude to stare, but she couldn't help but look at the long scars that ran down her uncle's body.

From fighting monsters, Father had told her once. He had said Uncle Kicker was one of the bravest wolves he had ever known, but that those stories were for later.

"Don't encourage them, Kicker," said Mother with a sigh.

"They don't need my encouragement, do they, brother?" Kicker said to Father. He was just bowing his head to Frost Feather, but Summer could already see that smile pulling on his lips.

"Not if they have your blood in their veins, Kicker," he said. Father then bowed his head to Summer and Sharp Tooth. They got to their feet and bowed back. "Not if they have Orion's blood."

"But they also have your blood, Watcher," whispered Mother. She walked up to Father and nuzzled him, whispering into his ear.

"Gross!" whispered Sharp Tooth. Summer giggled.

"Alright, alright, enough of that," said Father. "Come here, the two of you, and let's not forget your brother and sister."

Rose and Thorn had been playing nearby. They came running when Father called for them. Thorn came last, hopping on his three legs. *Three legs like Father's,* thought Summer, *and owl's eyes like Father's too.* They all gathered around, tucking themselves under his warm fur.

"Sometimes the best way to learn something important, the best way to remember it, is through a story."

A quiver of excitement rushed through Summer's fur. There was nothing she loved more than a story. Somehow, by some magic, they took her to places behind her eyes, places that were far away, where great and wonderful things happened to wolves just like her.

"Is this a new story, Father?" asked Rose.

"Are you in it, and Uncle Kicker?" asked Thorn.

"Are there battles in this one, Father?" asked Sharp Tooth.

"Yes, yes, and yes," said Father. He was still smiling, but his big eyes had gotten far away, like the way Aunt Windy's did when she was smelling for ghosts on the wind. "I haven't told you this story yet, but it is the tale of how we came to this Far Valley from the Old Forest. It is about our family, your uncle, your aunts, me – and our brother, Orion."

Orion! Another spark zipped through Summer. She heard the grown-ups talk about him sometimes. About the great deeds he had done.

"He was your brother too?" asked Sharp Tooth, screwing up his face the way he did when he wasn't sure if he believed something.

"Yes," said Father quietly. "He was the biggest, the strongest, the fastest wolf I ever saw. Faster even than the Far Runners of the Old Forest."

"I bet he pinned the rest of you down all the time, didn't he?" said Sharp Tooth, smirking at Summer.

"No," said her father, shaking his head. "No, he never pinned us down. He held us up, son. He held us all up."

"Where is he, Father?" asked Rose. "Is he – did he – *die?*" she whispered the last word.

"I don't know for sure. But if he didn't, I think he's off somewhere, having adventures and doing great deeds. But don't be too sad. I know I will see him again."

"How?" asked Summer.

"Look there, to where the sun is setting. Can you see the wolves? Running through the Sky Fields? Running before the sun in purple and gold and red?"

Summer squinted into the bright sunset. At first, she only saw the clouds, but after a moment, she *could* see them. They were huge – huger than anything she had ever seen – *wolves! Wolves running through the Sky!* "I can see them, Father!" she cried.

"That's where he will be," said Father. Summer thought there were tears glistening in his eyes. "Still running at the front of the pack. Still the fastest and the strongest. Still the greatest. My brother, Orion, Lord of the Wolves."

THE END

ACKNOWLEDGEMENTS

I suppose it's appropriate this book took such an arduous journey to publication. After all, that's what the story is about: *the journey*. Though it didn't get there the "traditional way" – whatever that means anymore – here it is, and I'm proud of it. It is my own, shortcomings and all. For good or for ill no one can take that from me. I hope it has found a way to burrow into your heart and mind, to the Watcher and Orion in each of our hearts, trying to find our place in this world, trying to understand what to make of our strengths and our weaknesses. Trying to understand what we should *do*.

But as all authors who write such paragraphs know and admit, storytelling is never a journey of one. There are allies who aid you along the way, wizards, warriors, conjurers, and tricksters, without whom you would never have reached the finish.

To Steve, Sam, Keith Patrick, and Richard, for being my longest, best, and most talented friends in Los Angeles, and for having long ago formed a powerful circle of our own. To Jenny, for helping me get through my lonely times in SD, and for not forgetting me when I moved away. And to Savanna, for eating M&Ms and writing, and for the pleasure of knowing such a gifted writer.

To the Wolfpack: Gretchen, Nadine, Brad, and Jenn, for giving me guidance along this book's perilous trek from page one to THE END. Thanks for letting me run with you.

To Lisa Abellera, Tamson Weston, and Julie Gray, for being professionals in the field, and yet still believing in a no-name dreamer like me. A special thanks to Lisa, for understanding when I had to travel my own path, and for cheering me on regardless. And also to Lora Lee, whose incomparable art has elevated all of my books.

To Matt, Brett, Laure, and Corinne, for constant support and encouragement, for sun and cornhole and volleyball, but most of all for friendship.

To all my friends in Kentucky, from the banks of the Ohio down to Big Blue Nation. I've never forgotten you. Thanks for not forgetting me. Special thanks to Dave, Chad, and Russ. TwentyOne forever.

To my mother, my sister, my brother, my Oma and my Opa. In the end, it is family that holds us together and makes us who we are. For a wolf has no home but the pack. I'm thankful for mine, each and every one, and for who they formed me to be.

And to everyone who came together at the eleventh hour, when I was feeling down and defeated, who helped bring this book to life. There were too many to list in full, but the names of twenty-one are on the page that follows. They are my Far Runners, the rescuers of this book from the abyss.

Most of all to the readers. There is no story without you, no adventure, no quest, no triumph. Thank you for letting me draw and paint and sing in your imagination for a while. It is my greatest joy.

~JMR
Sep 2016

The Far Runners – who helped make this dream a reality:
Tara DiGiovanni Murphy
Janie Olmstead Head
Elaine Martinez
Chris Good
Humberto Ibarra
John Goss
Lauren Fellows
Eunice Castaneda
Danielle Mahoney
Kate Nagy
Gareth Lee
Tarik Al-Alami
Kristian C Kennedy
Keith Patrick Tutera
Tammy McKnight
Heather Hughes D'Amico
Jim and Sonja Holley
Therese Raney
Jacqueline Pineda
Brad Gottfred
James Holley

65513568R10155

Made in the USA
Charleston, SC
30 December 2016

Index

Index